A Vince Torelli Mystery, Book 5: Southern Justness

By John Schembra

Writers Exchange E-Publishing

http://www.writers-exchange.com

Justness: The act of being just; righteousness: to uphold the justice of a cause.

Chapter 1

Judge Anthony Torelli was on his usual jog, and was halfway through the park. It was 7:40 in the morning, a cool and sunny day, the kind of Georgia day he liked. Three hours later he would be dead.

Anthony turned right out of the park and headed toward his house. There were pedestrians on the sidewalk, and, as usual when approaching them, he would go into the street and jog along the bike lane. In front of the Dunkin Doughnuts shop, the sidewalk was blocked by three men in suits, standing together talking. Anthony moved to the street to pass them, and before he got back to the sidewalk, a speeding sedan swerved into the bike lane, striking him from behind. Anthony flew up onto the roof of the car, and rolled off the trunk onto the street. The car kept going, and turned right at the next corner. Witnesses could describe the car, but none of them got a look at the driver. The three men who had been blocking the sidewalk split up and hurried away in different directions.

Vince walked into his Concord home after a long night at a messy homicide scene in the Bernal Heights neighborhood of San Francisco. He had a splitting headache that felt like something was trying to pound its way through his skull, was exhausted, and looking forward to hitting the sack.

He'd taken off his gun and badge when the chirping of his cellphone filled him with dread. Glancing at the screen, he saw it was the night watch lieutenant. Vince groaned, and reluctantly answered the call.

"We got a possible double homicide that's just been reported," the lieutenant said. "We need help, Vince. The other two inspectors are stuck at a gang shooting in Hunter's Point--there's three dead, and seven wounded-- and it looks like they'll be there all night. It's a mess."

Vince looked at his watch and saw it was after two a.m., and sighed audibly. *Jesus, why tonight?*

"Really? Isn't there someone else you can call? I've been on the job since eight yesterday morning."

"It's a slam-dunk, Vince. The suspect is holed up in the victim's house. Claims there's two dead inside and he's armed with a gun. The hostage negotiator is there, talking to him, and we've got the house sealed off. All you gotta do is show up and supervise until we can get him out. Whadda you say?"

"I say, shit." Vince sighed, and after a moment of silence, said "All right, I'll be on my way back."

Vince went to the bedroom and gently woke his wife, Maggie. "Hey, Babe. I've gotta go back. There's been another murder and they need me."

"Didn't you just get home?"

"Yeah. It's been a really crappy night. I'll be home in the morning." Vince leaned over and kissed her on the cheek.

"Be careful, Hon," Maggie muttered, half asleep.

She puts up with so much. God bless her.

Vince called the lieutenant while driving to the city, placing his cell on speaker so the LT could fill him in on the case.

"OK. Whatcha got for me?"

"Lemme see," the lieutenant said. Vince heard papers shuffling in the background.

"At 12:30 a.m., Jackson Miller kicked in the front door of his ex-wife's house, and beat her to death in her bedroom. Her mother--they lived together-- probably awoke to the daughter's screams and called 9-1-1. It's not clear what happened next, but according to Miller, she came into the room screaming at him, and whacked him with a baseball bat. He said he took it from her and hit her a couple of times, in, he said, 'self-defense'."

"Is he in custody?"

"Not yet. Miller claims to have a firearm, but denied shooting the daughter."

"So the negotiator's made contact with him." It wasn't a question. "Is it confirmed there's a hostage in the house?"

"Now he's saying the mother is still alive. Miller's refusing to come out, and won't let us come in to help the mother. The negotiator says he sounds drunk."

"OK. I'll be there in fifteen minutes. Call me if there are any further developments." *Sure doesn't sound like a slam dunk.*

Vince spent the next four hours at the scene while the negotiator tried to get Miller to come out. Vince took over for him when it became clear the negotiator wasn't making any progress.

At various times Miller would sob, yell, or threaten but finally agreed to surrender if they would give him a cheeseburger, fries, and a pint of Jack Daniels.

Vince agreed to Miller's demands, not telling him the Jack Daniels wasn't on the list. He told Miller it would be waiting for him at the police station.

At 5:20 a.m., Miller came out, with his hands in the air, yelling for them to shoot him, saying he didn't want to live. He was handcuffed without trouble, and transported to the PD by patrol car. He ate his food, drank a large Coke, without Jack Daniels, and fell asleep, slumped on the table.

Vince remained at the house for another forty-five minutes, until the forensics team arrived, then entered to view the murder scene. A paramedic had gone in after the house had been cleared of any other suspects, and found the mother dead. After the bodies were processed and removed, Vince left and went to interview Miller.

Vince arrived at the interview room at 6:45 a.m., and woke Miller. After advising him of his Miranda rights, Miller waived his right to an attorney, and told Vince what he had done. An hour later, Miller said he was tired and wanted to sleep. Vince told him he'd be back later to talk more with him, and turned him over to the booking officers.

It was after 8 a.m. when Vince got home. Too tired to do anything else, he set the alarm for one p.m., undressed, and climbed into bed with Maggie. He was asleep in less than a minute.

The alarm buzzer jarred him awake. Vince turned over, and groped along the nightstand until he found it, never opening his eyes. Unable to find the off switch, he yanked it loose from the plug. "God, I hate this alarm," he muttered, throwing it across the room.

Maggie had come into the room to make sure Vince was awake. She was all too familiar with his disdain for alarm clocks, and made sure she was out of the flight path if he threw it.

"So, by the flying clock, I gather you're awake." She walked over to the bed and pulled the covers off him, slapped him on the butt, and said, "Rise and shine, Inspector. Your breakfast is waiting."

Yawning, Vince asked, "Breakfast? Isn't it lunch-time?"

"I figured you'd want breakfast. Get in the shower, and don't forget to brush your teeth. Your breath reeks."

"I love you, too," Vince replied, climbing out of bed.

While eating, he told Maggie about the case.

"Sounds gruesome."

"It was a messy scene. This guy was huge, too. I'd hate to try to arrest him if he was uncooperative. I'm glad all his anger died out before he came out of the house. By the time I talked to him, he'd sobered up. All he wanted was food and whiskey."

Vince drank the last of his coffee and stood up. "Well, back to the grind, Babe. Got a lot to do, people to see, and I have to interview the suspect again. Then, I get to spend a few hours writing two homicide reports."

"Will you be home for dinner?"

"Don't think so. Keep it warm for me, OK."

"Sure." Maggie grinned at him, and said, "I'll do the same with your dinner."

Chapter 2

Vince was sitting at his desk, organizing his notes from the morning's interrogation of Jackson Miller. As Vince listened to the recording of the questioning, making more notes now and then, his desk phone rang, interrupting him. He turned off the recording and took off the ear buds.

"Inspector Torelli," he answered.

"Hi, Honey," Maggie said. "Got a minute?"

The slight catch in her voice told Vince something was wrong.

"Hey, Babe. What's up?"

"It's about your uncle Anthony. There's something I've got to tell you." The tone of her voice alarmed him.

"Got a call from your cousin Steven in Georgia a few minutes ago."

"Is everything all right?"

"No, it's not." Her voice cracked. "Steve called to tell us that Uncle Anthony had been struck and killed by a hit and run driver a few hours ago."

Vince felt like he had been punched in the gut.

"Aw, no. God damn it," he exclaimed.

"He was jogging in the bike lane when a car swerved into the lane and struck him."

"You said it was a hit and run?"

"Yeah. Steve didn't have any more info. He's been at the hospital since the morning. Your uncle died during surgery."

Vince sighed, fighting the tightness in his throat. "I'll see you tonight. Call me if you need anything."

"I will. Love you."

"Love you too."

Vince went to Lieutenant Simons' office and told him about his uncle's death. "I might need some time off soon, when I find out about the services and funeral. Maggie and I are planning to go to Georgia to attend them, and be with the family."

"No problem, Vince," Simons said. "We can make it compassionate family leave. How long will you need?"

"I'd say a week."

"OK. I'll get the paperwork started."

"Thanks, Boss."

As Vince turned to leave the office, the lieutenant said, "Damn. I'm so sorry, Vince."

Three days later, on Monday evening, Vince's cousin Steven called. After the usual few minutes of small talk, asking how everyone was, Steve got down to business.

His voice breaking, Steve said, "I set Dad's funeral for Saturday, five days from today, at 11 a.m." Vince heard him take a deep breath, then continue.

"There's gonna be a lot of people there--cops, lawyers, friends, family. He was very well thought of around here. It will be held at Saint Mary on the Hill Church. After the service, he'll be buried at Cedar Grove Cemetery."

"Isn't that where our grandparents are?"

"Yes, and his grandparents, great-grandparents, and about a hundred other Torellis."

"I believe it. I knew Augusta was where the family settled after immigrating here in the late 1800s. OK. Thanks, Steve. We'll fly in on Wednesday. Is there anything I can do to help?"

"I don't think so. My brother and I have everything pretty much in control."

"Did you learn anything new from the police?"

"Not really. The car was found in the parking lot of a warehouse outside the city. It had been torched."

"Was the owner identified?"

"Yeah, they traced the vehicle identification number to a guy here. He'd reported the car stolen the day before the accident. Said it was taken from the parking lot at his work--a car dealership on the other side of town."

"Text me the investigator's phone number. I'd like to give him a call before I come out there."

"Alright. Her name is Louisa Princeton."

"Thanks, cousin. Call me if you need anything. I'm so sorry for your loss, Steve, and please pass our condolences on to your brother."

"I will, Vince. Joey will appreciate it. We have room at the main house, and you're welcome to stay there." Vince politely refused, figuring there would be several other family members staying there, and it would be a bit crowded.

"OK, Vince. See you on Thursday. Love you, Cuz."

"Love you, too. Bye." Vince hung up, and sat down on the desk chair, elbows on the desk and head in his hands. He quietly wept for a bit, feeling the loss of his uncle.

After a few minutes, he went to the bathroom, splashed cold water on his face, dried off, and went downstairs to be with Maggie and the boys.

Vince went in to work on Wednesday and spent the day catching up on one of his pending cases. By the early afternoon, he had briefed another inspector on the needed follow-up on the murder of a man in a homeless encampment. Vince had narrowed the persons-of-interest to two men and one woman who lived there. He was certain one of them had committed the murder, and they needed to be interviewed. Bobby helped get their other cases, in which a suspect had been arrested, parceled out to other inspectors. All the cases lacked was routine follow-up, or witness interviews, and then taken to the D.A. for filing. Bobby would be the lead inspector for any new cases.

Once Vince was satisfied the workload had been properly delegated, he notified Lieutenant Simons he was leaving, saying he would be back in a week.

Vince spent that evening, after dinner, reminisced with Maggie, Scott, and Tony, telling them stories of his childhood, and the things he did with his Uncle Anthony.

"I've told you before, Tony, you were named after Uncle Anthony. Only thing was--he hated being called Tony. Insisted we all call him Uncle Anthony, not Uncle Tony.

"Some of my best childhood memories were when we lived in Georgia, and dad and Uncle Anthony would take us kids fishing at Lake Sinclair for the weekend. We would stay in a two-room cabin with one bedroom, a main room, and no indoor bathroom. Of course, the bedroom was for the adults. We kids would put our sleeping bags on the floor in the main room. It would get crowded, since there were six of us. There was a small sofa and one armchair in there that were up for grabs each night. We would have a lively game of rock paper scissors, and the winner would get the couch. Second place got the armchair." Vince chuckled at the memory. "Steven, being the oldest of the cousins, always seemed to win, and I can't remember any time he slept on the floor. Over the years, we pulled some pretty big large-mouth bass outta the lake."

An hour later, Maggie and the boys were yawning, and losing interest in Vince's stories. They called it a night, and went to bed.

After breakfast the next morning, Vince called Sergeant Louisa Princeton of the Richmond County Sheriffs Accident Investigation Unit. After introducing himself, he asked for the information on his uncle's hit-and-run accident. She provided him with the basic facts, and said the case was an active investigation.

Vince said, "I'm flying in Wednesday. Any chance we can get together and you can tell me more. You know, a little professional courtesy?"

"We're not allowed to share open cases with anyone. It's against department policy, but since you're family, and a cop, I don't think it would be a problem. When you get here, give me a call. We'll figure something out, OK?"

Chapter 3

Vince and Maggie checked in at the Double Tree Hotel on Perimeter Road, off Highway 520, after their five-hour Southwest flight from Oakland. Once in their room, Vince called Steven to let him know they had arrived. They made plans to meet for dinner at 7:00 at Raes Coastal Café, a couple of miles from the hotel.

Maggie went to take a nap, while Vince went downstairs to look the place over. He didn't notice a man reading a newspaper in the lobby as he walked through to check the hotel restaurant. He looked through the fitness room and pool, then spent a few minutes in the gift shop. Vince stopped in the bar for a beer before going to his room.

Two minutes after Vince sat at the bar, the man walked in and took a stool five seats away. Twenty minutes later, Vince was back in his room, and the man was in the lobby on his cell phone.

"He's in his room, now. Walked around the hotel, checking it out, then had a beer in the bar. Want me to stay here for a while?"

"Nah. He's not going to do anything tonight. Be back by seven in the morning. Have breakfast, but keep an eye out for him. I want to know if he meets Sergeant Princeton."

"Will do, Boss."

Vince and Maggie were at the restaurant bar with Steven and his wife, Barbara. After catching up on their lives over cocktails, the conversation turned to Anthony Torelli. Steve told Vince his dad was presiding over a violent domestic violence case, in which the defendant's wife barely survived the beating.

"Dad hated these cases. Maybe that's why he was so tough on the defendants when it came to sentencing, more than likely doling out maximum, or near maximum sentences." Steve's eyes looked a bit misty as he talked about his father.

"The victim's families loved having their case before him, while defense attorneys and public defenders would groan when finding out he was the presiding judge." He picked up his drink and took a long sip. "Around the courthouse, dad was known as a defendant's worst nightmare. Pleas for lenience fell on deaf ears, and he would excoriate them mercilessly during sentencing."

"I knew he was a tough judge--not afraid to throw the book at a defendant." Vince replied, smiling.

They were interrupted by the hostess advising their table was ready. As she led them to their seats, Steve ordered another round of drinks. Once seated, he picked up the conversation where he'd left off.

"Dad called me last week and told me some of the facts in his current case. The defendant, Robert 'Junior' Henderson, is the son of a prominent, well-known Augusta businessman, Morey Henderson. Morey owns six car dealerships, two Laundromats, a restaurant/bar, and three check-cashing businesses in the greater Augusta area. He plays golf with the mayor, and four of the city council are in his monthly poker group. Morey belongs to the West Lake Country Club where he hobnobs with the wealthiest, most influential people in the city."

"Really. It would seem Morey wouldn't be too upset at Uncle Anthony's death," Vince mused.

Steve smiled, and continued, "His businesses have done extremely well--he is rich enough to afford a 2.3-million-dollar home in the Lake Forest Road development. The son has three drunk driving arrests and a previous minor domestic violence charge that were never prosecuted. In this case, the injuries to Junior's wife were bad--she suffered permanent brain damage, leaving her unable to care for herself, and now has to have a full-time caretaker living with her--the D.A. couldn't bury it."

Their server arrived with menus and water, and said he'd be back in a few minutes to take their order. Once he left, Steve picked up where he left off.

"Morey is close to the D.A., and with generous campaign contributions to his re-election campaign, and public backing, he assured the D.A. would remain in office."

"Wow," Vince said. "Seems old Morey is the puppeteer, pulling the strings, eh?"

"Yep. Rumor has it he helped bury a messy sex scandal the district attorney was involved in."

"No wonder Junior skated on the charges."

Steven said, "Dad told me Morey is the real power broker in Augusta. What he wants the council to do, they do--from building projects, to revocation of rival business owner's licenses, and everything in between."

The server returned, and they ordered their food. The rest of the dinner conversation was Steve and Vince bragging about their kids, and reminiscing about their childhood in Georgia. Steve told them of his mother Alison's death from a stroke three years ago, and how his father had thrown himself into his work two months after her death, not letting the tremendous grief he felt take over his life.

"Dad knew mom wouldn't want him to give in to his sorrow, so he didn't." Steven chuckled when he told them how Anthony had kept the house the same as when she was alive, and hadn't removed any of her clothes or belongings.

A year ago, Anthony called Steve and Joey and asked them to come over the next weekend and help him clear out Alison's clothes and personal items. "It is time," he told them.

Maggie and Barbara laughed at their stories, and chimed in with their own tales of living with the cousins. After dinner, they retired to the bar for an after-dinner drink, then Steve drove them to their hotel. It was a pleasant night, shared with family, though a pall hung over them. Back at the hotel, Vince had a hard time getting to sleep after going to bed. He was feeling the loss of his uncle, a man he loved and looked up to. He got up, dressed quietly, and went downstairs to the bar for a nightcap. Vince was lost in his thoughts, and one nightcap turned into three before he went upstairs and got in bed. The alcohol dulled his thoughts enough for him to sleep.

In the morning, Vince called Sergeant Princeton, and she agreed to meet him for lunch at 12:30 in the hotel restaurant. Vince was eager to find out more about the accident, and hoped she would bring a copy of the report. Later that afternoon, he and Maggie were going to Uncle Anthony's house for a family get-together. The funeral was set for the next day, with a reception following the burial.

Vince arrived at the restaurant ten minutes early. Standing inside the door, he looked around the crowded room, trying to identify the sergeant. Knowing cops, he focused on the tables near the back that faced the entrance. He spotted a woman sitting alone, with her back to the wall, dressed in black slacks, black half-boots, a white blouse, and blue blazer. Her hair was pulled back in a tight pony-tail, and she wore little makeup. She was an ordinary-looking woman, and the way she scanned the room screamed "cop". Her eyes locked on his, and after a moment she nodded and half-smiled.

Vince walked over to her table. "Sergeant Princeton?" he asked, as he pulled out the chair across from her and sat.

"You must be Inspector Torelli," she answered, reaching across the table to shake his hand. "How was your flight?"

"It was OK. Please, call me Vince."

"Around the department, I'm known as Louie. Will your wife and kids be joining us?"

"No. She's in the fitness room, and the kids are staying with her sister."

They chatted about their respective careers until they got their menus. After ordering, Sergeant Princeton retrieved a large purse from the floor next to her chair. Placing it on her lap, she pulled a small stack of papers from it and said, "Here's a copy of the initial report, and witness statements. You'll see there isn't much. No one got a good look the driver, or could say how many people were in the car. It happened so suddenly, and the car was gone so fast."

"We believe the suspect, or suspects most likely stole the car and were out joyriding. Witnesses varied on their statements, but most thought there was more than one person in the car. According to them, the car was speeding and veered into the bike lane where your uncle was jogging, striking him from behind. There were no skid-marks, or other evidence the driver tried to swerve or brake before the collision. After hitting the judge, the car accelerated, swerved back into the traffic lane, and sped off."

"I understand there is no description of the driver, or occupants?"

"That's right, Inspector. We don't know how many people were in the car, or if they were male or female. One witness said there were two, another said three. Problem is, it happened so fast, no one got a good look."

Their server arrived, and they ordered their meals. Once he left, Louie said, "The car was found torched outside the city limits."

"I know."

"Who told you it had been found?"

"I got a call from my cousin, Steve, yesterday."

"Really. What else did he tell you?"

"Just the basics of the accident, and the lack of evidence and credible witnesses. Were you able to identify the owner?"

"Yes, through the VIN. It'd been reported stolen the day before the accident."

Vince knew the owner's details, and where it had been stolen, and wondered why Louie withheld that info. He surmised it was because he was a cop, and she didn't want him snooping around on his own, interfering with her investigation.

Louie continued, "There is one thing bothering me, though."

"What's that?"

"There were no skid marks. It was a clear, sunny day, with good visibility and light traffic on the street."

"So?" Vince asked.

"So, I found it odd the driver didn't see your uncle, and try to brake or swerve, before hitting him."

"Maybe he, or she, was distracted."

"Possibly, but one of the witnesses said the car swerved into the bike lane, not drifted. If the driver was distracted, they would have drifted. The witness made it clear the car swerved."

"Almost like they aimed for him?"

"I don't have enough evidence to say that--yet."

"Evidence be damned, Louie, what's your gut feeling?" Vince asked.

Louie didn't answer for a bit, then said, "Between you and me, and I mean just you and me," she repeated, "I think it was deliberate. Your uncle was murdered."

Vince didn't reply, causing Louie to ask, "I take it you feel the same?"

"Yes, I do. After what you've told me, I believe it was intentional."

"OK. I've got to say this, Vince. I better not see this in the papers, or on the news. You are the only one I've told my suspicions to."

"No worries, Louie. I won't tell anyone, even the family."

Louie sat back in her chair, and stared at Vince for ten seconds. "I believe you, Vince. You have a good reputation with your department. You're honest, hard-working, and smart. I'm impressed."

Vince grinned at her, and said, "Been checking up on me, have you?"

"Nothing personal, but I had to know what kind of guy you are. My meeting you here depended on that check."

"You talked to Lieutenant Simons?"

"Yeah. He said I could trust you."

"Nice to know. What are your next steps in the investigation?"

"Since we can't get any evidence from the car, it comes down to witnesses."

"You said they gave conflicting statements, right?"

"Yes, but there were more people there than came forward, and some of them had to see what happened. We'll be contacting our witnesses and talking with them again. Maybe they will remember something of importance, or provide a name of someone who may have seen something, and hasn't come forth yet."

"A daunting task, to say the least."

"Yep. It means we're back to basics--pounding the pavement."

"I'd like to see where it happened. That OK with you?"

"Sure. Since we've completed the evidence work, it's not secured anymore. You need directions?"

"No. I'll take Steve with me."

"OK. If you find anything, or have any ideas, let me know."

"I will. Please don't think I'm trying to horn in on your investigation. I want to look the area over."

"No worries."

Their server arrived with their food. While they ate, they told each other of their lives, and compared notes on their jobs--how they came to be cops, what they liked about it, their most challenging cases. Vince told Louie about his time as an MP in Vietnam, and how he decided to give civilian law enforcement a try, once his time in the army was up. "I went through the MP school at Fort Gordon, in '67. We got passes to go to Augusta, and must have taken the wrong bus, as it dropped us off in the sleazy part of town. After a few hours, we left, having re-named it Disgusta."

Louie, in turn, explained she became interested in becoming a cop when she was the victim of a mugging while in college. She became friends with the campus detective during his investigation, and followed it closely. She was intrigued by its complexity, and how the suspect was identified and arrested. In particular, she got a sense of accomplishment when her trial testimony resulted in a conviction. She applied for a civilian community service officer position with the sheriff's department, was hired, and six months later took the police officer test. The rest was history. She had been married, no kids, and after six years, divorced.

After lunch, they said their goodbyes and went their separate ways, promising to stay in touch. Vince felt he had made a lasting friend.

Chapter 4

Vince called Steve from the lobby and asked if he would show him where the accident had occurred. Steve had been there the day before, and didn't want to go back--it was too difficult to be where his father had been killed--but agreed to go with him.

"Thanks, Steve. I can pick you up in a few minutes, if you're free."

It was a short ride, no more than seven or eight minutes. Steve told Vince to park in the Dunkin' Donuts lot, and they would walk the short distance from there.

Standing on the sidewalk, Vince saw where his uncle had been hit. There was nothing to show a fatal hit and run had occurred. He looked both ways, and saw an ordinary street, traffic flowing smoothly at the thirty-mile-an-hour speed limit, and pedestrians walking on the sidewalk.

"You told Maggie it happened in the morning. What time was it?"

"About 7:45, why?"

"I'd like to come back here tomorrow morning and see what the traffic's like, and how many people are walking around. Want to come with me?"

"Can't. Gonna be too busy with the funeral and the reception. If you go, don't forget the funeral starts at eleven."

"OK. Maggie and I will be there. We'll see you tonight, at the house."

The next morning, Vince was at the accident site by 7:30, standing next to the sidewalk, watching the traffic. Vehicle traffic was light, and foot traffic was moderate. Vince thought pedestrians would increase the closer it got to 8:00, as he was two blocks from a large commercial area of several office buildings, cafes, restaurants, various shops, and a half a block from a parking garage. As people approached him, he asked if they had witnessed the accident last week. Most either ignored him, shook their heads no, or said they didn't. A few stopped to talk, saying they heard it on the news, and asked if he was family. When Vince said the victim was his uncle, they expressed their condolences to him, and then went on their way.

Vince remained there for another half hour, without finding any new witnesses. He was about to give up when a woman who had stopped to talk earlier approached.

"Excuse me, Sir, can I talk with you?"

"I remember you. Yes, please."

"I feel bad I told you I didn't see the accident. I'm sorry, but I didn't want to get involved."

"What changed your mind?" Vince asked.

"When I found out he was your uncle. I couldn't stop thinking how bad you must feel, and how frustrating it had to be."

"Well, thank you. I'm glad you came back. There's a coffeehouse over there," Vince said, pointing to a strip mall behind her. "Let me buy you a cup of coffee, and we can talk."

She smiled at him, and said, "OK. I'm Sharon, by the way."

"Nice to meet you, Sharon. My name's Vince."

Sharon looked to be in her mid-forties, with blond hair. She was attractive, and was dressed in a tan business suit. She was not heavy-- pleasingly plump was how he thought of her--and had a nice smile. Her makeup was tasteful, not overdone.

They crossed the street, and Sharon went inside to buy their coffees. Vince found a table outside the shop, and Sharon soon joined him with their drinks.

"OK," she started. "I was walking to work when the accident happened. It wasn't more than fifty feet in front of me."

"Did you see the car?"

"Yeah. I understand it was found all burned up a day or two later."

"That's right. What about the driver, and was he, or she, alone in the car?"

"Yes, he was the only one in it."

"Did you get a good look at him?"

"No, but I'm pretty certain it was a man. He was white and had dark, wavy hair. I got the impression he was thirty to forty years old."

"What was he wearing?"

"I don't know. After hitting your uncle, he stepped on the gas and took off very fast."

"OK. Did you see anything else that seemed odd, or out of place?"

"There was one thing. It seemed a bit unusual. Three guys in business suits, were standing on the sidewalk, blocking it. I think that's why your uncle moved off the sidewalk into the bike lane."

"Why did it seem unusual?" Vince asked, taking a sip from his cup.

"Well, I saw them for maybe thirty seconds before your uncle passed me, and they were standing there, not talking. They kept looking in my direction, and before your uncle ran by, they spread out so they were blocking the whole sidewalk."

"Hmm. That is odd." Vince's mind was churning. Could Uncle Anthony have been set up? "Did you see where they went after the accident?"

"No, I didn't. They must have left right after the collision."

Vince took a business card from his pocket and wrote his cell number on the back. He added Sergeant Princeton's number below his. "Here's my business card. My cell is on the back, as is the lead investigator's from APD, Sergeant Princeton. Would you call her in an hour or so?"

"Will I be in trouble for not coming forward sooner?"

"Don't worry, I'll square it with her. I'll call her and let her know she will be hearing from you today. If she asks why you didn't come forward, tell her the truth. Tell her you heard my cousin and I talking about the accident yesterday as you walked by, and when you saw me today, decided to stop and contact me. I'm sure you'll be all right."

"OK, I'll call her."

"Thank you, Sharon. I appreciate you coming forward, and you've been a big help."

Vince got her cell number before leaving. He called Louie while driving back to the hotel and told her to expect Sharon's call and gave her a summarized version of what Sharon told him. He offered his help with the investigation, and asked her to call him any time.

Vince believed there was enough information to change his uncle's death from an accident, to a murder investigation. He decided not to say anything to Steve, or the rest of the family, until Louie could say for sure it was a homicide.

Over two hundred people attended Anthony Torelli's service at Saint Mary's. The mayor, chief of police, city council members, a dozen high-ranking police officers, twenty-five APD officers, the D.A., and ten of his fellow magistrates, were there. The Lieutenant Governor was there, as well as various other politicians. Thirty-five family members sat in the front three rows.

The bishop said mass, and presided over the communion. The priest, a close friend of the family, gave the eulogy, and after the ceremony, during the open mic, numerous people spoke about Anthony, how they knew him, and the effect he had on their lives. After the burial at the cemetery, everyone was invited to a reception at Anthony's house. The day was warm, with clear skies. Dozens of tables and chairs were set up in the large back yard, as well as in the house. The catered food was set up on several long tables on the patio along the rear wall of the house. There were two well-stocked bars, one outside, and one inside.

One guest spent time on his cell phone, walking around the house and grounds, describing the event, and who was there. It was the same person who'd followed Vince around the hotel. "Yes, Boss. It's like a gathering of the who's who of Augusta. Torelli was a popular guy." He listened for a minute, then replied, "OK. I'll try to do a bit of eavesdropping. Can't guarantee anything, though."

Vince and Maggie were sitting at a table outside with Steve, Barbara, and Joey. They all deeply felt the loss of Anthony, though it seemed to hit Joey the hardest. He was inconsolable at the mass, sobbing loudly at times. At the reception Joey started drinking right away, and continued throughout the afternoon. He hardly ate anything, and within two hours, was drunk. He cried off and on, until Steve helped him into the house and an upstairs bedroom. Steve took off Joey's shoes and sport coat, laid him on the bed, and covered him with a blanket. Joey was snoring by the time Steve left the room to return to the reception.

As Steve sat, he spotted Louie walking with a plate of food. She saw him, and smiled, and he waved her over to his table. "Want to join us?"

"Thank you. Don't mind if I do," she replied.

"Please, have a seat," Steve said. Turning to the others he said, "This is Sergeant Louisa Princeton. She is the lead investigator in the accident." Steve introduced his wife and Maggie to her, then asked, "Any more news on the case?"

Louie shot a glance at Vince, and said, "A little. Yesterday I got a call from a witness. She was close to the scene, and was able to give a general description of the driver."

"That's good," Steve said.

"Yeah, knowing the driver's race, and approximate age will help a little. It's a start."

"Did your witness provide any other new info?" Vince asked.

Louie looked at him, smiled, and said, "Nothing else."

Barbara interrupted. "Let's not talk about this now, Okay?" Turning to Louie she said, "You're our guest, and not on duty the moment, so please, enjoy your dinner."

The man trying to overhear them, casually walked by their table several times, once stopping to kneel and tie an errant shoelace. He didn't stand out from the other guests walking around, and if he lingered a bit too long nearby, they didn't seem to notice.

By 6 p.m., most of the guests had departed. Vince, Maggie, Steve, and Barbara, retreated to the house, where they sat in the living room, talking over a nightcap.

As the eavesdropper was driving home, he hit his speed dial, and reported what he had heard at the reception.

"There wasn't much new stuff, Boss. Sergeant Princeton was there, sitting at the family table with the San Francisco Inspector, and Anthony's sons. If she had important information, she wasn't passing it on. She did mention she heard from another witness, but the information she had was general, nothing specific."

"Is the inspector helping in the investigation?"

"I don't think so, though he left the hotel early this morning, and was gone for two hours."

"Where'd he go?"

"I don't know. I tried to follow him, but there wasn't much traffic. I had to hang back so he wouldn't notice me. I lost him when I got stuck at a red light."

"God damn it. I pay you good money to do what I ask. You're supposed to be a professional, yet you make amateurish mistakes? Get your head out of your ass, or you'll be sorry."

"I apologize, and promise it won't happen again," he said. He heard the click as the call was disconnected.

Chapter 5

Vince was relieved the day was coming to an end. It was a difficult day, with the funeral mass, interment, and reception. He was tired, and emotionally drained. The family had settled in the living room, talking and looking at old family photos when Vince's cell rang. The caller ID indicated it was Louie calling. "Excuse me, gang, I've got to take this." Vince went into the parlor, closed the door, and answered the call.

"Hey, Louie, what's up?"

"We've had a bit of a break in the case I thought you might be interested in."

"Absolutely. What've you got?"

"After I left the reception, I got a call from one of my investigators. He'd been out checking the area of the accident for any cameras. He found four in the immediate area."

"That's good news."

"Somewhat good. Three didn't show the accident, since they were from businesses across the street. They were aimed to cover the sidewalk in front of the stores."

"So, what's the good news?" Vince asked. "Gotta be something, or you wouldn't have called me."

"The fourth camera was at the Dunkin' Donuts. It, too, was aimed to cover the sidewalk, but fortunately, the store was so close to the scene, it caught the three guys in suits as they walked by. I'm guessing they were the ones who blocked Judge Torelli's path. Two of the guy's faces were partially caught by the camera. A few seconds after that, the right side of the car goes by in the bike lane."

"Terrific," Vince exclaimed. "Did the video show the driver?"

"All we saw was the lower part of the passenger door, due to the steep angle at which the camera was aimed. It didn't show the interior, or the actual collision."

"Damn. What about the faces of the two guys?"

"One is about a three-quarter view, the other more of a side view."

"Is there enough to make an ID?"

"Maybe. The resolution isn't the best--we're having our lab try to enhance it. I'd like to meet with you, Steve, and Joey tomorrow, for breakfast. I'll bring the stills from the video to show you. It's a long shot, but I'm hoping Steve or Joey will recognize the guys."

"Sounds like a plan. I'll get hold of them and set it up."

"Good. There's a Cracker Barrel Restaurant on Parkwest Drive. They serve a good breakfast, and plenty of it. You need directions?"

"No, thanks. I'm sure Steve or Joey will know how to get there. What time?"

"How's eight-thirty sound?"

"That's fine. I'll let them know. I'll text you in a bit. Thanks, Louie."

"You're welcome. See you tomorrow."

Vince called his cousins, explained Louie's call, and request. They agreed to meet with her the next morning, and Vince texted her advising they would be there in the morning.

At the agreed upon time, they entered the Cracker Barrel store, and made their way to the restaurant entrance. Vince saw Louie seated at a table. She waved at them, and they joined her.

"How's it going?" Vince asked.

Louie replied, "It's going." Turning to Steve and Joey, she remarked, "Nice turnout yesterday. Good to see so many people paying their respects."

"Yeah," Steve replied. "Glad it's over, though."

"I can only imagine."

Their server arrived at the table with a full pot of coffee, asking if they wanted some. Once their mugs were filled, she left, and Vince said, "Nice work getting the videos. I hope you can identify the guys."

"I do, too. We don't know for sure if they have anything to do with this, however, it's a possibility we need to investigate."

"Can we see the stills?" Vince asked.

"Sure. Maybe one of you will recognize them." Louie pulled a manila envelope from her bag and spread out the photos on the table. Pointing to one, Louie remarked, "This is the best of them. Shows most of the guy's face. Despite being blurry, you can see his general characteristics. Check out his hair, see how it's combed straight back, with the front puffed up a bit?"

"Yeah, Vince replied. "Reminds me of the 1960's style."

"I think so, too," Steve added. "Like something out of that movie, 'Grease'."

Louie chuckled, "That's what I thought, too."

They stopped talking as their server brought their orders. While being served, Joey had picked up the photo, and was staring intently at it.

Louie noticed, and when the server departed, asked, "Joey, you seem to be pretty interested in the photo. You recognize him?"

Joey looked up, and said, "No. I've never seen him, as far as I can remember."

"OK", Louie replied. "Do you think he may be someone from your past? An old schoolmate, or somebody you worked with?"

"No, I don't get that feeling, sorry."

Louie turned to Steve and Vince. "You guys recognize him at all?" Steve said he didn't, but Vince said he thought he'd seen him recently.

"Can you remember when?" Louie asked.

"I'm not sure when, or where. My first impression is I saw him in passing somewhere. Might have been at the hotel, or perhaps at the reception. I can't say I definitely did see him. It might be he looks like someone I know." Vince stared at the photo for a few more moments, then pushed it toward Louie, and sat back in his chair. "Sorry, that's the best I can do."

"That's alright. It's encouraging you might have seen him. Here are the other two guys," Louie said, pointing to the other photos. "Like I said, one of them has his back to the camera, and the other's head is turned mostly away. You can see a small bit of his face, and it's blurry. Don't think it will help to identify him."

Vince, Steve, and Joey looked at the photos, but saw nothing they recognized.

Vince said, "It's almost as if they knew where the camera was. Seems like too much of a coincidence they turned away while passing Dunkin' Donuts."

"I wondered that myself," Louie said, as their food arrived. "Let's eat before our breakfast gets cold."

While they ate, Louie told them about the recent witness's statement she had gotten. Vince, knowing the information came from Sharon, the woman who'd approached him at the accident scene two days ago, acted as if it was news to him, too.

"I contacted the owner of the car. He said on the day before the accident, he'd parked it behind the dealership. He saw it was missing when he got off work. He called the department and reported it before getting an Uber to take him home."

"The cops didn't come to the dealership?"

"No. On a simple auto theft, we usually take a phone report, unless it's a carjacking. We're short on officers, like everyone else, and too busy to spare someone to take the report in person. It was entered into the stolen database within a half-hour of being reported.

"One thing, though. The car dealership is owned by Morey Henderson. He's well known to the department, and his son would benefit the most from Anthony's death. Judge Torelli was hearing the son's recent felony spousal abuse case. Oh, the car's owner is his nephew." She shook her head and chuckled. "Seems there's at least two coincidences connecting this to the Hendersons."

Steve replied, "Too many. Think they may be involved?"

Louie replied, "At this point, I don't know, but it warrants me having a conversation with Morey."

"When are you going to do it?" Vince asked.

"I have an 11:00 appointment with him. Why?"

"I'd like to go along."

"I was afraid you would say that. It's highly irregular, and my boss will have my ass if he knew."

"I know, and I really didn't hear a no in there. Does that mean I can?"

"On one condition--you say nothing, just sit there and listen."

"I can do that. What if he wants to see my ID?"

"I'll introduce you as a new detective, along as an observer. I won't mention your name."

"Sounds like a plan. I'm sure I've never met him, though he may have heard my name mentioned in some way."

"Let's keep our fingers crossed you're right. I'll pick you up at the house at 10:30, an hour from now. Dress like a detective--coat and tie."

Vince laughed and said "I'll be ready."

Chapter 6

As Louie drove to Morey Henderson's house, she reminded Vince, in no uncertain terms, to not participate in the questioning. "Remember, you are an observer only."

"I got it Louie," Vince replied, somewhat irritated.

Picking up on his tone, Louie looked at him and said, "Sorry, Vince, but I'm taking a big chance letting you go with me. I need assurance."

"You can trust me, Louie. I know what to do and what not to do. I promise I'll behave."

Louie and Vince were ushered into Morey's office by the butler, Thomas. "Mister Henderson will be with you shortly. Please have a seat. Can I offer you anything--coffee, water, a drink?"

"No, thank you," Louie replied. They sat in the two chairs facing the desk, which was massive--six feet wide by two-and-a-half deep, with four drawers on each side. It was constructed of highly lacquered black oak, as were their two chairs.

After the butler left, Vince asked Louie, "How long you think it'll be before he comes in?"

"I'd be willing to bet it will be at least fifteen minutes. He's letting us know this meeting is on his terms, and he is in control."

"I've met his kind before. You know what's the best thing about dealing with people like him, don't you?"

"Yeah. It's seeing their smug faces fall as I slap the cuffs on them."

Vince grinned at her, got up from his chair, and walked to the bookshelves covering the back wall. They, too, were constructed of black oak.

There was a settee against the near wall, and two more chairs with green velvet cushions at the far wall. A lighter green, plush carpet covered the floor, matching the drapes over the two windows. Everything was spotlessly clean and in order. There was a fresh, outdoorsy smell in the air.

Vince noticed several books on business and effective leadership, but most were the classic works--Moby Dick, Sherlock Holmes, The Old Man and the Sea, and all of the Edgar Rice Burroughs' Tarzan books, among others.

Vince turned toward Louie and said, "Quite the eclectic reader."

The office door opened thirteen minutes later, and Morey Henderson strode in. Dressed in a navy-blue suit, light blue dress shirt, and wearing a scarlet tie, Henderson looked the picture of success. Standing six feet tall, he appeared to be in good shape and exuded an air of confidence.

"Good morning, Detectives. Can I offer you anything?"

Louie answered, "No, thank you, Sir. Thanks for agreeing to see us. I'm Detective Sergeant Louise Princeton, and this is my trainee." Louie purposely did not provide Vince's name.

"Always delighted to help our law enforcement people. What can I do for you?" Henderson asked, sitting in his chair behind the desk.

"I've got a few questions about an employee of yours."

"Oh? Which one? I've got quite a few."

"The manager of your auto dealership on the west side of town, Sam Winthrop."

"Yes, I know him well. What's he done?"

"It's not what he's done, it's what happened a few days ago. I'm sure you're aware of the accident in which Judge Anthony Torelli was killed?"

"Yes, very tragic. I feel for the family."

Louie replied, trying to keep the sarcasm out of her voice. "Yeah, well, the car that killed him belonged to Mr. Winthrop. It was stolen the day before from the car lot."

"Really? I wasn't aware of that."

"Somebody used it to run over the judge and flee the scene. We recovered it outside the city the next day. It had been torched."

"I assume you were unable to recover any evidence from it." It was not a question.

"That's right."

"Too bad. I'm sure that puts a crimp in your investigation."

"It doesn't help. What kind of guy is Sam Winthrop?" Louie asked.

"I like him. He's a stand-up guy. Married, three kids, two dogs, and a house in the 'burbs. He's a good manager--started at the dealership when he was eighteen, worked his way up the ranks, earning the manager's job ten years later. I've known his family for thirty years. Are you thinking he had something to do with Torelli's death?"

"Not yet. I'm gathering information--making sure all the t's are crossed and i's dotted." Switching directions she asked, "Where were you at 7:30 in the morning on the day of the accident?"

Henderson laughed, "Do you mean do I have an alibi?"

"No, Sir. It's the t's and i's thing," Louie said, smiling.

"Well, Detective Sergeant Princeton, I'm a bit hurt by your question. To help with your--shall we say--punctuation issue, I was in the gym, right here in the house. Several servants saw me there, and you are free to question them if you want."

"Not necessary, Sir. No offense is intended, but your son, Junior has a lot to gain by the judge's death, and you've come to his rescue with his past law troubles. I hope this isn't one of those times."

"I understand," Henderson said, nodding slightly to Louie.

Louie stood, saying, "I've taken up enough of your time, Sir. We'll be leaving now. Thank you again for talking with me."

"Anytime, Sergeant." He pressed a button on his desk, and a few seconds later, the butler appeared. "Jamison will show you out. Good luck with your investigation."

On the drive to Vince's hotel, Louie asked, "Did you believe him?"

"Not really. I don't think he was directly involved in the accident, but he knows more than he's telling us."

"I got the same feeling. If nothing else, he arranged the car, driver, and the three guys blocking the sidewalk."

"You might be right."

The man was sitting in the hotel lobby, looking through tourist brochures, holding them high enough to cover most of his face, when Vince returned. Vince quickly scanned the room, through force of habit, and, not seeing anything unusual, continued to the elevators. The man had taken a room there earlier and brought two changes of clothes, an Atlanta Falcons baseball cap, and a pair of clear glasses, so he could alter his appearance. He wasn't paying for the room, and he took advantage of the amenities and room service. He'd registered as Jack Monroe, presenting a Georgia driver's license in that name. It was one of several fake I.D.'s he used. The room, and anything else, was being paid with a valid credit card in another false name.

He wondered why his boss wanted such a close watch on Vince. When Vince and his wife checked in, the man heard the clerk confirming they were there for a week. Not that he minded. It was easy work, and the money was good, so he'd asked no questions--just did as he was told.

The man moved to the bar, sat where he could see the lobby, and ordered a beer. Looking at his watch he saw it was 12:30. This was going to be a long, boring day. He was glad someone else was paying the bill. *At least the Packer/Falcons game is on.* He ordered lunch and settled in to wait, watch the lobby, and the game on the big screen TV on the wall at the end of the bar.

Vince was sitting in his room, rereading the report Louie had given him. The investigating officers, and Louie, were thorough in their work and with the reports. Try as he might, Vince couldn't find anything they might have missed.

"Shit," Vince exclaimed in frustration.

"Problem, Babe?" Maggie asked.

"Yeah. Nothing points to the accident being deliberate, but I know, in my heart, Uncle Anthony was murdered."

"Why?"

Vince turned to her and said, "I can't get past the three guys blocking the sidewalk, forcing him into the street. Seems too much of a coincidence. Sergeant Princeton showed us photos of them, and one looked familiar. I've been racking my brain trying to remember where I saw him."

Maggie said, "I'd say it had to be here. Makes sense since the photo was taken here, doesn't it?"

"Yes, it does."

"Might be you're trying too hard. Try relaxing, and retracing your steps since we arrived."

"Easier said than done, Babe."

Maggie came up behind him and draped her arms around his neck. "Maybe you should forget about it for a while. I can think of a good way to help with that," she murmured, planting kisses on his neck and working her way around to his mouth.

Later, Vince lay in bed on his back, listening to Maggie humming in the shower. Replaying in his mind all he had done at the hotel and elsewhere, he still couldn't remember where he'd seen the guy. The feeling of having seen him was stronger, and he was certain it had been at the hotel.

Maggie came out of the bathroom wrapped in a towel, drying her hair. "Hey, handsome. Want to buy a lady some lunch?"

Vince smiled and said, "Sure. That's the least I can do after you helped me relax."

Maggie chuckled. "I'll be ready in fifteen minutes," she said, as she dropped her towel and went back in the bathroom.

Twenty minutes later Vince and Maggie entered the restaurant and were seated in a booth facing the bar. From there he could see the bar TV and the football game.

"Cool," Vince exclaimed. "The Packers game is on."

"Are the Niners playing today?" Maggie asked.

"Yeah, but they're not on until one o'clock, California time. They play the Chargers." Looking at his watch, Vince saw it was a 2:15. "If the hotel gets the game, it'll be on at four."

As their server arrived with water and menus, Vince asked if he would be able to watch the 49ers game. The server assured him he would, and said the NFL channel was available on their TV.

Vince and Maggie enjoyed a leisurely lunch talking about his family and making plans to visit a few historical sites afterwards. Vince would glance at the TV occasionally to check the score. He was a Packer fan, as well as a 49er fan, and thought Aaron Rogers was the best quarterback in the league. The only time he didn't root for the Packers was when they played the 49ers.

Each time he looked at the game, a man sitting at the bar with his back to him, apparently watching the game, was in his line of vision. Vince paid him no attention, until the man turned to the bar. Vince got a look at a side view of his face. It took a few moments for Vince to realize the man was one of the guys in the photos Louie showed him at breakfast.

Vince interrupted Maggie, who was saying something about dinner plans. "Hold on, Babe, I've gotta make an important call. I'll be right back."

Vince went to the lobby and called Louie, keeping an eye on the bar.

"Hey, Louie. You're not gonna believe this, but the guy in the photo you showed us is sitting at the bar in my hotel."

"Seriously?" she replied. "Are you sure it's him?"

"Yeah, I'm sure--the guy whose face we could see. If you want to talk to him, now's your chance. Are you close by?"

"No, I'm home. It is Sunday, ya know. I'll be leaving right away, but it will take me at least ten minutes to get there. I'll send a couple of uniforms. They'll be closer. Can you see him?"

"Not from the lobby, but I've got eyes on the entrance. If he leaves, I'll know it."

"OK. Hang back and wait for our officers. If he leaves, don't confront him. Try to get a plate if he gets in a car. I'll be there as quick as I can."

"All right. I'll be in the restaurant with Maggie. I can see him from there."

"OK. I'll text you when I arrive. Look for the uniforms. They should be there soon." Louie disconnected the call, and Vince went back to his table.

"Everything OK, Hon?" Maggie asked.

"Yeah, fine. See that guy sitting at the bar, the one with the blue shirt?"

"Yeah, what about him?"

"He's a person of interest in my uncle's accident. Louie has been trying to find him, as a possible witness. She's on her way."

Maggie placed her elbows on the table, and cupped her face in her hands. "Oh. I get to witness a big take-down?"

Vince chuckled. "You might be disappointed. She only wants to talk to him."

A few minutes later, the guy noticed Vince staring at him. It made him nervous, and he decided to go back to his room. He drained his beer, and left. Reaching the elevators, Monroe saw Vince watching him from the restaurant entrance, pointing his cell phone at him, and he knew Vince had taken his picture. The doors opened, and he got on, pressing the close door button. As they started to shut, he observed two uniformed officers enter the lobby. Once the doors were closed, he pressed several of the floor buttons. At the third floor, he got off and headed for the stairwell. He ran down the stairs to the lobby level and opened the door a few inches. Looking out, he saw one officer in the lobby.

Vince and the other officer were at the front counter, which was not visible from the elevators. The officer showed the clerk the photo on Vince's phone and asked if she recognized the picture. She replied she did and that the guy in the photo was a guest at the hotel.

"That's Mr. Monroe, Jack Monroe. He checked in this morning. Booked the room for three nights."

She provided them with the driver's license info and told them Monroe was in room 307.

The officer thanked her, and they returned to the lobby to await Louie's arrival. As they walked toward the other officer, Vince's phone chimed, indicating he had a message. It was from Louie, saying she was there and was near the entrance. Approaching the other officer, Vince saw Monroe walking quickly toward the hotel entrance. Vince alerted the two officers, and the three of them started moving toward Monroe. When they were forty feet away from him, one officer called out, "Jack Monroe, hold up, we want to talk to you."

Hearing that, Monroe ran to the doors, bursting through as Louie reached to open them. Louie was looking down at her phone and didn't see Monroe coming. He ran full into her, knocking her down, and continued to a car backed into a space in the lot. Jumping in, he started the engine, dropped it into drive, and punched the gas before the officers and Vince could reach him. Monroe drove out of the lot at a high speed, nearly losing control as he turned, and racing down the street before the officers could get to their squad cars. It took them fifteen seconds to run to their squad cars, and take off after him. By then, Monroe had made a few turns and was out of sight.

Vince was twenty feet from Monroe's car as it sped by in the lot. He had his cell phone in hand and managed to snap two photos. Running back to Louie, who was still on the ground holding her left shoulder and groaning in pain, he knelt and asked if she was OK.

"Does it look like I'm fucking OK?" she shouted. Taking a couple of deep breaths, she said, "Help me up, Vince. Let's get inside the lobby." Once she was settled in an easy chair, Vince directed the receptionist to call 9-1-1 and get an ambulance on the way.

The ambulance arrived five minutes later, along with three more squad cars, one being the shift supervisor. Louie's boss, Lieutenant Franklin, was on his way, having been called at home.

The two officers who had driven after Monroe returned to the hotel ten minutes later, reporting to the shift supervisor they had lost the car, and never got close enough to get the license plate number. After a quick area search, they returned, concerned about Louie's injury.

Vince called Maggie, who had retreated to their room, and told her what was going on. "I may be downstairs for a while. I'll come up as soon as I can."

While Louie was being examined by the paramedics, Vince approached Lieutenant Franklin, and told him he had a picture of Monroe, and the car. Vince showed him Monroe's picture--a clear, full frontal of his face--taken when Monroe was waiting for the elevator. Since the car was moving fast as it passed him, those two photos were blurred. There was enough detail to see it was a white, medium-sized, four-door sedan, and Vince added it was a Lexus. The license plate was not visible, but there was a decal in the lower right of the rear window. Lieutenant Franklin said he would have one of his photo techs try to clear it up as much as possible. Maybe they would get lucky and be able to see what the decal was. He asked Vince to text him the photos.

As the paramedics were loading Louie into the ambulance, Vince went over to check on her. Louie said she had a dislocated shoulder, and a few scrapes and bruises. She expected to be treated and released in a couple of hours, and said she'd call him later that day. Louie could tell Vince was upset. "You doing OK, Vince? You look angry."

"Yeah, I am. Sorry you were injured, Louie. I wish I had done things different, gotten closer before confronting him. I might have been able to keep him from running."

"No worries. You were doing exactly what I asked you to do--not get directly involved. I'll be fine. We'll find this guy, determine what his connection is to the accident, and what he was doing at your hotel."

Vince shook his head as the ambulance drove away, and then headed upstairs to his room.

Two hours later, Vince's cell rang. It was Louie.

"Hey, Louie. How're you feeling?"

"Sore. Got some killer drugs from the doc, so it's not too bad."

"What's the diagnosis? You going home, or are you stuck there tonight?"

"Family's on the way to pick me up. I'll be wearing a sling for the next week, though. The doctor was able to get the shoulder back in place easily, so no surgery is needed. My bruises and abrasions are minor. Lieutenant Franklin said I am on light duty until the sling comes off, so I'm supposed to be in the office instead of on the street."

"That sucks."

"Tell me about it. Between you and me, what do you think the chances are that's gonna happen?"

Vince laughed and said, "How does slim to none sound?"

It was Louie's turn to laugh. "I'm gonna go now. The family walked in, and the painkillers are making me sleepy. I'll be in touch tomorrow."

"Get some rest and try to do what the doc says, OK?"

"Yeah, right," Louie replied, and disconnected the call.

Maggie, listening to the call, asked, "How's she doing?"

"Gonna be fine. She'll be on light duty for a week and wearing a sling, but other than that there shouldn't be any complications. Louie's a tough lady."

"Good," Maggie replied. "You want to watch the Forty Niner's game? We should be able to see the second half."

"Absolutely," Vince replied, pulling a chair next to hers.

45

Chapter 7

Monroe had crossed into Florida two hours earlier, and was heading to Jacksonville when his cell rang. "Monroe here."

"Where are you?" the caller asked.

"Almost to Jacksonville. Why?"

"I need to see you. You remember where I am?"

"Yes. I'll be there is an hour. Can I ask why?"

"No. Get here as quickly as you can." The call was disconnected.

Monroe didn't like the sound of that. It worried him his boss was troubled enough to demand an immediate meeting. The original plan had been for him to get to town, check into a hotel, and call the next day. No urgency. He wondered why it had changed.

As he neared the abandoned warehouse where his boss was waiting, Monroe phoned and said he'd be there in ten minutes. Pulling to the side of the road, he opened the glove box, took out a Walther PPK .380 pistol, and pulled the slide back an inch to confirm there was a cartridge in the receiver. It was his weapon of choice because his PPK was the same model used by James Bond in all the movies, and Monroe liked the mystique attached to the weapon.

Parking fifty feet from the warehouse entrance, he exited the car, placing the pistol in his waistband near his right hip. There were two men in ill-fitting suits standing on each side of the door, one blonde, and the other dark haired and a few inches taller. They turned toward him as he started walking. The blonde was wearing an ear-bud and speaking quietly into a small walky-talky. He put it in his coat pocket when done. Placing his hand under his coat where a shoulder holster would be, he watched Monroe approach. The other taller man had pulled his coat back from his hip, and Monroe saw a large, black, semi-auto pistol in a holster. The second man rested his hand on the butt of the gun, also watching as Monroe approached.

Monroe slowed his stride, wary of the men's behavior. Suspecting he was going to be attacked, he stopped walking twenty feet away and called out, "Where's the boss?"

"Inside. We're to escort you in," the blonde said. "Come on up."

Monroe was more than a mere muscle-head street enforcer--he had brains and knew a set-up when he saw it.

"I don't think so. Call on your little radio and ask the boss to come out."

"Not gonna happen. Let's go. Now, Monroe," the blonde ordered.

"I think I'll pass on that. I'm going to leave now. Please tell the boss I'll call later."

Monroe started to back away toward his car, keeping watch on the blonde, and his hand on his weapon. It was obvious to him the blonde was the one in contact with the boss, and if anything was to happen, he would initiate it.

Monroe was almost to the car when he saw the blonde begin to pull his pistol from the shoulder holster. Pulling his own pistol from his waistband, he and the blonde leveled their guns at each other at the same time. Monroe was a little quicker in pulling the trigger, firing four rounds. The blond fired at almost the same time, getting off three shots before reacting to being hit by Monroe's bullets. Clutching his stomach and dropping the gun, he stared at Monroe in shock, and began to fall.

Monroe turned toward the other man, saw he had his gun out and pointed at him. Before he could bring his own weapon to bear, the dark-haired man pulled the trigger. The first bullet hit Monroe in the thigh. The second hit his chest, destroying his heart as it passed through it, killing him instantly.

Joey was pacing in the living room, his thoughts in turmoil.

I wonder if they suspect anything. If they ever found out about my involvement, it would destroy the family. Stupid, stupid, stupid. How did I let them drag me in? Tears rolled down his cheeks as he realized what he had done, how he had been used. His grief was almost overpowering.

I shouldn't have told them all that stuff about dad. I thought it was a friendly conversation. I should have realized it wasn't when they brought out the drugs and whiskey. I'm so sorry, dad, I didn't know they would kill you.

Joey quietly left and went up to his bedroom, wondering if he should tell Steve, or Vince. Pacing the floor and thinking for an hour didn't result in a decision. Joey was too frightened of what would happen to him if he admitted what he had done--the family hating him, getting arrested, going to jail--all made him more restless and jittery. Joey did come to one decision--he snorted two lines of cocaine. An hour later, the effects were wearing off, and Joey had decided not to say anything.

Joey did think about taking one of the pistols, though. It made sense, what was written on the note, and he knew the threat to the family was real. A druggie friend overheard a conversation at the seedy bar they frequented, and called to tell Joey about the threats. Joey then wrote the warning on his laptop, printed it out, and put it on Steve's windshield. He feared the next victim on the list would be him, since he knew who was there when they talked about his dad, and could provide enough information for the police to track them down.

Not a good idea. I'll disappear for a while, until this mess blows over.

Joey headed downstairs to the study and walked in. Interrupting them, he said, "I need some cash, Steve."

"OK. How much? What do you need it for?"

"A thousand, for now. I need to get away for a while. This getting to be too much for me."

"Don't do that, Joey. Stay here. We can look out for each other."

"No, Steve, I'm going. Nothing you say will change my mind."

"You're sure about this?"

"Yeah. Just get the money, OK?"

"All right." Turning to Vince, Steve said, "I'll be back in a couple of minutes." Lowering his voice, he said, "Talk to him."

After Steve walked out, Vince said, "Don't leave, Joey. I don't think it's a good idea. The threat left on Steve's car is for real. You would be much safer here, with Steve and I, and armed." Vince walked over to him and put his hand on Joey's shoulder. "C'mon, Cousin, stay with us. Together we can protect each other."

"Stay with us? Are you moving in here?"

"Yes. I've extended my stay for a week, and after I get Maggie to the airport on Wednesday, I'll be coming here."

Joey hung his head and said, "I can't, Vince. I'll feel safer on my own."

Steve returned to the study and glanced at Vince, who was shaking his head no. "Here's the money, Joey. When are you leaving?"

"Soon."

Steve walked to his brother, handed him an envelope with the cash. "You need anything else, call me. If you won't change your mind, then be careful," Steve said.

Chapter 8

Vince and Maggie were at the Outback Steakhouse, waiting for Steve, Barbara, and Joey to show up for dinner. Vince looked at his watch and saw it was 6:20.

"They're twenty minutes late."

"Relax, cowboy," Maggie said. "They'll be here soon."

Vince had chosen the Outback for the simple reason it was his favorite restaurant at home. "I'm ordering a Bloomin' Onion. Can't wait any longer." Maggie smiled and shook her head.

Vince waved the server over, placed the order, and as the server left to get the appetizer started, the others came in.

Besides Steve, his wife, and Joey, there was a young woman with them. She looked to be in her mid-twenties, had long blonde hair, and a shapely figure. Dressed in a low-cut, form fitting red top, skin-tight levis, and black half-boots, she made an eye-catching entrance. As they approached the table, Maggie leaned over and whispered to Vince, "It's rude to stare, so pop your eyes back in your head."

"Hey Vince," Steve said. "Hope you don't mind, but Joey brought a date with him."

"That's fine," Vince said. "The more the merrier."

Maggie chuckled, and muttered to Vince, "The more the merrier? You're pathetic."

"Thanks, Vince," Joey said, as they sat. "This is Janice."

"Nice to meet you, Janice. I'm Vince, and this is my wife, Maggie."

"Sorry we're late," Steve said, "but I got a call from Lieutenant Franklin as we were leaving."

"Franklin?" Vince asked. "What did he have to say?"

"Three hours ago, a Port Wentworth Police Officer saw a white Lexus sedan parked on the shoulder of Highway 25. He stopped to check it, and it took off, leading him on a high-speed chase."

"I know where Port Wentworth is," Vince said. "A couple of hours south of us, near the South Carolina border."

"That's right. Lieutenant Franklin told me the officer called for help, and a couple of state troopers joined the chase."

Vince interrupted, "Did they get it stopped before it could cross into South Carolina?"

"No, the officers called the chase off. Franklin said it was getting too dangerous to continue."

Vince asked, "Isn't there an active BOLO for the car?"

"I think the PD put one out before they left the hotel."

"I wonder why the officer wasn't aware of it. I'll give Louie a call in the morning. She's probably got more info, and might be willing to share it."

Vince picked up his menu, opened it, and said, "Our server will be back in a bit. I'm having my favorite, the prime rib, medium rare."

They enjoyed their dinner together, talking about their jobs, favorite movies, and recent vacation trips. During the conversation, Vince noticed Joey seemed distracted. At times, he would look around the restaurant as if he was expecting someone. He picked at his food, leaving half of his steak uneaten. Steve noticed, too, and said, "Everything OK, Brother? Is your dinner all right?"

"What? Oh, yeah, it's fine," Joey answered. "I'm not very hungry. My stomach's been bothering me lately."

Vince thought Joey was still unsettled over his father's death. It's not something easily dealt with.

After finishing their coffee, they said their goodnights, and went their separate ways.

The next morning, Maggie called for room service, ordering coffee and the continental breakfast for two while Vince phoned Louie. After hearing Louie was very sore, though feeling better, he said, "I heard a Port Wentworth officer got in a chase with a vehicle matching our subject's car."

"That's right. Called it off when the speed topped ninety. It was getting too hazardous."

"I gather he wasn't aware of the want on the car." It wasn't a question.

"Can't blame him, though," Louie replied. "The car took off before he could get the plate, and he never got close enough to read it during the pursuit. As far as he knew, it was a suspicious auto."

"Damn, that's too bad."

"Yeah, I think if we ID the car and Monroe's real name, it would be the break we need. I'm certain this case is not an accident--it's a homicide."

"Have you told anyone else your suspicions?"

"No, for the simple reason it would be handed off to the homicide guys."

"You'll have to tell them soon."

"I will, but first I've got to convince my boss to let me work with the homicide crew."

"Think he will?" Vince asked.

"I think so. Franklin's done it before, and he's a pretty level-headed guy."

"I hope so. You know more about this case than anyone. Your boss would be crazy not to have you continue. By the way, any results in identifying Monroe? Did the picture I took help?"

"Not yet. No one in the department recognizes him. He may not be a local, or even from Georgia."

"You know what I don't understand?" Vince asked.

"What?"

"Why was Monroe watching me? Seems he, or whoever who hired him, would be better served keeping an eye on you and the other investigators."

"That's a question I had, too. More importantly, who is Monroe reporting to?"

"I'm sure you are doing a check on people my uncle put in prison. Anyone jump out as being particularly pissed at him? Could it be a family member of a convict?"

"Anything's possible. There's a long list of potential suspects who hate Anthony. He's been at this a long time, and we're working our way through it. It's a slow process."

Vince said, "I'm due to go home in two days, but I'm going to extend my stay for another week. I need to know for sure if Uncle Anthony was murdered. Maybe my staying will help break the case. I'm sure whoever is orchestrating this knows when I'm supposed to leave and might be worried why I didn't."

"We'll see." Clearing her throat, Louie said, "I think we can benefit from your help. A fresh set of eyes from someone without any connection to APD could be a benefit. Now, I know Lieutenant Franklin would not want you to get involved, so I'm not going to ask. I'll keep you updated on the investigation, and there may be times I'll ask you to do a small task or two. Are you interested?"

Vince smiled and said, "Absolutely. What kind of 'tasks' are you talking about?"

"Perhaps interviewing potential witnesses, or conducting surveillance."

"Happy to help. I'm assuming Monroe's room was searched?"

"Yep. Not much there--only a few articles of clothing."

"Any prints found?"

"Surprisingly, no. Looks like he was careful about what he touched, and it appears he wiped down the surfaces. There was only a new toothbrush, still in the packaging, clothes, no hairbrush-- nothing that could provide DNA. The crime scene techs vacuumed the floor and bed before housekeeping could destroy evidence. Maybe they'll get lucky and find an errant hair, or get the DNA from the clothes."

"Jesus," Vince exclaimed, "We need a break--a small piece of evidence, or a bit of luck. The case is going nowhere fast."

"I know. It's frustrating the hell out of me," Louie replied. "I've even had an investigator try running down the credit card used to pay for the room. It was a Visa card issued ten days ago to a Tom Anderson through South State Bank here in Augusta. The room booking was the first charge on the card, and I'd be willing to bet it would never have been paid. The address on the account comes back to the Masters Cinema movie theater. So far, a dead end there."

"Did the bank mail it to Anderson?"

"No, Anderson came to the bank to pick it up. The investigator is going to view the CCTV from the bank later today. We should be able to get a look at this Tom Anderson. I'll call you, if you want to take a look at it with me."

"That's great. Thanks. Let's keep our fingers crossed. Whoever this Anderson, or Monroe is, he's got to have a rap sheet and prints on file."

Later that afternoon, Vince and Maggie met Steve and Barbara in the hotel lobby, and while the women headed to the spa, the men went to the restaurant for lunch.

"How are you guys doing?" Vince asked.

"We're OK. I'm dealing with dad's estate, the house, and his life insurance. Thanks to my mom's life insurance the house is paid off, and dad was able to save money. Then there's his life insurance--a half a million. Joey and I are the only heirs and will split the estate."

"Are you still working in accounting?" Vince asked.

"Yeah, at the corporate headquarters of Brookfield Properties. Been promoted a couple of times. Now I'm the finance manager."

"Good for you. How about Joey? What's he doing these days?"

"Ah, Joey. He's working as the manager of a tire shop. Joey has a problem keeping a job. Poor guy can't seem to find what he wants."

"I wondered about that ever since I found out he was living with his dad."

"Joey's had a problem the last few years with alcohol and drugs. Dad's put him in rehab three times. He comes out clean and sober, but it never lasts--the longest time was a couple of years ago. Lasted nine months before falling off the wagon. I don't think he ever got over our mother's death."

"I know he's never been married. What about girlfriends?" Vince asked.

"There's been a few in his life, but they never stay for long. His drinking and drugging drove them away. Joey gets mean when he's loaded. You didn't know, but he's been arrested twice for drunk driving, and once for assault."

"Damn, sounds like Junior Henderson. Spend any time in jail?"

"No. Because he's a Torelli, the cops and district attorney were very lenient. He was put on probation for the assault, and lost his driver's license from his second DUI."

Vince started to ask a question, but Steve stopped him by raising his hand, palm toward Vince. "Before you ask, the answer is no. Dad did not exert any influence in Joey's cases."

Vince noticed Steve seemed distracted and nervous. "You OK, Steve? You seem upset over something."

Steve slid his chair closer to Vince, looked around the room, lowered his voice, and said, "I'm worried about the family, Vince."

"Really? How so?"

"I haven't told the police about this, but yesterday I found an envelope on my car, under the windshield wiper, with my name on it. I opened it and found it was a warning."

"What exactly did it say?" Vince asked, concern etched on his face.

"It said people were coming after us and that dad was the first."

"That's all? I assume it wasn't signed."

"You're right. Dad sometimes got threats, though they were usually in person from defendants after sentencing them. Once in a while he would get a threat through the mail. He told us not to worry about it, said it usually was a con's family pissed at him for putting their son, father, uncle, brother, sister, whoever, in prison. Nothing ever happened, but this is different. Dad was mentioned in the message, but the threat is directed at the family."

"Do you have the note?"

"Yeah. I kept it. I'm the only one who's seen it, or handled it. I put it in a sandwich bag."

"Good. You should call Louie and let her know. She'll probably send it off to the lab for processing for prints or DNA."

"All right. I'll call after lunch."

"I think you should treat this threat seriously. Start paying attention to your surroundings when you are away from the house. Keep an eye out for people who look out of place, or seem to show an unusual interest in you. Pay attention to cars behind you. If you think you're being followed, make a couple of random turns and see if they follow. Simple measures like those will make you safer."

"What should I do if I think I'm being followed?" Steve asked.

"Take a good look at the car so you can describe it in detail. In particular, look for damage, window stickers, peeling paint--anything that would make the car stand out, and identifiable. The license plate would be best, but may be the hardest to get. Be careful, and watchful. Do you have a handgun?"

"I don't, but dad"s are locked up in the safe."

"Are you familiar with them? Did your dad teach you how to handle them, and shoot?"

"Yes, when we were teenagers, Dad took Joey and me to the police range several times. After teaching us the basics, he had one of his friends in the police department, a range master, set up a combat course. It was good training, and fun. After that, we went a couple of times a year to practice."

"Good. To be safe, you should take it with you when you leave the house. Do you think you should tell Barbara about the threat, and about carrying the gun?"

"I'll tell her about the threat--Joey, too--but not about carrying the pistol. She is very anti-gun, and wouldn't be happy with me carrying it."

"OK. Let Joey know what I told you. We'll all get together and go over more personal safety tips. Later today good for you?"

"Sounds good. Did you bring your pistol with you, Vince?"

"No. Had no reason to. Now, I wish I had."

"I can loan you one of Dad's, if you want. He has holsters and extra magazines, too."

"Alright. Can I get it when I come by the house later?"

"That's fine. How about four? It's better Barbara isn't around, and she has a two-hour hair appointment at 3:30."

"Four it is," Vince said, as Maggie and Barbara walked in.

Chapter 9

Vince was in his room, watching the Atlanta Hawks take on the Miami Heat when his cell rang. He saw the caller was Louie and answered it right away. "Hey, Louie. What's up?"

"We caught a break in the case."

Vince sat up straighter and said, "That's good news. What happened?"

"I got a call from Jacksonville PD in Florida. There was a shooting in an industrial area a couple of hours ago. One dead, and from blood at the scene, it appears one more person was shot. Wanna guess who the dead guy is?"

"Jack Monroe," Vince exclaimed.

"Yep."

"That's good news. Has his real identity been determined yet?"

"Not yet. They're running his prints, and are distributing his photo throughout the department on the off chance one of the cops will recognize him."

"How did they know to call you? The BOLO on the car, and him?"

"Yep. Seems to me whoever hired him didn't want to chance Monroe getting caught, and maybe spilling his guts to the cops."

"Makes sense to me. Any ideas who he is?"

"Maybe a private investigator, or a freelance enforcer. Might even be with one of the organized crime families in Florida."

"I'd bet Monroe was a freelancer. I can't see a crime boss knocking off one of his own for that reason. They get his DNA?"

"Yeah, but you know how long it takes to get the report back. Hopefully, his DNA is on file."

"The prints and photo are our best chance to ID him," Vince said. "What about his car?"

"It's been impounded and is being processed for evidence as we speak."

"Good. Making progress. Say, did Steve call you today?"

"Yes. Told me about receiving the threatening note. He dropped it off a little while ago. We're processing it for the usual stuff."

"I told Steve to take it seriously, and he said he would. I know my uncle has a couple of weapons registered to him, and a concealed carry permit. Steve said he will be carrying one of the pistols for self-protection. I told him to see about getting an emergency concealed permit. I didn't tell him not to carry it in the meantime."

"OK. Umm, I didn't hear that last part, and let's keep it that way."

"Obviously, I am allowed to carry concealed in California, but I know Georgia doesn't reciprocate with us. However, federal law allows current officers to carry in all fifty states, regardless of state or local laws. I'm telling you this because I'll be carrying a firearm, one of my uncles."

"That's fine. I'm aware of the law. I wouldn't advertise it if I were you."

"I don't plan to. I'll keep it low key."

"Do me a favor. When you get the weapon, give me a call and provide the make, model, and serial number. I'll run it to show it's legally registered, so I can say I checked it out properly if I have to."

"You got it, Louie."

"OK. Gotta go. I'm gonna call Steve next, and I'll keep you updated on Monroe's ID. Talk to you later."

Vince arrived at his uncle's house a few minutes after four that afternoon. Steve ushered him in and took him to Anthony's study, where he had laid out three firearms, all semi-auto weapons, in their holsters.

"Here's Dad's guns. I'm taking the Smith and Wesson .40 caliber, since that's the one I trained with. There's a Beretta 92FS nine-millimeter, and a Colt Commander .45 ACP. Your choice."

"I'll take the Colt. Can't beat it for pure stopping power."

"OK. There are two extra magazines and a box of ammo in the drawer."

"Thanks, Cousin. I feel better being armed. Did Louie call and tell you about Monroe?"

"She did. This whole thing is taking a very serious turn."

"I know," Vince replied, then asked, "Where's Joey?"

"He's not coming down. I couldn't convince him he should be armed. He doesn't believe we are in danger, even after telling him about Monroe's murder, and the threats. Joey said he'd keep a low profile and hide out somewhere until this all blows over." Steve paused, took a deep breath, and continued. "I think he's using again. I noticed his nervousness and lack of concentration a month ago. I asked if he was using, and he became belligerent with me. Joey yelled a few choice things and stormed out. I have no proof, but I've seen this behavior before when Joey was on drugs."

"Jesus. Would it help if I talked to him?"

"I don't think so. Joey can be pretty stubborn at times. I sure hope this decision doesn't come back to bite him on the ass."

"Me, too, Steve, me too."

Joey called Janice and asked her to pick him up, then threw clothes and toiletries in a satchel, grabbed his jacket, and headed downstairs to await her arrival. He could hear Steve and Vince talking, but wasn't able to make out what they were saying. Setting his bag by the front door, he went to the study and walked in. Interrupting them, he said, "I'm leaving now. I'll be in touch."

Vince said, "I still don't think it's a good idea. You would be better off here with Steve and I." Vince walked over to him and put his hand on Joey's shoulder. "C'mon, Cousin, stay with us."

"I can't, Vince."

Steve walked to his brother and hugged him. "You need anything else, call me," he said, as he broke the embrace.

Joey half-smiled, turned, and walked out.

Chapter 10

The next morning Vince and Maggie went to Steve's house, to help him and Barbara pack clothes and essentials, and escort them to Anthony's. They planned to stay there until the investigation was concluded and the killer was in custody, and it was safe to return to their house. Steve sent his eight-year-old-son and eleven-year-old daughter to stay with his best friend, for their protection, and Barbara would follow them later that day.

Vince was armed with the Colt .45. The gun felt good on his hip. He examined it closely. He removed the bullets from the magazines and reloaded them. The holster had a spare magazine holder, allowing him to have easy and quick access to two spares. *This is a much better weapon than the old, beat-up Colt 1911 .45 I carried in the army.*

After Steve and Barbara were settled, Barbara prepared lunch for them, and they retired to the dining room to eat. During the meal, there was little conversation.

Maggie broke the silence by asking, "You guys think all this preparation is necessary? It's like you're at the Alamo waiting for Santa Ana to show up."

Steve chuckled. "Good analogy, Maggie. One thing my dad always said was, 'You can never be too prepared.' Besides, you know what they say about the best-laid plans, don't you?"

Maggie replied, "Oh, God. I can sure tell you and Vince are related," making Vince and Steve laugh. "Vince must have told me a thousand times that a plan is perfect until it is put into action. Then it turns to shit."

"I don't think it was a thousand times, Maggie," Vince remarked, trying not to smile.

"OK, I'll admit you're right, Honey. It wasn't a thousand times." Turning to Barbara she said, "It was more like two thousand."

Their moods lightened, and they enjoyed the rest of their lunch. Vince and Maggie then left to pack up the hotel room. The plan was for them to check out the next morning and load their luggage in the rental car. Vince would drive to the airport, making sure he wasn't being followed, and drop Maggie and the bags off. He would tell her in a loud voice he was going to drop off the rental car and she was to go through the TSA security line, and he would meet her at the boarding gate, in case anyone was listening or watching.

In reality, Vince would return the car, remove a suitcase borrowed from Steve, packed with Vince's clothes, and pick up a different rental reserved earlier that morning. He would park it in the short-term lot, and walk to meet Maggie. By the time he got to the terminal, he would know whether he was being followed. If not, he would retrieve the new rental and drive to Anthony's, again taking measures to throw off a tail. If he was being followed, Vince would drive around until he lost the tail.

Wednesday morning, Vince and Maggie headed to the airport as planned. Vince made one unscheduled stop at a 7-11 store, ostensibly to pick up snacks and a bottle of water for their flight home. In reality, it allowed him to see if anyone was following him. A few minutes later he was back on the road to the airport. Vince was certain no one had tailed him, and dropped Maggie at her terminal.

Vince exchanged the rentals, parked the new car, and walked the short distance to the terminal. He sat in a secluded area until Maggie's plane lifted off, then walked back to the rental car and drove to Steve's.

Vince called Louie to let her know he was staying at Steve's.

"Glad you called, Vince. I got word from Jacksonville PD. Is Steve there?"

"He's in the other room. I can get him, if you want."

"Get him in there with you. Joey, too. I want them to hear this."

"OK, but Joey's not here. He elected to hide out for a while. Hold on for a second." Vince yelled out, "Steve, Louie's on the phone and has some info for us."

"Be right there," Steve replied.

Louie said, "Put the phone on speaker so he can hear."

"All right. Here he comes." Vince pushed the speaker button and said, "Can you hear me?"

"Yeah. As I said, I got a call from the Jacksonville detective lieutenant working the shooting of our mysterious Mister Monroe. They've identified him through prints. Seems he's a Jacksonville local. The LT said they've been looking for him for a few months, as a person of interest in two homicides."

"Is he connected?" Vince asked.

"Not that they know. Word is he's a freelancer. Any dirty job that needed to be handled, he was the go-to guy. His name is Mulvaney, Michael Mulvaney, but he goes by Mickey."

"That's good news," Steve said. "Any chance they'll find out who hired him to follow Vince around?"

"It's not likely. Jacksonville is looking into his financials, utilities, and phone companies, hoping to get his address from one of them. I'm hoping he didn't use a fraudulent name with the utilities. They're checking the Monroe and Mulvaney names, and putting the squeeze on their informants for info on him."

"Sounds good," Vince replied. "You'll find out all that stuff soon enough."

"I'd like to know how Mulvaney knew you were here, and who hired him to follow you. More importantly, why was he following you?"

Steve answered, "Maybe because you're a semi-famous homicide detective and he, she, or they, are afraid you would figure all this out."

Vince grinned and said, "Oh, come on, Steve."

"No kidding, Vince. Last year, the Augusta Chronicle did an article on Dad and the family, and your name was prominently featured. The article described your trip to Tennessee to arrest that Albert Jackson guy, and how you were kidnapped by him. Remember, I sent you a copy?"

"Yeah, but my part wasn't 'prominently' featured. It was barely a paragraph long, and that guy was Aldon Jackson."

Steve chuckled and said, "I know. I'm jerking your chain a bit."

Louie broke in, "OK, guys. Get serious. It's an important issue. You have any idea, Vince?"

"Only one--this appears to be a kind of vendetta against the family, and whoever is doing it, felt the need to include me."

Janice drove Joey to the Rodeway Inn at Grovetown, a small town outside Augusta, where Joey checked in for a week. He'd stayed there before and was familiar with the rooms, all identically decorated. A brown and yellow carpet covered the floor, the walls painted a light yellow, and the bed centered against the wall. There were two prints of landscape paintings attached to the walls, and a small desk and chair by the back window. A dresser against the wall at the foot of the bed held a TV, and a phone and clock radio were on a small nightstand next to the bed. Just inside the entrance to the room was the bathroom door. The room was clean and neat, and after settling in, Joey left and walked across the street to a pizza place to buy a large pizza and beer. After he left, Janice waited a few minutes and made a call on her cell.

"We're in Grovetown at the Rodeway Inn. He doesn't suspect a thing. Joey thinks I care for him, and wants me to stay with him a couple of days." She listened for a minute, then replied, "I can't stand the little prick. He's usually whacked out on drugs or alcohol, or both."

Janice listened for another couple of minutes, interjecting a yes or no now and then, as she paced the floor. Lighting a cigarette, she took a deep drag and said, "Yeah. The cousin is on the way back to San Francisco. Yes, I'm sure. My boyfriend waited for him to show up at the airport, saw him drop off his wife, then drive toward the rental return. Ten minutes later, Torelli was back and went into the terminal. He watched the entrance until after the departure time of Torelli's plane. He's gone. I, for one, am glad. I sure didn't want that SFPD homicide guy here getting involved, especially since it's his family we're after. Could be the one that might figure out Joey's been a mule for you, running your drugs all over the county. For now, the cops think it was a hit and run accident. Yes, Boss, I know. I want it to stay that way, too. By the way, I'll get the bag from the desk clerk while Joey's gone. There should be enough junk in it to keep Joey drugged up for a few days."

Done with the call, she walked to the hotel office and asked if a package had been left for Joey. The clerk retrieved it and handed it to her. "I didn't say anything about it when you checked in, like I was told, and waited until you came back to get it. You got my money?"

Janice reached in her pocket and pulled out a roll of bills. Peeling off five twenties, she handed them to him. "Bet that's the easiest hundred you ever made. I got another hundred for you if you keep your mouth shut about us being here, should anyone, cops included, come 'round looking for us. It's yours when we check out."

"Yes, Ma'am," the clerk replied, grinning ear to ear.

Joey passed out on the bed after drinking five beers and taking the two 15 mg Oxycodone tablets Janice gave him. When she was sure he was out of it, she took the opportunity to call her boss again.

"He's sleeping. Yeah, two pills plus the beer was enough. What a light-weight. When do you want him to OD? It'll be easy enough--I can crush a few pills and put them in his beer, then have him take more tablets. This coming weekend? OK. Can I ask why then, and not tomorrow?"

Janice listened as the boss explained that Steve was next on the hit list. "He's the smarter of the two, and the more dangerous son. Once he's dead, Joey will be an easy mark."

"When's the hit on Steve?" Janice asked.

"Don't worry about it. You'll know when it's done."

"I'm supposed to be paid for this--five grand, right?"

"Five grand, yes."

"Still want me to dump his body in the St. Johns River?"

"Yes, off the Buckman Bridge, but not too far from shore. More 'gators are there than in the middle. If he floats around for a day or two, they'll get him. His body will never be found."

"Why not leave him at the hotel?" Janice asked.

"Are you that dumb? Didn't the clerk see you, talk to you?"

"Oh, yeah. I wasn't thinking."

"That's the problem. I'll be in touch. Don't do anything until I call."

Steve and Vince were sitting on the patio drinking a beer, talking. It was a warm, sunny day, not a leaf stirring. The buzzing and chirps of the insects seemed to float on the air. It was a calm, relaxing day.

"Why would anyone want to come after the family, Steve?" Vince asked. "I could understand going after your dad, but threatening the family makes no sense."

"Beats me. Joey and I have nothing to do with Dad's work."

"Something's not right. I still wonder why I was being followed. Someone talked to the wrong people, telling them I was coming to Augusta, and that I was a cop."

"Had to be someone close to the family. Maybe they read the newspaper article from last year and assumed you would be here for Dad's funeral."

Vince paused, sighed, and said, "I don't think that's it. I hate to say it, but I think it was someone in the family."

"Really?"

"Look, I think I was being followed from the moment Maggie and I landed here. I know I saw Mulvaney at the hotel an hour after we checked in, and he was at Uncle Anthony's house the day of the funeral."

"I don't recall seeing him. Was he at the funeral, or at the reception?"

"I didn't see him at the church or the burial, but I remember pointing him out to Maggie at the reception and telling her I saw him at the hotel. I thought he was a friend in town for the services."

Steve thought for a moment. "Joey and I talked to my aunt and uncle, and some of the cousins. I don't remember, but we may have mentioned you were coming in." Shaking his head, he continued, "I can't imagine any of them being involved with criminals. They're regular people, they're family, probably don't even have a parking ticket on their records."

"Sorry to ask, Steve, but what about Joey? You said you thought he was using again. Could he have talked to the wrong people?"

"I don't think so. Even if he did, they would be users like him, or low-level dealers. Not the kind of people who would come before Dad."

"Did you ever suspect Joey was more deeply involved with the drug dealers than just being a customer?"

"No, I didn't. The last couple of years we didn't see each other a lot. I was busy with my family and work, and any free time I had was spent with them. Joey would come over for BBQs, birthday parties, and the holidays, you know, the usual family stuff, but I don't think I saw him more than once a month. You think it could be Joey?"

Vince got up from the chair and walked to the end of the patio. The lush, green lawn stretched out in front of him a hundred feet. He thought for a moment, turned to Steve, and asked, "Do you know where Joey is staying?"

"At a motel somewhere outside Augusta. That's what he's done in the past."

"Does he have a favorite place to hide?"

"I don't think so. He spreads it out all around Augusta and the county." Thinking for a second, Steve said, "There is one place I know for sure he's stayed in the past. The last time Joey took off, he was gone for two weeks, and when he came back to Dad's, I found a receipt in his jacket. It was from the Rodeway Inn. I asked him about it, and he told me he liked the place--it was clean, comfortable, and not expensive."

"Where is it located?"

"I don't know. He didn't mention where, other than it was out of town, and I didn't think to ask. I've called him, but his cell goes directly to voice-mail. I left a few messages."

"Let's see if we can find him. I'm worried about him, Steve."

"I am, too. I'll get my laptop."

Five minutes later, they learned there were three Rodeways in Augusta. Steve called them, but none had rented a room to Joseph Torelli.

Steve said, "I wonder if he registered in a different name?"

"Maybe," Vince answered, "But an ID is needed to check in." Vince thought for a moment. "What's Janice's last name? Maybe she rented the room."

"Hmm, didn't think of that. Her last name is Roberts. I'll call them back."

No reservation was found in her name.

"OK. Let's try looking outside Augusta," Steve suggested. Running a second broader search for Rodeway Inns near Augusta, Steve found two in the city of Grovetown, a few miles west of Augusta. He brought up the websites of the two and said, "I'll call this one, you call that one," pointing out the phone number.

Neither place had a guest under Torelli or Roberts checking in during the last two days.

"Looks like we need to drive out there," Vince said. "Got a recent photo of Joey we can take with us?"

"Yeah. You think he registered under a different name?"

"Probably. I'm sure he paid cash, and probably slipped the clerk fifty bucks not to check their ID's."

"I'll get the photo. It's about fifteen miles from here and shouldn't take more than a half-hour."

"Don't forget your pistol."

Chapter 11

Steve and Vince were no more than a mile into their drive when Vince spotted a gray van behind them in his side-view mirror, three cars back. That, by itself, wasn't what made him suspicious. There was nothing about the van leading him to believe it was following them. What did alert him was that he saw a gray van parked on the corner of a side-street a hundred yards from Anthony's house, with at least two people in it.

"Turn right at the next corner, Steve."

"What? Why?" Steve asked, puzzled by the request.

"I think we're being followed. See the gray van a couple of cars behind us?"

Looking in the rearview mirror, Steve said, "Yeah, so?"

"I saw them parked on the side-street near the house. There're at least two people in it. It seems odd they would now be behind us. Make the turn."

Steve turned and continued driving at the speed limit, glancing at the mirror every five seconds and saw the van make the turn.

"They turned."

"I know. Let's take the next left. Speed up a bit and after you do, drive faster."

"OK." Steve chuckled and remarked, "I should've let you drive."

Vince kept an eye on the van as they took the next side-street, and Steve stepped on the gas. A car was backing out of a driveway ahead of him, and Vince told him, "Go around it."

Steve yanked the wheel to the left and swerved, barely missing the car's back end. The driver must have seen him coming and slammed on the brakes, blasting his horn at the same time. The car came to a stop partially blocking the road, causing the van to slow and go up on the opposite curb to get around it.

"Step on it," Vince said, as he shifted in his seat, released his seatbelt, and drew his weapon. "Turn left again, then right the first chance you have. Pull over to the curb as soon as you can. Go, go, go. When you stop, I'll jump out. You stay in the car, with your weapon ready."

"But ..." Steve started to say.

"But nothing. Trust me, and do what I ask," Vince said sharply.

Steve made the turn, accelerated, then turned right a short block down, his tires squealing, and immediately pulled over to a stop.

Vince opened his door, half rolled and half fell out, stayed low, and ran to the car parked behind them. He crouched down between it and their car, and peered around the headlight. A few seconds later, the van came around the corner.

As it approached, Vince readied himself, and at the proper time, jumped up with his pistol pointing at the van over the hood of the car.

"Stop right there or I'll shoot," he shouted.

Taken by surprise, the driver braked hard and came to a stop ten feet from Vince.

"Hands where I can see them. Now," He commanded.

Both the men slowly raised their hands. The passenger was holding something in his right hand that Vince couldn't clearly see, due to the sun's glare on the windshield. Vince moved quickly to the passenger side where the window was down, still covering the men with his pistol.

"Easy, Inspector," the passenger said, slowly moving his right hand toward Vince, displaying a police badge and ID.

"You guys cops?"

As he slowly handed Vince his ID out the window, the passenger said, "Yeah. Believe it or not, we're supposed to be protecting you."

"Well, you're doing a fine fucking job. Did Louie set this up?"

"She did. Didn't she call you?"

Having checked the ID, Vince handed it back and holstered his weapon. He called out to Steve to let him know everything was OK. Steve waved at him and got out of the car, also holstering his weapon.

Walking to the van, Steve exclaimed, "Son of a bitch, Vince. I'm shaking like a leaf. What's with these guys following us?"

"Meet Detectives Steney and Borden, our guardian angels."

"Are you kidding me?"

"Louie set it up, and was supposed to call us. I think she would've called you."

"I didn't hear from...wait a minute. My cell rang at the house when I went to get Joey's picture. I was in a rush and didn't answer it." Steve took out his cell and dialed up his messages. He listened a moment, then said, "Aw, shit. I have a message from her. She called to let us know there would be two plainclothes dicks in a gray van following us around, as a precaution."

Turning to the two detectives, he grinned, "Sorry, guys."

The passenger, Steney, replied, "No worries, shit happens, right? By the way, how'd you get on to us?"

Vince answered, "I saw the van parked by the house, with you two in it, as we drove by. Didn't think much about it until I spotted you following us."

"We thought you knew we were there." Looking at Borden, Steney said, "We were wondering why you were making all those turns. Surprised the hell out of us."

"Sorry for the mix-up. Can't be too careful."

"Where you headed?"

Steve said, "To find my brother, and try to convince him to come home."

"You know where he is?"

"We think so. He may be at a hotel in Groveland, a Rodeway Inn."

Borden asked, "Want us to go with you?"

Steve turned to Vince and said, "Vince?"

"Sure. Would be nice to have back-up. Stay a few cars behind us and watch for a tail."

"Will do. By the way, Vince," Steney said, "Nice move, setting us up like that and getting the drop on us."

As Steve was driving to Grovetown, Vince kept his eyes on the traffic. He was able to relax a bit, knowing the two detectives were behind him. They parked in the check-in driveway at the first Rodeway, and the van parked in the lot. Steney and Borden remained in the van while Vince and Steve went into the lobby.

At the counter, Steve rang the bell, and a minute later the clerk came out. They saw he was a short, plump, balding guy in his mid-thirties, wearing thick, horned-rim glasses. His white dress shirt was wrinkled, and had food stains on the front, as did his tie. He needed a shave, and what hair he had needed trimming.

"Good day, gentlemen. How can I help you?"

Vince placed Joey's picture on the counter and asked, "You recognize this guy? He would have checked in yesterday."

The clerk looked at the photo briefly and replied, "No, I don't. He's not a guest here. Why?"

"He's family, and we want to talk with him. Do you work dayshift all the time?"

"Uh, yes, yes I do," the clerk stammered, "Why?"

"Could he have checked in when you were off? Maybe one of the other clerks took care of him."

"I, I, I suppose that's possible." He swallowed hard, and a line of sweat sprouted on his forehead.

Vince and Steve looked at each other. "You're sure you haven't seen him?" Steve asked.

"Pretty sure. Are you guys cops?"

Vince flashed his badge and said, "I am. Why?"

"Uh, no reason. Well, then, if there's nothing else I can do, you have a good day." The clerk walked to the back room, and they returned to the car.

"Drive out to the street and let me out. Park out of sight of the office and wait."

"What're you gonna do, Vince?"

"I want to see what the clerk does when he thinks we're gone. I won't be long."

Vince was watching the lobby from the parking lot, standing behind a truck. The clerk was not visible, and Vince took the time to look over the cars in the lot. He didn't recognize any, and turned his attention to the office as the clerk walked out, scanned the lot, and made his way to one of the rooms. Knocking on the door, he waited for a minute, then knocked again. When no one answered the door, he went back to the office. Vince went to the room and saw it was number 114.

After getting in the car, he told Steve to head for the other two Rodeway Inns. As they drove, Vince said, "If we have no luck at the other two, let's come back here. That guy sure seemed nervous, and he barely looked at Joey's photo before denying he was there."

"I noticed, too. He's lying. He couldn't get rid of us soon enough."

"We'll let him calm down while we check the other motels. If we come back, I'll bet he shits himself when he sees us."

Laughing, Steve said, "That's a sucker's bet."

What they didn't know was the clerk had called Joey's room after he saw their car leave, and getting no answer, left a message. He thought to knock on the door in case they were sleeping. *This is something they would want to know, and maybe there will be another fifty in it for me.*

After checking the other two hotels, Vince and Steve decided to stop for a quick lunch. They pulled into a Chic-Fil-A, and were joined by Steney and Borden.

After eating, Vince looked at his watch. "Let's go back to the first hotel. It's been almost an hour. The clerk's calmed down by now, so let's go rattle his cage a bit."

When they arrived at the Rodeway Inn, Steve parked in the same place in front of the office. They saw the clerk at the counter, working on the computer. He looked up, smiling as they entered. When he saw it was Vince and Steve, the smile disappeared. "Oh. It's you. I already told you that guy and his girlfriend aren't here."

They looked at each other, and Steve leaned over the counter. "Girlfriend?" he asked. "We never mentioned my brother was with his girlfriend."

The clerk sputtered, gulped, and said, "You must have. Um, how else could I know that?"

Vince said to Steve, "You know what I really hate? People who lie to me. It angers me, and makes me want to break their nose." He turned to the clerk, who backed up two steps, sweating again. Drawing his gun, Vince slammed it flat down on the counter and said, "You wanna start telling us the truth, bucko?"

It was as if the flood gates burst open. The clerk, visibly terrified, began to talk, telling them Joey had checked in the previous day with a hot gal, and they had rented the room for a week. She paid him a hundred bucks to deny they were there, should anyone ask. He admitted he tried to warn them, but they must have left early this morning. He was in tears by the time he finished.

Vince and Steve listened without interrupting until the clerk ran out of things to say. The clerk was shaking, and breathing like he had run a marathon.

"You think he's telling us the truth, Vince?"

"Maybe part of it was true. Can I slap him around a bit, 'cause he pisses me off?"

The clerk, hearing this, said, "I'm sorry, I'm sorry. After you were gone, I left them a phone message you had been here looking for them. I thought they weren't in the room 'cause they didn't answer, but five minutes later, I hear a car peeling out of the lot. I saw it was their car. They're really gone, now. I swear."

Vince smiled at the clerk and said, "Now, that wasn't so hard, was it? And think of all the grief you avoided by telling the truth." Turning to Steve, he asked, "They left in Janice's car, right?"

"Yep. A gray Ford Focus. It should be in the registration book, right?" Turning to the clerk, Steve said, "Let me see it."

"Yes, Sir. I'll get it for you."

Vince copied down the make, color and license plate of Janice's car. "We're gonna go now, but if we have any more questions for you, we'll be back. I expect you to be truthful when we do."

"Of course, absolutely, Sir," the clerk stammered.

"Good. Give me the key to room 114. We wanna take a look through it."

After getting the key and a description of the car, which matched Janice's car, Vince holstered his pistol and walked out with Steve, pausing at the door, he turned and scowled at the clerk, who visibly wilted. With a growled, "I'll leave the key in the room," they left.

They found nothing to indicate where Joey and Janice had gone. The room was a mess--empty beer bottles and food containers littered the desk and floor. The bed was unmade, and a lid from a container of cheese puffs was over-flowing with cigarette butts. There were burn marks from cigarettes on the desk and dresser, and the air stunk of stale smoke.

"How the hell could they trash the room like this in one day?" Steve said. "What now, Vince?"

"Let's head back to the house. We'll keep calling him--hopefully, he'll call back soon."

"I hope so. Joey's vulnerable right now, and if he's using again, he won't be thinking straight."

"I'll call Louie when we get back. She can do a search of the nearby cell towers, and see if his phone pinged any of them. At least it will show he was in the area, and if any of the hits were after we went to the hotel, we'll know he still is. Maybe Louie can put out a BOLO for him."

"Good idea. I hope it works.

Chapter 12

In the pizza restaurant across the street from the hotel, Joey and Janice watched his brother and cousin through the front window as they went in the lobby, then to the room Joey had rented.

"What are they doing?" Janice asked.

"Don't know. Maybe searching the room for something. Whatever it is, take a look at the clerk." Janice could see him standing in front of the main door, looking toward their room. "He looks terrified." She chuckled, and said, "Whatever they said really upset him. He looks like he's gonna cry."

"We'll wait until they leave, then find another place to stay. Your car's parked around back, out of sight, so unless they drive around there, they won't know we're here."

"Why don't you want them to know where you are?"

"It's not that so much. I don't want whoever killed my father to know. I'm scared, because what I did makes me a big target, and I've put Steve and Vince in danger. I'm so ashamed, I don't think I could face them."

"What did you do?" Janice asked.

Joey looked at her, wringing his hands, as tears welled up in his eyes. Despite her dislike for him, Janice felt a pang of pity. She knew it was Joey who inadvertently provided the information that made the hit on the judge possible.

Janice placed her hand on Joey's shoulder and patted him gently.

"I need a jolt, Janice. You got any more coke?" He sniffled, then wiped his nose on his sleeve. "I miss my dad so much. I am so sorry for talking about his morning routine." Looking at her, he said, "You know that mule that works the area by the Jersey Bar?"

"Yeah. They call him Donkey, right?"

"That's him. One night a while back, I was drinking with him and another guy, doing a couple of lines. I got pretty wasted and don't remember much about what we talked about, but I do remember thinking it odd they were so interested in my dad's routine. I'm pretty sure I told them about his daily jogging, and they must have passed it on to the wrong people."

"You know who those 'wrong people' are?"

Wiping his tears away, he took a shuddering breath and said, "No idea."

Janice handed Joey a small baggie of white powder, and squeezed his shoulder. He put his hand over hers, half-smiled, and muttered, "Thanks. I'm going to the head. Be right back."

Janice knew who was going after the family, and why. A month earlier, her ex-boyfriend, Jeff Martin, showed up at her apartment with a proposition. If she would play babysitter to a guy for a couple of weeks, there was $5,000 in it for her.

"Who's the guy?"

"Joey Torelli. He's the son of Judge Anthony Torelli. You know who the judge is?"

"Name sounds familiar, but I don't think I know him. What's the judge got to do with anything?"

"You know my buddy, Sammy Peters? He married one of the Henderson girls. She's related to Morey Henderson--don't know how, but she's a distant relation. Might be a third cousin or something like that. Anyway, two years ago, Sammy and another guy got nabbed in an armed robbery of a little mom-and-pop deli. The cops arrived before they left, and the other guy took a couple of shots at them. They returned fire and Sammy was hit twice. He's now paralyzed from the waist down--he'll never walk again."

"That's too bad. Must be tough being in a wheelchair in jail."

"Tell me about it. That's not the worst part. Sammy never fired his gun, but one of the guy's bullets hit the owner's wife, killing her. The D.A. charged Sammy with the old lady's death under the felony murder rule."

Janice asked, "What's that?"

"It means if someone dies during a felony, like robbery, the robber can be charged with the death, even if he didn't kill them."

"That don't sound right."

"It's true. They charged Sammy and he got the death penalty. He's rotting on death row now. Judge Torelli was the one who sentenced him, even though Sammy's attorney pleaded with Torelli to show mercy, because of his condition. He ignored the pleas, and sentenced Sammy to death for the killing. Torelli added twenty-five years for the robbery, said Sammy didn't deserve mercy. The old lady died during the robbery that he was part of."

"Well, that sucks."

"That's not all. Sammy's mother had a heart attack and almost died when she learned of the verdict. One of his brothers went on a three-day drunken rage and attacked a cop with a knife. He was shot and killed. There's only one son left. The family was nearly wiped out, all because of the judge."

Janice lit a cigarette, took a deep drag, and didn't say anything, knowing it wasn't the judge's fault. She knew the Peters family, and was surprised they all lived this long without being killed or sent to prison.

"Is Morey Henderson involved in the judge's death? Did he put out the contract on the judge's sons?" Janice asked.

"No. Seems Mama Peters stashed away a chunk of money over the years. She's the one running it from her house in South Carolina. She's hired some local thugs to carry out the murders."

Janice believed Jeff. The few times she'd talked to her "Boss", it was always a woman. She began to realize Mama Peters was blaming the Judge, and by extension, his family, for her own failure as a mother. Janice felt the responsibility lay with her, and her dirt-bag sons, not with the judge, and began having second thoughts about her involvement. She felt bad for the Peters family, but they only had themselves to blame.

She pitied Joey, too, but for a different reason. He had nothing to do with the Peters' losses. She realized it was wrong to target him and his brother. His dismay and grief over his father's death were palpable. When the time came, she didn't know if she could go through with the plan to kill Joey by making it look like an overdose.

Janice was not a nice person. Caught forging stolen checks at the local mall at eighteen, she was convicted of a misdemeanor and spent a year in the county jail. After she was released, and on probation for a year, she turned to prostitution to support herself. Several times, Janice set up a trick to be robbed by her pimp. Those robberies went unreported. The men chose to avoid the embarrassment to themselves, and their families, and since all of them were businessmen from out of town, they didn't want to chance their boss would find out. Not having to return to testify in court was another reason.

Janice thought about calling Mama Peters and appealing to her to stop her efforts to kill the Torelli's. She didn't think that would happen, but felt she had to try. After Jeff left, she called Mama Peters.

Vince called Louie as they were driving home, and told her what they had learned about Joey's whereabouts. Vince asked if she would put out a BOLO for him and the car. "He's definitely at risk, Louie. I think the threats are real, and should be taken seriously."

"I've got news on that note."

"Hold on, Louie. I'm putting this on speaker so Steve can hear it."

"OK. We checked for prints on the envelope and note, and got several good latents. We didn't get any hits, so, on the off chance it came from someone in the family, I had them compared to Steve and Joey's elimination prints. A couple of prints on the envelope were identified as Steve's, but four of them on the note and two on the envelope were Joey's."

"Ah, shit." Vince responded.

"That's what I said. Seems Joey knows more about this threat than he let on."

Steve interrupted, "You think Joey has something to do with it?"

"I don't know," Louie replied. "But I do know he has gone from being a potential victim to a person of interest. I agree with you, Vince. We do need to find him. Give me the info on the car, Joey's particulars, and his cell number, and I'll get the BOLO out right away. By the way, my captain pulled Steney and Borden from the investigation. He didn't feel we needed them to babysit--a waste of resources, he said, at least at this point. You two are on your own."

"Well, that sucks."

"I know, sorry."

"Not your fault. Steve and I are gonna keep looking for Joey. If you get any info on where he is, please let us know. We'll do the same for you. By the way, I don't believe for a second Joey had anything to do with the hit on my uncle, or this threat. Why would he warn us, leaving his prints all over the note? I think he's smarter than that."

"You may be right, but I gotta check it out, and the only way is to find him, and interview him. Could be he was high, or drunk, when he wrote the warning, and not thinking clearly. I know you two are worried about him, but be careful where you tread. This is an active investigation, and you shouldn't get involved. Looking for Joey is OK. I don't have a problem with that, and I will let you know what I can, when I can. That's the best I can do. If you find out anything at all, you have to tell me."

"We will. And thanks, Louie. Talk to you soon." Vince disconnected the call and turned to Steve, who had pulled to the curb.

"I don't believe my brother is involved in dad's death. It can't be true."

"I don't believe it either. Let's go home and continue our search."

Chapter 13

Janice was on the phone, talking to Mama Peters, trying to reason with her. After a few hours of thinking about what she had gotten into, she realized she didn't want to kill Joey. Yes, she thought of him as a pathetic loser, but he wasn't a bad guy, and didn't deserve to die because of his father's job. She'd decided to get out of the whole thing.

"C'mon, Boss. Joey had nothing to do with your troubles."

"What? Are you getting soft on me? That fucking judge sentenced my boy to die, and I lost another son because of it. Vengeance is mine, and I will take out his two sons, and anyone else who gets in my way."

"I was thinking maybe this isn't the right thing to do. After all, the judge is dead, so how is this gonna hurt him? Seems kinda useless to me."

"Useless or not, it's what I want. If you aren't up to it, let me know. I've got others who would be only too happy to take your place, and maybe I'll send them out today."

Janice heard the menace in Mama Peters' voice, and knew she was stuck. If she said she wanted out, she was as good as signing her own death warrant.

"No, Boss. I'll do my job, but I want more money."

Mama Peters laughed, and said, "Now you're gonna try to squeeze me, huh? Tell you what, Joey's life ain't worth more. You'll do it for the five grand, and like it."

"Yes, ma'am."

"Good. I'll call you tomorrow. Where are you staying?"

"We were at the Rodeway Inn in Grovetown, but his brother and cousin, the San Francisco cop, tracked us down. I don't know how they did it, but the clerk let us know they'd called asking about us."

"So, what did you do?"

"We packed up and left. Later that day, we saw them at the hotel, searching our room. When they left, we waited a half-hour, then drove to Aiken, South Carolina, and checked into the Econo Lodge. I think we're safe here."

Janice lied about where they staying, not wanting Mama Peters to know where they really were. After their last conversation, she realized how unstable Mama Peters was, and didn't want her to have second thoughts about Janice doing the job. She suspected Mama Peters would send someone to kill Joey, and probably her too. They checked in to the Motel 6 on Boy Scout Road in Augusta, using Janice's fake ID in the name of Maria Mariposa.

Later that afternoon, they went to the Cook Out Restaurant a short distance away for barbecue and beers. Joey hadn't been drinking or using, and seemed more alert and composed, less morose. During the meal their conversation was like one between two friends out for the evening. Janice learned a lot about Joey, his likes and dislikes, hobbies, family, and dreams. She began to see him as a regular guy, nothing special, but not the pathetic loser she once thought he was.

"Now you boys better git goin', and no stops 'til you get there--no bars, no whorehouses, understand?"

"Yes, Mama."

Walking up to the car, a ten-year-old Dodge Charger with rusting mag wheels, and faded, navy-blue paint, Mama Peters waited as Billy and his two friends, Chester Williams and Floyd, stashed the weapons in the trunk, along with an ammo can with extra rounds. They had an AR-15, converted to full auto, a replica AK-47 semi-auto rifle, and an old WWII M-1 .30 caliber carbine. Each of the them also had a semi-auto pistol tucked into their belt, covered by their jacket. They got in the car, and Billy started the engine. Mama reached in the window and grabbed Billy's ear, twisting it until he cried out in pain.

"What you doin' that for, Mama?" he asked, pulling his head away, breaking her grip.

"Wanna make sure you don't fuck this up, Billy. You my last son, and as useless as you are, I don't wanna to lose you, too. You be careful, you hear?"

"Yes, Mama."

"You boys remember the plan?" she asked, addressing Billy and the other two. "You get there, set up in the hotel, and when the boy comes out, kill him quick."

"Why we goin' after him? Isn't Janice supposed to take care of him?" Billy asked.

"I don't trust her. Last time I talked to her she was tryin' to get me to drop the hit, may be getting' soft on Joey. We may have to do her, too. All right, go now. Call me when you find him. I might have more instructions for ya'll."

"What about the other brother, Steve, and that cop cousin?"

"Don't up worry none 'bout Steve. I got plans for him. Leave the cop be, unless he gets in the way or tries to stop you. We don't want to kill no cop unless we has to--that would piss off the local cops and bring a lot of heat lookin' for the killer."

"Listen up, Billy. Drive safe, at the speed limit. Don't want no cops pullin' ya'll over."

"OK, Mama, I got it. Call you in a few hours."

In an act of defiance, Billy floored the gas and burned rubber down the street.

Mama Peters shook her head and spit out her wad of chewing tobacco. "Goddamn kid. Ain't never been worth a shit."

Four and a half hours later, Billy turned into the parking lot of the Aiken Econo Lodge. Pulling into the arrival lane, they all got out and headed toward the entrance.

Chester and Floyd were dressed in dirty Levi's, filthy t-shirts, worn dirty clod-hopper shoes, sweat stained baseball caps, with messy, greasy looking hair, and a three-day growth of beard. Billy ordered them to stay outside. "You two look like thugs. You'll need to clean up when we get to our room. I'll go in and register, and find out what room they're in." He entered and paused a moment, looking around the lobby, then approached the clerk.

"Good afternoon, sir. Need a room?"

"Yeah, I do. Need two beds and a rollaway. There's three of us."

"We can manage that. It's $70 with the rollaway. Sure you need it? The beds are queens."

"Yeah, I'm sure. We'll only be here for tonight." Billy placed four $20 bills on the counter, then said. "We want to be close to my brother and his girlfriend."

"I'll do my best. What's his name?"

"Joseph Torelli. Could be under his girlfriend's name, Janice Roberts."

Looking through the registrar, the clerk said, "Don't see anyone with either of those names here. I checked the last three days. Sorry guys. You sure you got the right place?"

"Positive. He told me he checked in yesterday."

"I don't have them registered here. You know what car they were driving?"

"A gray Ford Focus."

"Hmm. I can't recall seeing a car like that recently. You're welcome to look through the lot, but I'm sure they aren't here."

"Thanks, anyway. We'll take our room. Can we have one that looks out at the lot?"

"Sure. Here you go, room 127. I'll have the rollaway brought over." The clerk put the money in the cash drawer, took out a $10 bill, and handed it to Billy.

Ten minutes later there was a knock on their door. Billy opened it and saw a young porter standing there, with the rollaway behind him. "Here's the bed, sir, and a pillow. There's linens, too."

Billy stepped out of the way as the porter pushed it into the room. "There you go." Looking around he said, "Need help bringing in your luggage?"

"No thanks. It's in the car. We can manage." Billy handed him a $5 tip, and locked the door after he left.

While Chester and Floyd made up the roll-away, Billy walked to a small convenience store a half-block away. He bought a pack of razors, shaving crème, and three plain t-shirts. He suspected Chester and Floyd didn't have toiletries with them. From the look of their scruffy beards, and the foul breath and body odor he had to endure the whole trip up from Jacksonville, he added two toothbrushes, toothpaste, and a can of deodorant.

When Billy got back to the room, he tossed the bag of purchases on the bed. "Ya'll go shave, shower, brush your teeth, and use the deodorant. There's a clean t-shirt in there for you. You stink, and look like a couple of back-country hicks. I don't want people noticing you because of it. When you're done, we'll get something to eat. There's a little diner a block up. While you're cleanin' up, I'm gonna take a walk around the parking lot, see if I can find the car."

"What we gonna do if they ain't here?" Floyd asked.

"We'll keep watch on the lot, all night if we have to. If they don't show up today, I'll call Mama and she'll tell us what to do."

Billy walked through the lot in front of the hotel, along the sides, and the back. He didn't see Janice's car. *Maybe they're out to dinner, or sumthin'. We'll keep an eye out tonight, and get them when they come back.*

Janice couldn't stop pacing in the room. She had a bad feeling Mama Peters already sent someone to kill Joey, and was scared for her own life. She regretted getting involved with her, not only due to her fear, but because she had a change of heart. Janice didn't believe Joey, or Steve, should die because of their father's ruling. She knew, deep inside, it was not justness. Mama Peters was not being equitable, or right--merely vengeful.

"Hey, Joey. I've got an errand to run. I'll be back in an hour. You stay inside, OK? Watch TV."

"Alright. See you later."

On the drive to Aiken, Janice called her ex-boyfriend, and asked what kind of car Billy drove.

"He's got an old blue Charger, and a beat-up red and white Ford Pickup. Why?"

"No particular reason. Just curious."

"What's going on, Janice?"

"Nothin'. I'll call you tomorrow." She disconnected before he could ask any more questions.

Janice drove the twenty-five minutes to Aiken and parked two blocks from the Econo Lodge. Walking the rest of the way, she stopped across the street from the hotel and scanned the lot, spotting a parked dark blue charger. She walked past the Econo Lodge, then crossed the street and along the side lot, then the rear lot. There were no other cars matching the description of Billy's. She returned to her car by a different route, and drove to an office complex lot across the street from the Econo Lodge. Parking close to the street, she chose a space partially screened by shrubbery with a clear view of the hotel's parking lot, Charger, and the two rooms on each side of it. She slumped down on the seat and watched to see if Billy was there. Janice new she would recognize him even though she hadn't seen him in six months. She left the engine on, cranked up the A/C, and tuned the radio to her favorite country-western station. She called Joey and told him she would be back in an hour or so, and reminded him to stay indoors.

A half-hour later, she saw the door of the room in front of the car open and a person carrying a blanket come out, walk to the back of the car, opened the trunk. Recognizing Billy, she watched as he spread the blanket in the trunk. Two other guys she didn't know came from the room and joined him. With their backs to her, they blocked her view of the trunk, but it appeared they took some things out and put them on the blanket. Billy folded the blanket over the items, lifted the wrapped bundle out, closed the trunk lid, and the three went back into the room. Whatever was wrapped in the blanket was around three feet long. Janice didn't know what the bundle was, but suspected it was weapons.

She realized that Mama Peters had sent the three of them to the Econo Lodge to kill Joey, and probably her. It angered, and scared her. Janice decided the best thing to do was get Joey, and take him home to his brother and cousin.

Janice left the lot and headed to the Motel 6, her heart racing. She didn't have Steve's cell number--she'd get it from Joey when she got back to the motel, so they could call Steve and tell him he was coming home. Janice knew Joey's best chance of survival, and hers too, was with his brother and cousin.

When Janice opened the motel room door, the stench of vomit hit her like a slap in the face. As she entered, she saw Joey passed out on the bed, his clothes smeared with vomit, and a pool of it on the bathroom floor. *At least he tried to make it to the toilet.* She tried to wake him by shouting his name and shaking him, but he only grunted and moaned.

God damn you, Joey. I'm trying to help you here.

Janice found an empty soda cup, filled it with cold water, and poured it over Joey's face and head. He didn't react at all, and she knew they were going nowhere that night.

Janice saw an empty fifth of Jim Beam whiskey on the floor next to the bed. She stood there and shook her head, then went over to undress him. She piled Joey's clothes, along with the soiled bedspread at the door and managed to get him under the covers. Rolling him on his side in case he vomited again, Janice grabbed the clothes and spread, and took them to the motel laundry room. While they were washing, she went back to the room, propped the door open and open the windows, then cleaned the bathroom floor with the hotel towels. She put them in the plastic laundry bag and set them outside the door.

It was nearly midnight by the time she finished cleaning the room. Retrieving Joey's clean clothes, she folded them and put them in the dresser drawer. She got the extra blanket from the closet and spread it out over the bed. The smell of vomit had dissipated and was almost gone. Janice was wiped out, and after undressing to her underwear, poured herself into bed. Joey was softly snoring next to her as she fell into an exhausted sleep.

That night Billy, Chester, and Floyd took turns watching the front lot for any arriving cars. Chester took the first three-hour shift, Floyd had the second shift, and Billy the last.

Not a single car drove into the lot after 10:00 p.m.

At 7:15 a.m., Billy walked through the parking lots looking for Janice's car, again with no luck. He returned to the room and woke the other two at 7:25. While they were dressing and washing up, Billy called Mama Peters.

"Hey, Ma. Janice's car wasn't here when we arrived, so we watched the lot all night. No luck. We checked with the clerk when we got here, and he said there weren't nobody here named Torelli, or Roberts. What you want us to do?"

"Guess you'll have to come home. That bitch lied to me. We'll have to find another way, 'cause it's obvious she cain't be trusted."

"All right, Mama. We'll get some breakfast and be on our way in an hour."

Billy stopped at The Waffle House Restaurant not far from the hotel for breakfast. All three ordered the same meal: ham, eggs, hash-browns, toast, a stack of pancakes with lots of syrup, and black coffee. After fifteen minutes, there was little left on their plates. They spent the next twenty minutes drinking coffee, talking, and laughing loudly, drawing annoyed stares from other customers.

As they left the restaurant and were walking to the car, Billy's cell phone rang.

"Hey, Ma. What's up?"

"Get your asses over to the Motel 6 on Boy Scout Road. Your buddy Hooter spotted Janice's car there fifteen minutes ago."

"Really? How'd he find her?"

"He was there with a whore, and saw her car parked in the lot when he was leavin'."

"Damn. You were right, Mama, she is a lyin' slut."

"Stop yappin' at me and get goin'. Joey's got to be with her, so don't waste no time."

"We're leavin' now. Be there in 30 minutes."

"Good. And Billy, take 'em both out."

Chapter 14

Janice woke at 7:30 a.m., took a shower, fixed her hair, and applied makeup. She woke Joey at 8:15.

Sitting up, he yawned and rubbed his eyes. His mouth felt dry and furry, and had a foul taste. He was exhausted, even though he had slept nine hours.

"Ugh. I gotta clean up." Looking at Janice through blood-shot eyes, he half-smiled and headed to the bathroom. Twenty minutes later he had brushed his teeth, used mouthwash, showered, and dressed in his clean clothes.

"Did you wash my clothes?"

"Duh. Couldn't leave them filthy with puke."

"I puked? I don't remember that."

Janice smiled at him. "You were passed out when I came back last night. You threw up all over yourself. What a mess. Where'd you get the whiskey?"

"I don't know. I remember drinking last night, but most everything is a blank."

"Well, don't worry about it." Janice took a deep breath and said, "I'm taking you home, Joey. Back to your brother and cousin."

"No. It's too dangerous. That's the whole reason I left, to protect them. That's not a good idea."

"All you've done is put yourself in danger." Taking his hands in both of hers, she pleaded with him. "You'd be much better off with them, much safer."

She paused for a moment, then continued. "I've got a confession, Joey. I was hired by some evil, crazy people to keep an eye on you. I didn't know until a week ago they wanted me to kill you, to make it look like an accident."

"An accident?"

"Yeah. An overdose on oxycodone. I was to give you two pills, and when you were loopy, crush eight more, and put it in a soda. Ten would do the job."

"Why didn't you?"

Janice looked away and muttered, "I couldn't do it. I realized you and Steve didn't deserve to die because of your father. It was wrong, and so unfair. I even called her and tried to get her to stop, but she wouldn't. Now, I think she wants me dead, too, because I know too much."

"Who is 'she'?"

Ignoring the question, Janice started moving through the room with a sense of urgency, gathering what few belongings they had. "We need to get going, Joey. They may be coming for us right now."

"How could they know where we are? We didn't tell anyone."

"I don't know, but I know people are coming. I lied when she asked where we were. I sent them to a hotel in South Carolina, but that won't stop them. As soon as they realize I lied, there will be a bunch of their friends looking for us. It's only a matter of time until one finds us."

By the time they were ready to go, it was 8:45. They piled into her car, and she drove out of the lot headed for the highway. As she drove, she called Steve and told him she was bringing Joey home. As she related the events from the last two days, she failed to notice the faded navy-blue Dodge Charger drive past them, heading the opposite way, toward the hotel.

Unfortunately for her, Billy spotted her car as he drove by. He slammed on the brakes and pulled a U-turn, accelerating to catch up to her. He stayed two cars behind as he followed.

"What the fuck, Billy?" Chester shouted from the back seat.

"They passed us goin' the opposite way. I saw the car, and recognized Janice driving. You two get the guns ready. Check to make sure there's a round in the chamber, and they're ready to fire." Before leaving the hotel, they had put the wrapped-up weapons on the floorboard behind the front seat by Chester.

He did a quick check and found all three were ready to go. Keeping the AK-47 for himself, he handed the AR-15 and M-1 carbine to Floyd, who placed them on the front floorboard at his feet.

"Where they goin'?" Chester asked.

"I think they are heading for Torelli's house. I'm pretty sure it's not far away. Mama said the judge lived in this neighborhood. When they stop, I'll pull over across the street. We'll get out and open up. With the firepower we got, we're bound to get 'em. Fire a full magazine, get back in the car, and we'll get the hell outta here."

Five minutes passed before Janice turned off the main street into Torelli's neighborhood, then turned right onto the judge's street. Janice slowed as she neared the house, and parked in front of the porch steps. Beeping the horn twice to let Steve know they had arrived, she turned off the engine and grabbed her purse. Janice didn't see the Charger park across the street one house down from Torelli's.

Joey got out and moved to the back door. Opening it, he bent over and reached inside to get his bag, saving his life.

Billy parked across the street and left the motor running. He grabbed the AR-15 from Floyd, flipped the selector switch to fully auto, and got out of the car. Chester and Floyd took their cue from him, and got out with him. They walked to the front of Billy's car, raised their weapons and opened fire on Janice and Joey.

Billy fired the AR-15 in short bursts, until the magazine was empty, while Chester and Floyd fired single shots as fast as they could pull the trigger on their semi-auto rifles. The shooting echoed down the street, startling the neighbors, who had the presence of mind to call 9-1-1.

Janice didn't stand a chance. In seconds, she was hit with four bullets, the final bullet a head shot that killed her. Glass from the window shattered and sprayed the inside of the car. Janice's blood splattered the passenger window as she slumped on the front seat, dead.

Joey reached inside the backseat when the shooting started and instinctively threw himself face down on the seat. He was sprayed with bits of broken glass, and heard the deadly tattoo of bullets hitting the car. He covered his head with his arms, screaming in terror. Bullet fragments from rounds that penetrated the car through the back door tore bloody grooves on his arms. The wounds were painful, but not serious.

Steve had opened the front door when the shooting started. He drew his pistol and dove to the porch floor. Vince was right behind him, crouching down. They both saw the three shooters across the street and began returning fire. Vince fired at the closest shooter, Floyd, firing several shots. He saw him jerk and double over, turn and stumble back to the car.

Steve was shooting at Billy, who had run back to the car when Steve and Vince started firing at them.

"C'mon, Chester, we need to go, now," he yelled.

Chester fired the rest of his ammo, and turned to run to the car when Steve fired at him.

One of Steve's bullets struck him in the back of his shoulder, half spinning him around. Chester dropped his rifle, scrambled the last two steps to the car and fell onto the passenger seat. Before he could sit up and close the door, Billy punched the gas and peeled out down the street, out of the killing zone.

Vince ran down the steps, out into the street and aimed at the Charger speeding away. Cursing to himself, he held his fire, knowing he wouldn't be able to hit the car. He holstered his gun and ran to Janice's car, where Steve was helping Joey out. Vince could see Janice had fallen over, and from the amount of blood on and around her, knew she was dead.

Running to where Steve had sat Joey on the sidewalk, he saw blood on his head and his arms.

"He's OK, Vince," Steve said as Vince crouched beside them. "Got wounds to his arms. They're bleeding, but don't look too bad."

"Get him inside while I call 9-1-1."

People were coming out of their homes, now that the shooting had stopped. Two rushed over and said they had called the cops and an ambulance, and offered their help. Vince told them to go home and wait, and shouted to the others out on the street to do the same. He said the police would be there shortly, and would be contacting them for their statements after the scene had been secured.

Vince dialed 9-1-1 and identified himself as a San Francisco PD homicide investigator. He gave the dispatcher a brief account of the shooting, and a description of the Charger. The dispatcher advised several police units were on the way, and an ambulance was enroute.

Vince went in the house and saw Joey sitting on a chair, with Steve pressing a dish towel on Joey's arm, applying pressure to stop the bleeding. Joey was conscious, and alert, moaning from the pain.

"He's OK. I checked him and couldn't find any wounds other than on his arms."

"What about the blood on his head?"

"Must have come from his arms." Steve addressed Joey, saying, "You're OK, kid. The bleeding's slowed, and an ambulance is on the way."

Joey grabbed Steve's arm. Weeping, he said, "I'm so sorry, Steve, so sorry. All this is my fault."

"Hush, Joey. It'll be all right. We'll talk after we get you to the hospital."

"How's Janice? Is she OK? Can I see her?"

Steve looked at Vince, who shook his head 'no', and Steve knew she was dead.

"I don't know," Steve replied. "She's been hurt, but the paramedics are almost here. They'll take care of her."

The sound of sirens getting louder announced the arrival of help. Vince went out on the porch to meet the officers, and get the EMTs to help Joey.

Chapter 15

Six hours later, Vince and Steve were released by the sheriff's department after being questioned by investigators about the shoot-out at the house. They had been separated, placed in separate interview rooms, their weapons seized as evidence--routine investigative procedure--and a set of elimination prints taken from both. The investigators treated them as victims, and kept them updated on the investigation, to that point.

The forensics team located forty-three bullet casings on the street where Billy's car had been parked. They found eighteen holes in Janice's car, and located another twelve bullets embedded in the porch and front of the house. With the four that hit Janice, thirty-four had been accounted for. That left nine. Most of the recovered bullets were too badly damaged for comparison, though there were a few that had possibilities. There also was a small amount of blood at two locations where the shooters stood. Samples were collected for typing and DNA profiling.

Chester's AK-47, recovered at the scene, turned out to be stolen in a burglary in Augusta.

Janice's body had been transported to the morgue, awaiting an autopsy, collection of bullets from her body, and other evidence. Her autopsy was scheduled for the next afternoon. Her car was impounded for evidence collection, and towed to the Richmond County Sheriff's impound lot.

Joey was interviewed at the hospital after his wounds were treated, receiving eight stitches in one arm and four in the other. He was discharged, and called Steve's cell. Steve didn't answer, so he left him a message to come get him at the hospital.

While being driven home by a patrol officer, Steve checked his phone and found the message from Joey. He told Vince, and when they were dropped off, they went to the hospital to pick him up. They found him sitting in the waiting room, awake and alert, having been given ibuprofen for the pain. A uniformed officer was standing nearby, keeping watch over him until they arrived.

Joey was glad to see them, and the first thing he asked was how Janice was. No one had told him she was dead.

Steve sat next to Joey and said, "Got bad news, bro. They killed her. She didn't have a chance."

Joey's eyes opened wide, and the tears welled up. He sobbed softly, covering his eyes with his hand. "Did she suffer?"

"No. It was instant. She never felt a thing."

"Oh, God, what have I done?" Tears were flowing freely down his cheeks. "I'm sorry, I'm so sorry. This is all my fault."

Steve looked at Vince, then asked, "What are you talking about?"

Between sobs, Joey said, "It's all my fault, dad's death, her death, the shooting, everything."

Vince stepped up to him, and put his hand on Joey's shoulder.

"Whatever you did, or said, it's not your fault. These people were after you, Janice, and probably Steve and me. This would have happened regardless of anything you did."

Joey looked hopefully at Vince, his sobs lessening. "You really think so?"

"I do, and I know Steve feels the same."

Steve nodded his head as Joey looked at him. "Tell you what, let's go home. It's been a long, trying day. Don't worry about anything." Leaning in, Steve whispered in Joey's ear, "I love you." Joey turned away, and continued to sob.

Vince saw the tears in Steve's eyes as they left the hospital. He said nothing on the ride home.

Once they were home, Joey trundled off to bed, and Steve and Vince retired to the judge's office. It was a large room, painted a light yellow, which Vince estimated to be twenty-five by twenty feet. There was an antique, dark-oak rolltop desk set perpendicular to a large window, looking out over the grounds and forest west of the house. The floors were lacquered and polished yellow oak. Tastefully covering the high-traffic areas were throw rugs of autumn colors. A six-foot-high bookshelf, also built of black oak, filled with legal books, lined the entire wall behind the desk. Three over-stuffed brown leather chairs were arranged along the opposite wall.

Six paintings by Bev Doolittle decorated the walls, and with the rest of the decorations and knick-knacks, the room ambience was of comfort and coziness.

The sun shining brightly into the room in the afternoon negated the need to turn on the room's lights.

Steve and Vince sat in two of the three over-stuffed easy chairs. Steve asked, "How long did the detective say it would be before we could get the guns back?"

"He gave us a receipt and mentioned they would be released in a week or so."

"Well, that leaves us with one sidearm. Dad has two shotguns and a .308 deer rifle, but I wouldn't want to be parading all over the place with one of those--they're hunting guns and are very long."

"How about friends of yours? Does anyone have a pistol we could borrow?"

Steve thought for a moment, then said, "Let me make a couple of calls."

A half-hour later, Steve's friend, Carl, pulled up in front of the house. Grabbing a Harvey's Supermarket bag, he exited the car and walked to the front door. Steve opened it before he could ring the bell.

"C'mon in, Carl. Thanks for helping us out."

"No sweat, bro. I heard about the shootout on TV, and it will be all over the papers tomorrow. Glad you guys weren't hurt."

"Yeah, me too. Joey got a couple of minor wounds, but Vince and I weren't the targets. You know Joey's friend, Janice, was killed, right? Joey was lucky to escape with his life."

"Yeah." Carl handed the bag to Steve, saying, "Keep 'em as long as you need to." He put his hand on Steve's shoulder and said, "I can stick around for a few days, in case you need backup."

"I appreciate the offer, but I don't think it will be necessary. We doubt the shooters will be back. I think Vince and I wounded two of the three. If they want to go at us again, they'll have to recruit new shooters."

Vince added, "If they're still gunning for us, the attack will be somewhere else, so we're gonna stick close to home as much as we can."

"OK, but the offer is still open. Call me anytime if you need help."

"I will," Steve replied. "Thanks again, my friend."

After Carl left, Steve took the two pistols from the bag. He kept the Glock .40 caliber, and gave Vince the Ruger 9mm. There were spare magazines and a full box of bullets for each.

"Great," Vince stated, "I feel better, now. What about Joey?"

"I think he'll agree to be armed after today. He'll use Dad's Beretta. He's used to it."

"He any good with it?"

"Yeah. He put a lot of rounds down range with it, and he's a decent shot."

"I hope so--it's a lot different shooting back at someone shooting at you."

"He'll be OK. There's a lot more to him than you think."

"Well, he's a Torelli," Vince replied, smiling.

Sergeant Louisa Princeton, was part of the investigator's meeting on the shootings at the department's Bureau of Criminal Investigation. Sitting at a table in an interview room with two detectives, Ballesteros and Carlson, who were handling the shooting. As she was the lead investigator in Judge Torelli's death, it made sense. She could offer insights on the hit-and-run, and her contacts with the Judge's family, that weren't in any reports.

"We've got a BOLO for the suspect's vehicle, and a call for witnesses, other than the neighbors," Ballesteros said. He still had a slight Hispanic accent, left over from his English as a second language classes from years ago, and had a "bulldog" reputation in the criminal investigation unit.

"Did you get a good description of the car? Louie asked.

"Yeah. Several wits said it was an older, dirty Dodge Charger, black or dark blue, No one got a plate number, and one guy said there were no plates on it. It's a rusty junker, with loud mufflers. I pretty sure it's got bullet holes in it."

Detective Carlson chimed in, "And before you ask, Louie, yes, we did get descriptions of the shooters. Only problem is, they were sketchy, and no two witnesses agreed on the descriptions. There are indications at least one of them was wounded."

"That come from witnesses?"

"No. The shooting was over in less than thirty seconds. By the time people came out of their houses, it was mostly over. That info came from Steve Torelli, and his cousin Vince, the SFPD homicide investigator. They returned fire, and were pretty sure they got some hits. There was blood collected from the area the where the suspects stood. Couldn't be Janice's or Joey's."

"We've got the BOLO out to the Georgia state police, and all other PDs in Georgia," Ballesteros offered. "Also, we've sent the info to South Carolina agencies within 200 miles of Augusta. Someone somewhere is bound to spot the car. All the hospitals and emergency clinics in Augusta have been notified to report it if they get any patients with bullet wounds, though the mandatory reporting law requires it."

"Guess we'll have to wait, and hope for the best." Louie said. "From the facts of the case, it doesn't appear these guys were professionals. If they were, they wouldn't have stood in the middle of the street spraying bullets everywhere, and Joey would be dead, too."

"You may be right." Carlson stood, and said, "If there's nothing else, we've got more people to interview."

"Nothing from me," Louie replied. "If there's anything I can do, let me know."

Billy was in a panic as he drove south on Highway 25. Looking at his speedometer he saw his speed was 92 mph. He forced himself to slow down to 70 as he approached the town of Millen, 50 miles south of Augusta. It had been less than an hour since their ill-fated ambush of Joey and Janice.

In the front passenger seat, Chester had a rag pressed against his shoulder next to his armpit, to stem the bleeding. The bullet hit him in the back of his shoulder, broke his shoulder blade, and exited the front. It was a painful wound that bled freely. Chester was slumped in the seat, moaning.

"I been shot, Billy," he complained. "I think I'm gonna die."

"You ain't gonna die. Keep that rag pressed against it."

"What about Floyd?"

"I don't know. He's layin' on the back seat. I ain't heard him moving around since we left, and he ain't said nuthin."

"He dead?"

"How the fuck would I know? We'll deal with him when we get back to Mama's. She'll know what to do."

Billy called Mama Peters as he drove, and told her about the shooting, and that Floyd and Chester were both wounded.

"The judge's fucking son, and, I'm guessin', his cousin, the SF cop, opened up on us from the porch."

"What about Joey, and Janice? They dead?"

"I don't know. We shot the hell outta the car, but don't know if we hit them."

"Jesus Christ, Billy. You sure screwed things up."

"It weren't my fault."

"Yes, it was, dumbass. You should've known better than to attack Janice and Joey in front of the house. You were supposed to take care of them at the motel. Damn you!"

"I'm sorry, Ma. What do I do now?"

"Get your ass down here, and we'll take care of it. Don't fuck this up any more than you already have, Billy," Mama Peters said, and disconnected the call.

Billy knew he would need gas before much longer, and chose a gas station off the highway outside Millen. Parking at a self-serve pump, he went to the trunk, opened it, and took out two blankets.

Giving one to Chester, he told him to cover-up and stay in the car. Billy checked Floyd, lying on the back seat, and found he was dead. He covered his body with the other blanket.

Billy filled the tank, then went inside to pay for the gas, a half-dozen bottles of water, and a six-pack of beer. He used cash, heeding Mama's instructions to not use a credit card--too easy to trace.

Twenty minutes further down the road Billy pulled off the highway. The realization that Floyd was dead and Chester, wounded and now unconscious, might die, overwhelmed him. He couldn't hold in his frustration and anger any longer.

Holding the wheel with both hands, Billy hung his head, and sobbed as tears ran down his cheeks.

Chapter 16

As Steve was preparing dinner, Vince called Maggie to see if she was aware of the shootings. When she answered, it was clear she already knew.

"What the hell is going on, Vince? I turn on the news, and what do I see? A video of Uncle Anthony's house, cops everywhere, and a shot-up car parked in front."

"It's OK, Babe. Steve and I are fine, but Joey was slightly wounded."

"Tell me what happened, and no B.S., Torelli."

Vince described the attack on Joey and Janice as they arrived at the house. He said he believed two of the three shooters were wounded, and that they all got away.

"I don't think they expected Steve and I to come out shooting. They were there to get Joey and Janice, and were totally focused on them."

"You sure you and Steve are not hurt?"

"Yeah. They weren't aiming at us."

"How about Janice? Did she survive?"

"No, she didn't, poor girl. She didn't stand a chance. Janice died sitting in her car."

"Oh, I'm so sorry to hear that. How's Joey taking it?"

"He's devastated. Keeps saying it's all his fault."

"What? How could it be his fault?"

"He won't say. When we ask him, he retreats into himself and stops talking. I'm hoping he'll open up soon, 'cause there may be something important he isn't saying that could help in the investigation. Look, Babe, I gotta go. I'll call you tomorrow, and don't worry--Steve, Joey, and I are OK, and safe for now."

"All right. I love you, cowboy. Don't do anything stupid, OK?"

"I won't. I'll be home in a few days, a week at most, I hope. Love you too."

Twenty minutes later, Steve called him in to dinner. "I checked on Joey. He's sleeping, so I didn't wake him, he needs the rest."

Vince and Steve sat down to a dinner of roast chicken, roasted red potatoes, asparagus, thick slices of buttered French bread, and a bottle of Malbec to go with the food. Halfway through the meal, there was a knock on the door. Steve and Vince looked at each other, grabbed their pistols, and moved to the front room. Standing on each side of the front door, Steve called out, "Who's there?"

"It's me, Louie. Can we talk?"

Letting her in, Steve asked, "You got good news? Any ID on the shooters?"

"Not yet. We're working on it." Louie didn't seem surprised they both were armed.

"We're in the middle of dinner. Want to join us? There's plenty," Steve said, leading the way to the dining room.

"I'll pass, though it smells terrific. You cook this?"

"Yep."

"Maybe I will have a little."

Vince prepared a plate for Louie and they sat at the table, not talking, concentrating on the food. When done, Steve cleared the dirty dishes, and returned with another bottle of wine. He poured Vince and Louie a glass, then sat and filled his glass.

"So," Vince started, "What's the evidence telling us?"

"Well, there were over forty rounds fired by the suspects. Casings collected at the scene show three different weapons--.223 caliber from an AR-15, .30 caliber, likely from an M-1 carbine, and 7.62 caliber from an AK-47. Thanks to you guys, by the way, for your descriptions of the guns. We also recovered a replica AK-47 at the scene, dropped by one of the shooters."

Vince chimed in, "These guys were strictly amateurs. With the firepower they had, Joey should have died, too. It was their shitty tactics that made them fail."

Steve added, "It was a piss-poor setup, attacking in broad daylight like that. They didn't even use cover. That's why we got two of them."

"Any registration info on the AK serial number?"

"Yeah. It was reported stolen two years ago in Florida. We checked the owner's background, and he's clean as a whistle--no criminal record. Only thing he's got is a speeding ticket. We've got the local PD going out to interview him, but I don't think we're going to get anything useful."

"Damn," Vince exclaimed. "Seems you can't get a break on this."

Louie chuckled. "One thing about this is the gun was stolen in a burglary in Jacksonville. Same city, Vince, where the guy following you around was killed. Ballesteros and Carlson will be cross-checking that info with anyone from the area sentenced by Judge Torelli. We're working on it, and eventually, something will break the case wide open."

"I sure hope so, and soon," Vince replied. "I'm due back at work in five days."

Once Billy regained his composure, he became very angry with Steve and Vince. He blamed them for Floyd's death and Chester's wound. It never crossed his mind that none of this would have happened had they not set out to assassinate Joey and Janice, on the orders of his mother.

Before he resumed driving, Billy checked on Chester. His wound was still seeping blood, he was semi-conscious and moaning. Not knowing what to do, Billy dialed his mother's cell,

"Where are you?" she demanded.

"On my way home."

"What about Chester and Floyd?"

"Floyd's dead, and Chester ain't doing too good. What should I do, Ma?"

"Shut up and let me think." There was silence on the line for half a minute, then she said, "You know the Graves Mountain Mine?"

"Yeah. Gramps used to take us up there to get crystals and rocks. What about it?"

"On your way home, ya need to dump your car. There's a dirt road a half-mile past the entrance to the mine that goes up into the hills. Turn left and a mile in, there's an old retention pond that was part of the mine property a long while ago. It's pretty deep. Nobody goes there now, so that's where you dump the car."

"What about Floyd, and Chester?"

"Leave them inside. Find a good place above the pond to drive the car off into the water. Roll the windows down half-way, so it sinks. Before you do that, don't forget to take the plates off, and the VIN tag. Keep them with you, but leave the weapons inside with the bodies. Once the car sinks, walk on back to the main road. I'll send someone out to pick you up there."

"Chester ain't dead, Ma."

"Not yet, he ain't. He'll probably die before you get there, but if he don't, finish him off."

"Kill Chester? Ma, I can't do that. We been friends since grammar school."

"Just do it. We can't take him to the docs, or a hospital. They'd report it to the cops, and we'd be done for, understand?"

"Yeah, yeah." Billy took a deep breath and said, "OK, I'll do it, if I have to."

"Good boy. I'll see ya when ya get here."

Two hours later, Billy stood at the top of a thirty-foot cliff, watching as the Charger rolled down the slight slope and off the edge, dropping into the water. He'd checked on Chester before rolling it down the slope, and found he had died somewhere between Millen and the mine.

Billy watched as the Charger hit the water, saw the large splash it made, and ripples moving out across the pond. The car sank slowly out of sight, carrying the bodies of Floyd, and Chester. Bubbles burst on the surface as it filled with water and disappeared into the depths. Billy waited a few minutes to make sure the Charger was not visible in the rust-colored water, then, satisfied it wasn't, began the mile trek back to the main road, carrying the grocery bag from the gas station with the beer, license plates, and VIN tag. It was hot out, with a cloudless sky and a merciless sun beating down. He would drink three beers before getting to the road twenty-five minutes later.

Once at the road, he sat in the dust waiting for his ride to arrive, drinking another beer. Twenty minutes later, a black Chevrolet SUV arrived, and stopped next to him. As he stood, the driver rolled down the window and

Billy recognized him. He smiled at the driver, and said, "What the hell are you doing here? I thought you were in jail."

Robert "Junior" Henderson grinned at him. "Out on bail. A stroke of luck, eh, the judge getting killed in that hit-and-run?"

Billy walked around the SUV and got in the passenger seat. Closing the door, he felt the welcoming cool air from the car's air conditioning. "Ah. That feels good." Looking at Junior, Billy remarked, "Yeah, a real convenient stroke of luck, if you ask me."

Junior chuckled. "My case has been continued until it gets assigned to another judge. My attorney said it will take at least two months, so I'm free until then. So, what happened when you messed up the hit on the Torelli's?"

Billy told Junior how Floyd and Chester were killed. "I don't even know if we got Joey. We got off a lot of shots, but once Steve and his cousin came out and started shooting at us, we had to get the hell out of there."

"I heard about it on the radio, and Joey ain't dead. It said he was wounded, but it wasn't serious. The news said a woman with him was killed, but they didn't give her name."

"That was Janice. Too bad about her, but she would recognize me, so she had to die."

"Aw, man. I knew her. She is, er, was, a hot little piece."

Billy asked, "Were you involved in the judge's death?"

"Kind of."

"What do you mean 'kind of'?"

"Can I trust you to keep your mouth shut?"

"Of course."

"All right. I don't know who set this up--I think it was your mom--and I don't know who drove the car." Junior paused for a moment. "All I did was block the sidewalk with a couple of my buddies."

"Who told you to do that?"

"My dad. Had us clean up, put on suits and ties, gave each of us a briefcase, and said to be on the street at a certain time to block the sidewalk."

"Did he say why?"

"No. I had no idea they were going to kill the judge."

"What did you do after he was run down?"

"Got the hell out of there. Too many cops know me, and it wouldn't have been good to be seen there. I went home and confronted my dad, but he claimed not to know Torelli would be killed."

"You believe him?"

"No. How could he not know what was going to happen? I know my father--he's no dummy. I wouldn't be surprised if he was up to his neck in the murder."

"Huh," Billy said. "I thought it was all my mom's doing. She's really pissed about my brother Sammy, being paralyzed and on death row. Judge Torelli's the one who sentenced him to death."

"I don't blame her. I'd want him dead if I was in her shoes."

"Speaking of which, I better call her and let her know we are on our way."

Mama Peters was angry. She had little tolerance for Billy's incompetence, and it showed as she paced her office, reviling him at the top of her lungs.

"I sent three of you out on a simple task--kill two people-- and now only you are left to report back. How the hell did it end up this way?"

"But, Ma, I didn't expect anyone would be shooting back at..."

"Shut up, you fool," she shouted. "Three of you, with rifles, against two unarmed people, and you couldn't complete the task? Jesus Christ, Billy, if you weren't my son, you'd be at the bottom of that retention pond with Floyd and Chester."

Billy stood there, hands in his pockets, hanging his head, said, "I'm sorry, Ma. Joey's family took us by surprise. There's nothing we could do about it."

"Nothing you could do about it, eh? What about shooting back at them? Did that ever cross your mind? You might have got them, or at least chased them back in the house, then gone after Joey. How hard is that to figure out, you dumb ass."

Looking up at her, Billy replied, "It won't happen again. Give me another chance, Ma, and I'll get them all."

"No. I'm done with you. You need to disappear for a while--I don't want you around here. Your cousin, Marty in Texas, has agreed to put you up for a month or so."

Resigned to his fate, he asked, "How am I gonna get there? My car is gone."

"You'll be taking the train. I've got your ticket, and the train leaves tomorrow morning. You stay there, do what Marty says, and stay out of trouble. Keep a low profile, Billy. I don't want you raising a ruckus or getting in trouble with the cops, you hear? We've gotta lay low for a while."

"Yeah, Ma. Don't worry, I'll behave."

"You better, boy, you better."

The threat in her voiced came through to loud and clear.

Chapter 17

It had been six weeks since the attack, and Vince was back at work in San Francisco. He was on administrative leave the first ten days after returning, while the sheriff's department investigated his role in the ambush. Predictably, it was determined he, and Steve, were justified in their response, ruling it self-defense. Since the weapons they used were legally registered to Judge Torelli, there was no problem there. The Sheriff even sent a commendation letter to the SFPD Chief on Vince's quick response and actions that day, saying it was highly likely he and Steve thwarted the ambush and saved Joey's life.

The SFPD Chief was not happy with the whole situation, and made that clear to Vince during a one-on-one meeting. He did not like his officers being involved in shoot-outs away from San Francisco.

Vince stood humbly in front of the chief, not responding other than to say "Yes sir" a few times. He knew the chief wanted to vent, and nothing more would come of it. He appeared repentant during the dressing down, and apologized when the chief was done.

Lieutenant Simons and the other homicide inspectors were curious when Vince returned, and pestered him to tell his side. Vince, wisely, declined until he was done with the chief. At the end of that day, he was taken to dinner by his squad, including the lieutenant. They went to Capp's Corner, an iconic landmark Italian restaurant in San Francisco's North Beach that had been in business since 1960, where he was plied with drinks and unending questions.

He got home after midnight, after breaking away from the "celebration", having limited himself to three beers.

Vince talked with Steve every few days, and made it a point to talk with Joey, too, mostly to check up on his recovery. Vince was interested in not only his physical recovery, but his progress on getting straight.

Steve regularly texted Vince with updates, and Vince was happy to hear Joey had stopped drinking and using drugs. Steve said Joey seemed to have come out of his depression, though he still professed guilt about his part in their father's death, unwitting as it was.

Life for Steve and Joey had returned to near normalcy. Steve sold his house and moved into his dad's place with his family, and Joey. After being sober for a month, Joey had gotten a part-time custodian position at the courthouse. Things were looking up.

Vince kept in regular contact with Louie, and she reported they had made little progress on the judge's death and the ambush at the house. She found six video cameras on businesses within two blocks of the murder scene. Hoping one of them would have caught a better picture of the car, or the three men that blocked the sidewalk, Louie spent hours reviewing the videos from one hour before until fifteen minutes after the judge was run down, with no luck. There were whispers that Junior Henderson was involved, but everyone she, and the other investigators, interviewed said it was only rumors. Louie vowed she would not give up, and promised Vince the APD would ultimately solve both cases.

Mama Peters was sitting in the office lobby of Salvatore "Sonny" Rufigio, the current Capo of the Jacksonville branch of the Trafficante crime family. Billy had returned home from Texas two days earlier, and she felt it was safe for her to look for other means to exact her revenge.

The office was, ostensibly, for the entertainment arm of the crime family businesses. On the surface, Sonny handled the day-to-day operations of six gentlemen's clubs, which were merely facades for the actual business in the back rooms. Prostitution, drugs, and stolen property were available there, bringing in several millions of dollars every year to the family. A lucrative extortion racket thrived involving the Jacksonville VIP's who were foolish enough to patronize the back rooms. Sonny had high-ranking police officials, judges, and even an assistant D.A. under his thumb. So much so, none of his clubs had been successfully raided by the police, state authorities, or even the FBI, thanks to those who had a lot to lose by not doing what Sonny commanded.

After waiting for over an hour, Mama Peters was ushered into Sonny's empty office, and told to take the chair facing the empty desk. "Mr. Rufigio will be in shortly," his secretary said, before turning and leaving the room. As she left, she did not shut the door. Her desk was positioned so she could see anyone sitting in the chair.

Fifteen minutes later, Sonny emerged from a back door, walked up to Mama, and shook her hand. "To what do I have the honor of your visit, Mrs. Peters?"

Sonny knew who she was--a back-woods hillbilly and small-time criminal. She'd come to him three months earlier asking for help with the assassination of Judge Torelli. Sonny listened to her request, asked a few questions, then politely declined to help. He told her he was not in the murder business, especially if the target was a public official, judge, or cop--it would bring too much unwanted heat on his businesses. Mama Peters left disappointed.

Sonny had no doubt Mama Peters, at some point, would be arrested for the Judge's death, and would spill her guts trying to work a deal with the D.A. She would hand him over on a platter, if it benefitted her.

Mama was fuming while Billy drove her home. Upset at that "Guinea bastard's" refusal to help, Billy had to listen to her rant, punctuated with a liberal dose of profanity. After she calmed down, Mama directed Billy to turn toward the east side of Jacksonville.

Billy was shocked by her order. "I don't think that's a good idea, Mama. You know what Eastside is like. It's a bad place, very dangerous."

With high unemployment and low income, if you weren't from the neighborhood, it was very likely you would become the victim of a violent crime before you could drive through it.

"I know that, dumb-ass," Mama shouted. "Do what you're told and leave the thinkin' to me." Mama pulled out her cell phone and dialed a number she knew by heart.

"Clive? Mama Peters here. I need a favor. Can you meet me at the little market on Franklin and Third Street? Yeah, as soon as you can. Got a job for ya, if you're interested."

She listened for a few moments, then replied, "OK, I'll be there in fifteen minutes."

Mama and Billy arrived ten minutes later. She wanted to be there before Clive and his boys, in case he was planning to set up an ambush. She directed Billy to park where she could see the driveway to the parking lot, and the areas from which anyone on foot could enter. While they waited, she retrieved two pistols from a bag on the floorboard, and checked they were loaded and ready to fire.

Handing one to Billy, she told him, "Keep this out of sight, but ready to go. I'll watch Clive, you watch the others with him, but don't do nuthin' unless I say, 'guess that's it, then'. If you hear that, start blazin' away at the others. I'll handle Clive. Keep the engine runnin', in case we gotta get away quick."

Billy didn't answer, and Mama looked at him. Seeing the terrified look on his face, she reached over and backhanded him in the face, hard enough to cause a small cut on his lip.

"Hey," she shouted. "You hear me, boy? Snap out of it."

A small trickle of blood came from his lip, and a red mark appeared on his cheek. Billy rubbed his cheek as he looked at her. "Ow, Ma. What was that for?"

"I need you to concentrate on what we're doin' here. Clive's always been OK with me, but to be safe, we need to be prepared in case this goes sour."

"I got it, Ma. Jesus, that hurt."

"Oh quit yer whinin". Mama Peters saw a silver Ford Explorer turn into the lot, stop for a moment, then turn in her direction.

"Here he comes. Be ready."

Clive Rutherford was known as "The King of Eastside". Nothing of a criminal nature went on there without his approval. He, and his gang of 'collectors', made sure The King got his twenty percent cut. The criminal gangs knew better than to try to get around the cut, having learned what happens to those who had tried. Not only did they forfeit all of their loot, they often disappeared, their fate unknown.

Clive was fifty-seven years old. His physical appearance was intimidating, due to his daily two-hour workout in his home gym. He rarely smiled, and his perpetual frown made him look like he was angry all the time. He was by no means a good-looking man. With his dark brown skin, shaved head, pock-marked face, mustache, goatee, and ever-present bodyguards, the drug dealers, pimps, and crooks were nervous in his presence. What they didn't know was he had cultivated and practiced the look to perfection. It made others think twice about trying to cheat or cross him.

Clive himself never victimized the people in Eastside, but outside the community, most everything was fair game. Wisely, he didn't deal in drugs, as he knew the drug suppliers were much larger, better armed, and more murderous when it came to interlopers trespassing into their operations.

The majority of his activity was comprised of running a lucrative fencing operation, doing for-hire thefts and burglaries, and taking on the occasional murder-for-hire.

The Explorer pulled up parallel to Mama Peters' car. Clive lowered the bullet-resistant window a few inches, and looked over at her.

"Hello, Mama, Billy. How're you doing?"

"We're hanging in there. Thanks for meeting with me," Mama replied.

"You said you needed a favor. I'm assuming this has something to do with the death of judge Torelli, and the attack at his house."

"Damn, Clive," Mama exclaimed, "How'd you know that?"

Clive signaled the two bodyguards in the back seat of the car to get out. One took up position at the right rear of her car, the other by the right front. Billy saw them standing watching him, their hands on the pistols in their shoulder holsters.

Clive rolled his window down a few more inches, and said, "I've got my sources. What can I do for you?"

"Well, you know what happened at the house, right? Billy here fucked it up, got two of my shooters killed, and didn't get the job done. The judge's sons are still alive."

"Wasn't killing the judge enough? I know it was you who set it up."

She didn't deny it. "No, it ain't enough. Because of him, one of my boys is in a wheelchair, sittin' on death row, and another is dead. I wanna even the score. Take his two boys down. Then we'll be even."

"I hear the cops are goin' all out to find who killed the judge. There's a lot of heat in Georgia, South Carolina, and even here in Florida. If you're smart, you'll drop it right now. You won't win, ya know. The cops will find out it was you, then there's no hiding from them. It may take them a while, maybe even years, but they ain't gonna stop 'til you're in prison or dead."

"Don't matter none to me. I'll worry about it when the time comes."

Clive nodded, and said, "Your choice. What do you need from me?"

"I need a good shooter. Someone who can take out a man from some distance away."

"Is there more than one target?" Clive asked, knowing what the answer would be.

"Yeah--both the Torelli boys."

"I hear there's a cousin with them, a San Francisco cop."

"He's gone. Went home about a month ago. He was one of them that shot up my shooters."

"That's good. This ain't gonna be cheap ya know."

"I'm willing to pay fifteen grand for the two of them."

Clive chuckled. "Fifteen grand each is more like it. It's thirty, if I decide to accept the job."

"Shit, Clive. You're bleedin' me. How about twenty-five?"

"Nope. Take it or leave it, Mama, it's your choice."

Mama thought for a few moments, sighed, and said, "Guess I ain't gotta choice. All right, thirty it is."

Clive smiled. "I'll call you tomorrow with my decision. I gotta check with my boys, and see if the guy I'm thinking of is available."

"OK. I'll be waiting for your call."

Clive called the two bodyguards back to the car, rolled up his window, and told his driver and chief of security, DeWayne White, to drive on.

As they drove away, Clive said to DeWayne, "What do you think? Is this something we should get involved with?"

"I'm not sure, Boss. Let me do some checking around before you decide, OK?"

"All right. I've known Peters for a few years, and we've had moderately lucrative interactions. I don't like working with her 'cause she's so unpredictable--never know when she will go nuts. She's one bat-shit-crazy bitch."

"Yeah, I'm aware of that. I wanna check and see if it's possible to get to the Torelli's. After Billy's fucked-up ambush, they may be too well protected. If it was me, I wouldn't do it for less than fifty grand. The shooter is going to want at least fifteen, maybe twenty. That leaves you with a very slim profit margin."

Clive replied, "I know. I'm thinking tomorrow I'll call her and say the Torelli's are well protected, and the shooter is demanding twenty-five for the two hits. I'll tell her I need forty to make it worth my while."

DeWayne asked, "What if she agrees to the forty grand?"

"Well, then, I'll have to decide whether we do it or not. Right now, I'm not feeling too good about it."

They rode in silence for a while, until Clive said, "I need a drink. Pull in up here at Big Mac's Bar. I'm buyin'."

Chapter 18

It was Steve's turn to pick the kids up at school, and he used the opportunity to stop at the market for much-needed groceries. He pulled into the driveway, and, with the kids' help, started unloading the bags and carrying them into the house. Steve paid no attention to the silver Explorer parked across the street, and the man sitting inside.

DeWayne, wearing an orange safety vest and white hard-hat, had been parked at various locations for the last hour, waiting for someone to return to the house. Every fifteen minutes, he would move the car to a new place, in case the neighbors started wondering what he was doing there. He'd been parked across the street from Steve's house for ten minutes before Steve returned.

DeWayne had earlier scouted the area for a vantage point from which the shooter could see the front of the house. There was nothing within blocks high enough to see over the other homes for a clear shot.

He parked several houses away and walked past the house. Wearing the orange safety vest and white hard hat, and carrying a clipboard with papers attached, he knocked on the front door to confirm no one was home, then, looking around to see if anyone was watching, casually walked up the driveway and peeked over the fence. He made a mental note to find a way into the woods behind the house. He returned to his car to watch the house.

DeWayne waited another five minutes, then started the car, preparing to drive away, when he saw Steve's son come out the front door, bouncing a basketball, and head towards the hoop in the driveway. Steve followed him out and backed his car into the street, parking it in front. He walked back to the driveway, and for the next twenty minutes they shot hoops, then played a couple of games of Horse.

As Barbara arrived home, she tooted her horn, and they moved out of the driveway, making room for her to park. DeWayne watched as they greeted each other with hugs, then went into the house. *How touching. Too bad it has to end.* DeWayne made a pistol with his thumb and forefinger, pointed it at Steve, whispered "bang", and drove off to find a way into the woods in Steve's backyard.

Driving back to Jacksonville, DeWayne called Clive to report what he had found.

"No way a shooter could get to Steve or Joey from the front of the house without being seen. It would have to be a close-in shooting, and after Billy screwed it up, the neighbors could be worried there may be another attempt. While I was in the neighborhood, I saw a couple of them looking out their windows, keeping an eye on the street, and the cops drove by four times in an hour."

"So what do we do? Call it a day? Let Momma Peters know we don't want the contract, or what?" Clive asked.

"There is one way a shooter could get to them, and that's from the woods in the back of the house." DeWayne paused, waiting to see how Clive would respond.

"Go on."

"I found a path through the woods, a jogging trail, that comes out a couple hundred yards down from Torelli's back yard. There's public access from the streets behind the house, so the shooter could park close by and walk in, then move off the trail until he's behind the house. From there, it's about a hundred-yard-shot. Piece of cake for our guy."

"OK. I want you to stay there a couple of days and watch the back of the house from the woods. See if Torelli routinely spends time in the back, how much time he spends in the yard, that sort of stuff. Find out if the brother, Joey, is staying there. Once you've got the information, come on back, and we'll let the shooter know the plan."

"You gonna tell Momma Peters we're taking the contract?"

"Yep. I'll call her today."

"All right, Boss. Call you when I'm done here." DeWayne made a U-turn and headed back toward Augusta, glad he hadn't gone very far before having to turn around.

Later that day Steve was on the phone with Vince. "Been nothing shaking here, Vince. No suspicious cars driving by or people hanging around. The usual traffic--my mailman, a service person or two, delivery people. I'm hoping they gave up on us."

"You may be right, Steve, but don't let your guard down. It's been six weeks since the first attack, and based on that, someone wanted you and Joey dead really bad. I'm worried they're biding their time and will be back for another try."

"I hope not, but I'll keep a close eye on things."

"How's Joey doing? He staying straight?"

"Yeah, as far as I can tell. I don't see him much, but when I do, he hasn't been drunk or high. He's not living here anymore."

"Really? Where is he?"

"He's staying at a friend's place outside the city. Matter of fact, the friend is his AA sponsor. He even got Joey a better job at a Walmart warehouse. Hard work, but the pay is decent. Best part is Joey works the four-to-midnight shift. Makes it easier to stay out of trouble."

"You hear from him much?"

"Yeah, couple times a week. We meet for breakfast or lunch once in a while."

"Is he being careful? Keeping a close eye out?"

"Says he is. Not hitting the bars or clubs anymore. I believe Janice's death was a real wakeup, and he's not over it. Talk about being scared straight. When we meet in a public place, he's very nervous--constantly looking around. There's a few of his closest friends who know where he is."

"Well, that's not a bad thing. How are you doing?"

"Oh, so-so. I'm worried they will come back for another try at me."

"Ya know they won't come at you from the front again. Not after the disaster of the first try. The only other place would be from the rear, through the woods. Have you thought about getting a couple of outdoor wireless cameras?"

"I looked into cameras for the front of the house, but haven't gotten them yet."

"Check Amazon for outdoor security cameras for the backyard. There are ones that are wireless, have motion sensors, night-vision, and can transmit images to your phone or computer, up to 500 feet away. You should get a set."

"I'll look into it."

"When you get them, emphasis on 'when', have them installed just inside the woods. That way if anyone is trying to ninja up to the house, you'll be warned early."

"I'll call Louie tomorrow. She should be able to recommend a security company."

"Good idea. I gotta go, Steve. Maggie and the boys are home. You stay safe. Talk to you later."

"Later, Cuz."

Over the next three days, DeWayne spent eighteen hours lurking inside the tree line behind Steve's house, watching the backyard. He was there at 3 p.m. each day, an hour before Steve or Barbara arrived home from work, and stayed until 9 p.m. before returning to his hotel.

With his binoculars, he could see glimpses of the family moving about the kitchen and a sunroom through the windows. They didn't seem to be stationary long enough for the shooter to aim and shoot accurately. But then DeWayne knew he, himself, wasn't proficient in long-range shooting, or familiar with rifles. His weapon of choice, a Smith and Wesson .40 caliber semi-auto pistol, wasn't accurate beyond 25 to 30 yards.

DeWayne learned Steve would come out to the patio some evenings after dinner with coffee and a cigar, and sit there until he finished them. He was outside for around 20 minutes before going back in after the sun set.

Perfect. You're making it easy for us, Torelli.

Steve followed this routine for two of the three days. DeWayne decided to stay another three days, two of which would be on the weekend, to determine if Steve spent more time outside on Saturday or Sunday. He found the time he spent in the backyard or patio was erratic, and usually because he would be watching his kids playing. DeWayne felt the best chance for the shooter would be on a weekday evening.

DeWayne called Clive on Sunday afternoon and reported what he found out, and his recommendation.

"I think the shooter will have a better opportunity to hit his target and escape on a weekday evening. I've noticed there aren't many people wandering around the woods then, and few joggers. What I see the most is people walking their dogs, but they stay on the path. I watched from directly behind the house, and it is a good 200 feet from the path. The woods are pretty thick there, with bunches of undergrowth, so he could stay hidden if anyone happened to get near him."

"That's good news. I'll call the shooter tomorrow and get it set up with him. If he takes the job, he'll be in Jacksonville in a few days, so come on back, and you can fill him in on what you learned."

"OK, Boss. I took photos of the area, too. They might help him get familiar with the area." Looking at his watch, he saw it was nearly 5 p.m.

"I'm gonna checkout and get my dinner, so I should be back in town by 10 tonight. Want me to check in with you when I get there?"

"Nah. Go home. I'll see you tomorrow morning."

"You got it. See you then."

Chapter 19

Steve took Vince's advice and called Louie, who recommended a security company she was familiar with, SecurePro Systems. Steve called them and set up an appointment for Monday afternoon to discuss what he wanted. A representative came out and spent two hours with him, going over the different available products designed to keep an eye on the rear yard.

Steve decided on a wireless system of three motion detector cameras with night-vision placed in the woods. They would be a few feet inside the tree-line, facing his backyard, and would activate if anyone got within fifty feet. The cameras were spaced 100 feet apart and could pick up anyone or anything coming toward the house from the trees. Set on the tree trunks five feet up, there would be little foliage and branches blocking the camera's view, or interfering with the motion detectors. The equipment was miniaturized and disguised to look like the tree's bark, minimizing the chance they would be noticed.

Two more similar cameras were to be attached to the back corners of the house, covering the field to the left and right, and one more, with a fish-eye lens, was placed on the front eave, covering the street and approach to the porch.

The technician and installers showed up at Steve's at 8:30 a.m. on Wednesday, and went right to work. By 11 a.m., all the equipment was installed, and Steve, who had taken the day off from work, spent the next hour-and-a-half with the technician downloading the app to his phone, desktop computer, and laptop. The tech showed him how the system worked, and played the distinctive ping notification whenever they went active. They checked the resolution, coverage, and focus, of each camera, making slight adjustments as needed, until they both were satisfied with the results. Testing the system took another twenty minutes, with Steve and the tech walking into range of the cameras, hearing the ping and seeing the video come up on Steve's phone.

Steve was satisfied with the results, and felt good he had heeded Vince's advice. With the house alarm, and video cameras, he felt they were well protected inside and out.

Clive had DeWayne pick up the shooter, known only as Ronin, at the Augusta airport Wednesday afternoon. DeWayne saw Ronin waiting outside the terminal, recognizing him from his physical description and a description of his clothes Clive provided. Dewayne pulled to a stop next to him.

Ronin was an ordinary-looking guy, a bit short at 5'6", and slight of build. He wore tortoise shell glasses, and his thick, light brown hair was neatly combed. He was dressed in Levis, and wore a light blue polo shirt. People passing by didn't give him a second glance. Ronin's appearance gave others the impression he was a nerd.

A suite was already reserved for him at the Hilton Doubletree Hotel under the name Robert Jones, and a rental car for him was parked in the lot. While driving Ronin to the hotel, DeWayne told him of the layout of Steve's house, and the woods to the rear. He gave Ronin a Google maps printout of the area, with the trail through the trees highlighted.

As they pulled up to the lobby entrance, DeWayne handed him a piece of notepaper and said, "Here's the address of Clive's Augusta office. Be there by 8 a.m. We'll have the money ready for you as agreed--half now, half when the job is done. All the info you need will be ready then, including the two targets' photos. Don't be late."

"Don't worry about it. I'll be there on time."

"Good. Enjoy the rest of the day."

As Ronin retrieved his duffle bag from the back seat, DeWayne said, "Oh, yeah. Here's your car keys." Tossing them to him, he added, "It's the black Chevy parked across from us."

Ronin nodded and walked into the hotel without another word.

Ronin was at Clive's office at 7:45 the next morning, Thursday. He had risen at five a.m. and driven to the woods, parking where Dewayne had indicated on the map. Making his way through the trees, he stopped ten feet back from the meadow, and watched Steve's house and the area through binoculars as the sun rose. He saw the two security cameras mounted on the back of the house, and recorded it on a small notepad. An hour later, he was back in the car, driving past the house a couple of times, familiarizing himself with the neighborhood. Ronin parked three houses down from Steve's and watched as the neighbors left for work, or to take their children to school, meticulously recording the address of each and the time they left. He noted when Barbara left with the two kids in tow, and noted her car make, model, and color. When Steve left ten minutes later, he did the same with his vehicle.

Looking at this watch, Ronin saw it was 7:20, and left to keep his appointment with Clive.

Ronin wasn't worried about DeWayne or Clive seeing his face. The theatrical makeup he used made him look paler than his normal olive coloring, and aged him ten years. His hair was much darker than the light brown he had dyed it. His glasses had clear lenses, as he didn't wear them in real life. Once he was done with Clive, whether he took the contract or not, he would change his appearance again, and would not be recognized as Ronin. If, by chance, he was recognized, then Clive and Dewayne would have to be eliminated.

After Clive and DeWayne finished their briefing, Ronin said, "Let me think on this for a day. I want to scout the area more. I'll call you at noon on Friday and let you know. It's twenty grand for the two of them--half up-front, non-refundable, the rest when the contract is completed."

"I'll have the money here on Friday."

Ronin nodded, and left, headed back to Steve's neighborhood. He spent the rest of the day thoroughly scouting the approaches in the front, and rear of the house. He quickly ruled out an attack from the front--it hadn't worked the first time, and he knew it wouldn't work if tried again.

Ronin noted the security cameras covering the front of the house. DeWayne hadn't mentioned them during their meeting, and, wondering how long they had been there, called him.

"Hey, DeWayne. I see a couple of cameras on the front of the house. Have they been there long?"

"No. In fact, there were no cameras, front or back, a week ago."

"You sure? I saw two on the back this morning."

"Yeah. I scoped out the back with binoculars, and specifically looked for cameras. There were none that I could see, and there were none on the front of the house, either."

"So, it's safe to assume they were added in the last few days. That could mean the local police know something, or Torelli had that stuff added. Why would he all of a sudden install cameras?"

"I can't answer that."

"I'm gonna take another look at the back, see if there are more cameras there. Call you back in a while."

Fifteen minutes later, Ronin was crouched in the brush at the edge of the forest with his binoculars, searching for cameras. He saw the two on the corners of the house, and noticed they were not covering the field, only the sides of the house.

Why no surveillance of the field? Makes no sense, unless..., Ronin shifted around to face the forest. Within two minutes, he'd located two cameras aimed at the house from behind him.

Shit. Goddammit. Now they know I'm here.

Ronin thanked his stars he had the foresight to wear a plain black baseball cap, as he pulled the brim down to help cover his face. He casually walked into the forest, his head down as if he were looking for something on the ground. Once he felt sure he was past the cameras, he walked straight back to the car, and left the area. He could only hope his face, disguised as it was, couldn't be seen.

He called Clive while driving to the Doubletree. "There's surveillance all around the house--too much to chance taking him out there. Give me another day to find an alternative location. Tomorrow, I'll follow him to his work. That might be the best chance we have. By the way, does anyone know where Joey Torelli is?"

"Not yet. We're working on it. I've got all my crew on the look-out for him. Let me know what you decide. One day, Ronin, and that's it. A yes or no is all I'm looking for." Clive disconnected before Ronin could reply.

Fuckin' asshole. One day I'll be coming for you, Ronin promised himself.

When Steve got home from work an hour after Ronin left, he fired up his computer and reviewed the video recordings. Nothing from the front cameras, and he turned his attention to the field recordings. Since those were motion-activated, and time-stamped, he didn't have hours of video to watch. The recordings lasted a few minutes at a time, until they turned themselves off after two minutes without detecting any motion.

He saw a couple of joggers running along the fringe of the trees in the morning--they appeared to be two young women--and kids walking to the trees, kids he recognized as neighbors two houses from him. The rest of the day revealed deer, coyotes, a small group of wild pigs, and an armadillo visiting the field. The last video showed a man walk past the camera to the forest's edge, and crouch in the brush, looking toward the house.

The view showed him from the back. Once crouched down, the camera picked up the back of his head. When Ronin turned his head slightly, Steve saw he was looking through a pair of binoculars.

Steve paused the video, and dialed Louie's number.

"Sergeant Princeton. Can I help you?"

"Hey, Louie, It's Steve."

"Hi, Steve. Everything all right?"

"Maybe, maybe not. I've been reviewing the surveillance videos, and the last one from an hour-and-a-half ago picked up a guy crouched in the brush at the edge of the forest. He was watching the back of the house with binoculars. According to the time stamp, he was there for twelve minutes until he turned around and spotted the camera."

"Did it pick up a good shot of his face?"

"Pretty good. He must have spotted it as soon as he turned. There is about a two-second view before he pulled his cap low on his head and looked down."

"Could you tell if he was armed? Would have to be a rifle at that distance."

"Didn't see one. He left immediately, turning away from the camera as he did."

"Well, that's something. Can you forward the video to me? I'd like to view it with the lead investigator in your dad's homicide."

"Detective Farrell? I talked to him two days ago, letting him know about the cameras. He told me to send any suspicious videos to him."

"No worries. I'll let him know I talked with you, and the video is on the way. It'll be OK this time, but from now on, better send them to him first. Don't want any hurt feelings, ya know. You have his department email?"

"Yeah, I do."

"If you get any more recordings like that, let me know, OK? I'm staying on top of the case, and am helping with the investigation."

"Good to know. It's been a few weeks without much progress."

"I know, and I'm sorry. We are trying our best, but there isn't much turning up. We need someone to come forward, a witness or something. Farrell has a meeting with the narcotics undercovers tomorrow. I'll be there. We're going to see if any of their informants could help. Somebody's got to know who's involved. I'm going to increase our patrol presence behind your house--more drive-bys, more walk-throughs of the trees. If we can't catch him, we can at least take away that avenue of attack, if he is involved."

"Sounds good. I'll send the video to Farrell, and you. Talk to you soon."

After disconnecting the call, Steve went upstairs and got his hunting rifle. He spent the next few minutes dusting it off, checking the mechanism, and loading it. Taking it downstairs, he put it on the top shelf of a small pantry in the kitchen, out of sight, but readily available.

Chapter 20

Joey had been working hard at the warehouse, volunteering for overtime and extra shifts, then returning to the apartment he shared with his AA sponsor in Evans, a small town ten miles northwest of Augusta. Joey liked Evans because it was a quiet, family-oriented town with little crime. He'd been clean and sober for over a month. Though he still longed for a stiff drink most every day, living with his sponsor, helped him resist the urge, and stay sober. His life had returned to normal, and he felt happier and calmer than he had in quite a while. He and his sponsor, James Holmgren, got along well, and had become fast friends.

There was a small 24-hour diner off Highway 104 that served the best breakfasts in the area. A gravel lot around the weathered building was the parking lot. The building had been built in 1931, serving first as a saloon, then, seven years later, a hardware store. After WWII, a former marine, fresh from the Pacific front, bought it and turned it into a diner. He ran it until 1980, when he deeded it to his son, the current owner.

The light blue paint outside was peeling, and the inside was in desperate need of a good cleaning and fresh paint. The locals didn't seem to mind, and the diner did a brisk business. Joey would stop there after work once or twice a week, and had become known to the owner and employees as a regular. He had even dated one of the night shift servers, Sherie MacDonald, a couple of times. He liked her, and felt she returned the feeling. It was a budding romance.

This night, Joey got off work at two A.M. Tired and hungry, he decided to stop at the diner, have breakfast, and visit with Sherie before heading home. He called his sponsor to let him know so he wouldn't worry, as was his practice.

Joey pulled into the lot and parked in front. There were only three other cars in the lot, and he saw four people inside. As he approached the door, one of the customers was leaving. Joey pulled the door open and stood aside as the guy left, glancing at Joey and muttering, "Thanks."

Joey recognized him as one of the people he used to hang around with during his drinking and drugging days. He averted his face, hoping he wouldn't recognize him.

Though Joey had gained twenty-five pounds, cut his hair, and shaved off the scraggly beard, the guy stopped next to him, and asked, "Hey, don't I know you?"

"I don't think so. Maybe you seen me here a couple of times."

His brow furrowed as he replied, "Nah, that's not it. You look a lot like a guy I used to hang with a couple of months ago."

"Sorry, pal. I got into town a week ago."

Joey turned to enter, and heard him say, "Joey. That's it. You're Joey Torelli. Where you been, Bro?"

Joey kept walking, saying over his shoulder, "Got the wrong guy, pal."

He kept walking and took a seat at the counter, resisting the urge to turn to see if he was gone.

Sherie came up to him and said, "Breakfast, or somethin' else, handsome?"

"Just coffee for now. Do me a favor. Don't be too obvious, but take a look outside. Is the guy that left still out front?"

As she poured him a glass of water, she looked out the window. "Yeah. He's standing out there staring at you, scratching his head. Oh, wait. He's walking away, toward a car." She put a mug on the counter. Grabbed the coffee pot, and poured Joey a cup.

"He's driving out of the lot, but took one last look at you. What's going on, Joey?"

"Some bad people are trying to find me." Joey grabbed her hand and said, "If anyone comes in here and asks about me, by name or description, don't let on you know me. Tell them you never heard of anyone by that name. You don't know me, understand?"

"Let go Joey, you're hurting me."

Joey looking startled, dropped her hand. "I'm sorry, Sherie. You don't know these people. They're dangerous, and if they find me, they will kill me."

"Want me to call the cops?"

"No. I'll call them when I get home. Promise me you'll do what I asked."

Taking both his hands in hers, Sherie said, "I promise, Joey."

Joey took a swallow of his coffee, put money on the counter, and left. He looked around before going to his car, but didn't see any vehicles with someone inside who might be watching.

Driving out of the lot, he went back to Evans. Joey started making random turns, checking his mirrors for any cars following him. After ten minutes and a dozen turns, Joey was sure he wasn't being followed. He encountered one other car going in the opposite direction that whole time. Relieved, Joey took back roads to the apartment.

The next morning, Joey called Steve and told him about the encounter at the diner.

"He knew me, Steve--called me by name. God damn it. What should I do?"

"Don't panic, little brother. You're sure you weren't followed home?"

"Yeah, I'm sure."

"OK. Don't go back to the diner. If anyone comes looking for you, that's where they're gonna start. How many people at the diner know where you live?"

"Just one, a server named Sherie. We've gone out a few times. She's been at the apartment once. I warned her not to let on she knows me."

"Does she know why?"

"Not specifically, only that there are dangerous people looking to hurt me."

"Can she be trusted to do what you asked?"

"Yeah, I think so."

"All right. You want to come home?"

"No. I think I'll be OK here."

"I can have a friend meet you and give you one of our guns. Before you refuse, let me say you need to be able to protect yourself. How do you know that guy won't call whoever it is that's trying to kill us, and let them know he saw you?"

"I don't. I remember the guy. He's not too smart."

"What's his name?"

"His street name is Banjo. I never heard his real name."

"Banjo? That's odd."

"Not really. He can play the banjo pretty well, so the nickname stuck. I remember him saying he once was in a bluegrass band."

"You need to call Louie and tell her all this. Maybe she can find him. Somebody on the PD might know a Banjo. He might be one of the guys who ambushed you and Janice."

"Yeah, I was planning on calling her. I gotta go, brother. Got a double shift today. I'll talk to you later."

"Tell Louie to call me when you're done with her."

"Will do."

After leaving the diner, Banjo, whose real name was Forrest Monroe, couldn't shake the feeling he had seen Joey. Yeah, he looked different--heavier, no beard, short hair--which, along with the half-pint of Jack Daniels he'd drunk, made him unsure it was Joey. When he got home, he had a few more Jack Daniels, and fell asleep on the couch.

When Banjo awoke, with a raging headache, he headed back to the diner for his cure-all breakfast. Nothing like a big plate of eggs and grits, a side of ham, and several cups of hot, strong coffee to fix what ails you.

It was nearly 10 a.m. when he took a seat at the counter. Sherie and the rest of the night shift had gone home four hours earlier. She told the day cook about Joey, and to not let anyone know Joey was a customer, or even that they knew him. He said he would pass it on to the others as they arrived.

The diner's busiest time was from 6:30 a.m. to 10 a.m., when it was packed with diners on their way to work, and the cook and staff were nearly overwhelmed hustling to fill orders. As busy as he was preparing the kitchen and cooking the breakfasts, he forgot to pass the info on to the day shift as they arrived.

A heavy-set, older woman in her powder-blue waitress outfit, her name-tag pinned above her ample bosom identified her as Elsie, came carrying a coffee pot. She was in her 50's, forty pounds overweight, with short gray hair and an abrupt manner. She asked Banjo what he wanted, and once he told her, she chuckled and asked, "Had a tough night, did ya?"

"Don't start on me, Elsie. I ain't in the mood."

"You always 'ain't in the mood' these days."

"Yeah, yeah. Get the order going, will ya?"

Elsie sneered, and poured his coffee, making sure to slop a bit on the table, then strolled off to place his order. She could tell Banjo was hungover by looking at him. He was a regular at the diner, coming in three or four times a week, ordering the same thing each time.

Elsie didn't get the warning, so when she delivered Banjo's food, and refilled his coffee, Banjo asked her if she knew a customer named Joey. She said, "Yeah. He usually comes in late at night. Nice guy, though a bit quiet."

"If he comes in at night, how'd you get to know him?"

"I used to work that shift, up 'til a month ago. Got used to seeing him in here."

"You know his last name?"

"Not really. I think it was Tor-something."

"Torelli? Could that be it?"

"Yeah, I think so. Torelli. Why you askin'?"

"He's an old friend of mine. We lost touch six months ago. Want to get back in contact with him. You know where he's living?"

"Said he had an apartment in Evans."

"You wouldn't have a phone number for him?"

"I don't, but, according to scuttlebutt, he's been seeing Sherie, one of our night waitresses. She probably does."

"Great, I'll come back tonight, if she's working."

"Should be. This is her last night before her days off."

"Thanks, Elsie. You been a big help."

"Sure. Keep that in mind when you leave the tip."

Banjo finished his breakfast, then sat in his car to make a phone call to Junior Henderson. Junior's cell went to message, so Banjo left him a message.

"Junior, it's Banjo. Call me back when you get this. I've got information you might want. It's about Joey Torelli."

As Banjo drove to Augusta, his cell rang. He saw by the caller I.D. it was Junior Henderson calling.

"Hey, Junior. Thanks for calling me back."

Without so much as a hello, Junior said, "What's this about Joey?"

"I know there's people looking for him, and I think I found him."

"Why you calling me? I got nothing to do with that."

"Thought maybe you could pass the information along to whoever wants him, cause, you know, who your dad is. Let them know I'm the one who found Joey, in case there's a reward."

Junior paused before responding.

"You still there, Junior?"

"Yeah, yeah. Tell ya what. Tell me what you know, and I'll ask around. If it pans out, I'll be sure to mention your name, in case there's a reward."

"Thanks, man. I really appreciate it."

Banjo was glad to tell Junior what he knew, thinking he might get a fat reward from someone. He turned the radio up and sang along to the latest Sugarland tune as he drove.

Junior called the Peters house immediately after ending the call. It was known in the local crime circles Mama Peters was looking for Joey Torelli, and there was a $5,000 reward for information on his whereabouts. Billy answered and Junior told him about Banjo's call.

"He's pretty sure he saw him at the diner, Billy. It's that joint off 104 outside Evans. Let me talk to your mom."

Junior waited while Billy went to the kitchen and gave the phone to his mother. "It's Junior Henderson, Ma. He wants to tell ya something."

Mama Peters wrote down the information, thanked Junior, and assured him he would get the reward when they found Joey. She, in turn, called Clive, who notified Ronin.

Ronin pulled into the diner parking lot at midnight. Entering, he saw he was the only customer. Ronin took a stool at the counter, and signaled the short, blonde counter server over. Her name tag identified her as Lois.

"Good morning, sir. What can I get you?" she said, placing a menu and coffee mug in front of him.

"I'll have coffee, and maybe one of those pastries," he said, pointing at the bear claws on display at the end of the counter.

Lois poured his coffee, then put a bear claw on a plate and served the pastry to him.

"There ya go, sir. If you want anything else, let me know."

"There is one thing, Lois. I'm looking for an old chum of mine that may be living in Evans. His name is Joey, Joey Torelli. I don't know his address, or phone number, but another friend or ours said he thinks Joey is dating one of the ladies that works here. Her name is Sherie. Would she be working tonight?"

Lois had gotten the warning from Sherie, and though surprised at Ronin's question, covered her reaction well.

"It's her night off. She'll be back tomorrow night."

"Would you have a phone number for her? I'm passing through and will be leaving tomorrow, and I really am anxious to see him."

"Sorry, sir. We're not allowed to give out the employee's phone numbers."

"Oh, that's too bad. Guess I'll have to wait to talk to her until next week, on my way back to Atlanta. Thanks, anyway."

Ronin watched Lois as he ate the bear claw and drank his coffee. She glanced at him a few times but looked away if he saw her staring. After a few minutes, Lois went into the kitchen. Ronin walked through the swinging door and saw Lois near the rear door, her back to him. She was quietly talking on her phone and was unaware of his presence. He crept closer until he was a few feet behind her and could hear what she was saying.

"No, I've never seen him before. He said he knew you were seeing Joey, and that a friend told him that."

Lois listened for a moment, then replied, "Of course. I didn't tell him anything. Don't worry. OK, I'll see you tomorrow."

Lois ended the call, and as she put the phone in her pocket, Ronin slipped an arm around her neck and clapped his other hand over her mouth, stifling her startled scream. She started to struggle. Pulling her back against his chest, he whispered in her ear, "Quiet, now. We're going out back to talk. You cooperate and no one gets hurt."

Ronin guided her toward the door and had her open it. Once outside, he said, "I'm going to remove my hand from your mouth. Don't scream, or I'll cut your throat, understand?"

Lois nodded, weeping as he took his hand away. "Please, don't hurt me," she cried.

"Shh, shh, Lois. Tell me what I want to know and you'll be fine." He took a switchblade from his pocket, held it in front of her face, and hit the release button, causing it to pop open. Holding the blade against her neck, he walked her to a cluster of trees fifty feet away and said, "Now, I want the truth."

Chapter 21

Vince was sitting at his desk, rereading a cold homicide case. With his feet on the desk, he flipped through the report, yawning, bored out of his mind. He and Bobby had wrapped up their most recent case, and the few open cases they had were stalled while they looked for new information.

Cold cases often were boring grunt work, but a necessary evil. Sometimes a detail missed earlier could provide the link to solving the case. On his third cup of stale coffee, he found his mind drifting to his uncle's homicide.

Looking at his watch, Vince saw he had been reviewing the report the last thirty minutes. It seemed like hours to him. He yawned again and stretched.

Vince and Bobby spent the last few days chasing down potential leads from the tip line and re-interviewing witnesses to see if they remembered anything that would help in the investigation. They learned nothing new.

The highlight of the week was the call Vince got from Steve, who told him of the chance encounter between Joey and Banjo, and asked if Vince thought Joey was in danger.

"Well, yeah. You both are. Seems things have been too quiet there. I find it odd that whoever came after you two would give up. No, I think they're still looking for Joey."

"There's been nothing here other than that one time the cameras recorded the man in the woods. They must know I'm still here at the house. Why haven't they come after me?"

"I don't know. Maybe they want to locate Joey first then go after both of you at once."

"Would it be ok if Joey came out to stay with you for a while? After a week or so, if things haven't been resolved, we can move him to a hotel."

"He can stay with us as long as he needs. Why don't you ask him? You and your family could come out for a visit, too. It would be nice, and get you both out of the area for a while."

"I'll think about it. I'll go by and see Joey today. Call you later, Cuz."

Bobby overheard the call and asked, "That your cousin?"

"Yeah. Our weekly update."

"Anything new on your uncle's case or the ambush at the house?"

"No, and that worries me. I can't believe whoever ordered the hit gave up after the botched attack."

"I know. Had to be the same person who set up your uncle."

"We're trying to get Joey to come out here for a while. It'll be safer."

"Think he'll agree?"

"Don't know. Steve's gonna go see him later today."

"Well, good luck with that."

Ten minutes later, Vince's cell rang. Looking at the caller I.D. he saw it was from Louie.

"Hey, Louie. What's up?"

"Hi Vince. I just finished a call with the narcotics lieutenant. One of their snitches was at a bar last night with some other shitheads, and overheard Joey's name mentioned."

"Really? That's good, right?"

"Could be. Being the good snitch that she is, she joined the conversation, and learned that dirtbag called Banjo claims he saw Joey at a diner outside Evans."

"Where's that?"

"It a small town about ten miles from Augusta. Anyway, Banjo said he was pretty sure it was Joey. He'd cleaned up a bit, and put on weight, but he knows it was him."

"I take it this Banjo character didn't get Joey's address."

"No, but earlier today we got a report of a homicide at that diner."

"No shit?"

"No shit."

"Coincidence?"

Louie chuckled, "I don't believe in coincidences. I know it's connected."

"Did you call Steve?"

"Yeah. Told him everything."

"What ties the homicide to the info on Joey's location?"

"Steve does. He told me today Joey's been seeing one of the servers at the diner--a gal named Sherie."

"Is she the victim?"

"No. It was another server, an older woman named Lois Sampson. Farrell and I are on our way to the Columbia County Sheriff's Office, since they are handling the investigation. Their detective agreed to meet with us. We're almost there, so I'll call you back later."

Louie and Farrell learned the victim was found after a trucker stopped at the diner for breakfast, and saw no one inside. After calling out and getting no response, he went into the kitchen, saw the cook asleep in the office, and woke him up. They searched the diner, then outside, and found Lois's body by the woods, in a large pool of blood.

"The medical examiner determined her throat had been cut. She hadn't been dead long--less than an hour."

"Any suspect info?"

"No. The diner was empty, and the cook was asleep in the office when it happened."

"What's your take on this, Louie?"

She paused in thought for a moment, sighed, and said, "I think whoever killed her was looking for information on Joey, either where he lives, or about his girlfriend. I'd bet this guy is a hunter, a for-hire killer, and probably good at what he does."

"Makes sense to me. Well, whatever he learned won't help him. Steve was planning to pick up Joey this morning. Hopefully, he'll be on a plane to California later today. He'll be safe with me."

Ronin drove slowly by the apartment building with the headlights off. It was 1:25 a.m. With no street lights along the curb, and with a half-moon in the sky, almost totally dark.

"Which apartment?" he asked.

Sherie said, "It's number twenty-three." The words came out slurred. The swelling to her mouth, the broken nose, and the two missing teeth made it hard to speak clearly. Her eyes showed purple bruises, and dried blood caked her chin and the front of her clothing. The pain was a throbbing ache.

Ronin had tied her to the seat with several wraps of strong rope. Her arms were secured to her sides, and the knots were on the seat back where she couldn't reach them. Unknown to him, Sherie had arched her back a couple of inches and taken deep breaths while he was knotting the ropes, giving her two inches of slack.

Once past the apartments, Ronin pulled into a lot with an abandoned building, its windows and doors covered with plywood. Graffiti marked the sides, and a faded sign on the roof read 'Jefferson's Coin and Jewelry'.

He parked in the rear, close to the building, so the car couldn't be seen from the street. He got out and walked around to the passenger door. Opening it, he grabbed the roll of duct tape on the floor.

"This is to keep you from calling out," he said, as he wrapped it twice across her mouth and around her head. "I'll be back soon. Be a good girl, and this will all be over, and I'll release you."

Sherie was weeping, and having a hard time breathing. Her broken nose had swollen, and was filled with clotted blood.

Ronin shut her door and started walking to Joey's apartment, pulling on a pair of thin leather gloves. He was not concerned about fingerprints in the rental car--he planned to torch it, with Sherie's body inside, when he finished here.

Ronin climbed the stairs to the second floor, paused, and looked around. He saw no one on the sidewalk, or in the lot, not unusual for a small town after dark.

He drew the silenced .22 Colt Diamondback revolver, and holding it down along his leg, walked up to Joey's apartment door. He could hear music from inside, and someone moving around. Ronin knocked on the door, and heard a man's voice say, "Wait a minute." Twenty seconds later, the door opened, and James Landers asked, "Can I help you?"

Ronin saw the man was clean shaven, and had short dark hair. The photo he had of Joey showed his hair several inches longer and disheveled, and he sported a scraggly beard. The description Banjo provided had Joey clean-shaven, with his hair cut short.

Ronin raised the Colt and fired two shots into James' chest. He stumbled back, a hand pressed to the wounds, a look of shock on his face, then crumpled to the floor. Ronin took a step inside and shot him again in the head. Backing out of the apartment, he placed the gun in his waistband, closed the door, and casually walked away.

Sherie waited until Ronin was out of sight before pressing her body into the seat, causing the rope to sag a bit. Within a minute, she was able to wiggle one of her arms up and out from the rope. Once it was free, the rope was looser, and she quickly got her other arm out. She managed to pull the rope around her, and when the knots were in front, untie them.

Sherie was terrified she wouldn't escape before he came back. Trembling and sobbing, she opened the door and slowly got out. Though shielded from view by the building, Sherie crouched over and ran through the tall grass in the field, keeping the building between her and the apartments, while pulling off the duct tape over her mouth. The faint light from the moon allowed her to see the darker shapes of trees. Twenty yards from the car, she stumbled into a dry creek bed, falling three feet, landing on her hands and knees. The hard dirt and rough stones cut her hands, and tore her jeans at the knees, causing abrasions to the exposed skin. Sherie grabbed her knees, crying out from the pain. She clapped a hand over her mouth to muffle the sound of her sobs, and, looked around. Terrified, she got to her feet and ran along the creek bed as fast as she could.

Sherie didn't know how far she'd run when she came to a small bridge arcing over the creek. She climbed the bank and saw the bridge connected to a hard-packed gravel path. She stopped to catch her breath and listen for any sounds of pursuit.

After a couple of minutes listening to the silence, Sherie felt it was safe for her to continue. She ran along the path toward a cluster of houses a short distance away, dodging around a swing set, slide, and monkey bars. Sherie realized the path lead her through a small neighborhood park, and once out of it, she ran up on the porch of the first house she came to.

The house was dark, and Sherie began banging on the front door, calling out for help. Not thinking her assailant might hear her, she continued her pleas while trying to open the door, until the porch light came on and the front door opened a couple of inches.

Sherie cried out in relief, and began sobbing, trying to talk at the same time. The owner saw her bloodied face and clothes and opened the door wide. Sherie pushed her way past him into the house, slamming the door behind her and turning off the porch light.

"Call the police," she said, before collapsing to the floor.

Chapter 22

Vince awoke to the jarring ring of his cell. He groped along the top of the nightstand to answer it, but only succeeded in knocking it onto the floor. The continued ringing, and the clatter when it landed on the hardwood woke Maggie.

"Answer your phone," she said, turning over and pulling the covers over her head.

Vince saw the clock next to the bed read 5:20 a.m. He yawned and turned on the nightstand lamp, located the phone, retrieved it, and answered with a growl. "This better be damn important, calling me so early in the morning."

"Wake up, Torelli. We've had a break in the case, and its 8:20 here."

"Louie?"

"Yes. You awake, now?"

"Give me a minute." Vince sat up in bed. He shook his head and rubbed his face with his hand, trying to clear the cobwebs.

"Did I hear you say there's been a break in the case? Which case?"

"The attack on Joey at the house, the death of your uncle, and I'd be willing to bet, the homicide at the diner."

Fully awake now, Vince got out of bed, went into the living room, and sat on the couch. "Did you call Steve?'

"I just got off the phone with him. Thought I'd give you a courtesy call."

"Thanks. Tell me about it."

"There's a lot to tell." Louie took a deep breath, then continued. "Last night, the sheriff's office got a call from a citizen in Evans saying a young woman had pounded on his door, screaming for help. He opened the door and saw her face and clothing covered in blood. She was very distraught-- crying, and disoriented. He took her in and called the police and an ambulance. She'd collapsed, and was semi-conscious when they arrived. She was able to tell him she'd been kidnapped and beaten. Wanna guess her name?"

"Sherie?"

"Sherie."

"Son of a bitch."

"My words exactly. I'm at the sheriff's office, heading to a strategy meeting. Steve knows everything, so call him, and if you have any questions, give me a ring in a couple of hours."

Vince called Steve and told him Louie had called.

"The sheriff's office searched the neighborhood, and the surrounding area for the suspect, but came up empty-handed," Steve said. "Sherie gave them a description of the car, but the killer must have fled in it before the deputies arrived."

"No doubt. Damn. You know where Sherie is?"

"She's at University Hospital in Augusta, the trauma center." Steve paused for a long moment. "Is Sherie's abduction connected to the murder at the diner?"

"Louie's sure of it. She thinks the victim at the diner, Lois something, gave up Sherie's name and address to the killer, and he went after her."

"I thought so. Was Sherie able to tell them anything else?"

"Louie said she was in pretty bad shape, and severely traumatized; kept slipping in and out if consciousness. The doctor said any further questioning would have to wait until later today. Sherie needed x-rays, and treatment for her injuries, plus the doc gave her pain-killers."

Steve paused, sighed, and said, "We have another problem."

"What's is it?"

"Joey doesn't want to leave. Flat out refused after I told him about Sherie and Lois."

"What the hell is wrong..."

"Easy, Cousin. He's moving back to the house. He's pissed, and worried about me. Said we could watch out for each other."

"He has a point." Vince thought for a moment. "OK, but make sure neither of you goes anywhere unarmed."

"We've already discussed that. If we have to go somewhere, we will go together."

"Good plan."

An hour after talking with Steve and Vince, Louie was sitting in the briefing room with Detective Farrell, strategizing the direction of the investigation. The sheriff homicide investigators wanted to link the murders of Lois Sampson, Judge Torelli, and Janice Roberts, with the abduction of Sherie MacDonald. They were all aware of the attack on Sherie. In a moment of lucidity at Johnson's house, she told the responding officers she was forced to give the killer Joey's address, an apartment in Evans, not far from here.

As the meeting broke up, Holmgren said he was going back to the apartment with a signed search warrant. Farrell asked if they could tag along.

"Sure. Now that I have the warrant, I could use the help."

Louie asked, "Did you do a cursory search last night?"

"Yeah. A quick walk-through around 3:00 a.m. It was sealed after that until the CSI team arrived. They stood by while I got the warrant signed. They took all the photos, and printed everything they thought important. The medical examiner released the body an hour ago."

As they followed Holmgren to the apartment, Louie tuned her police radio to the sheriff's frequency. Monitoring the broadcasts, she heard one of the detectives confirming the victim had been shot twice in the chest and once in the head--a classic professional hit.

"You catch that?" she asked Farrell.

"Yeah. Think it might be connected to our other homicides?"

"A professional hit? Nothing yet connecting it to the others? Don't know who the victim is? No doubt--it's connected."

Farrell smiled and shook his head. "Sounds logical to me."

The apartment had been secured by the first two deputies arriving at the scene. Yellow police line tape encircled the area, three marked patrol cars blocked the driveway, and six deputies searched the area around the apartment, and where Ronin had parked, for evidence.

The apartment was a typical low-cost rental. With two bedrooms, it wasn't unusual to find four or five people living in a unit, sharing the rent and other costs. Every room was painted a pale yellow, and furnished with cheap furniture.

As Holmgren led them in, he was saying, "These apartments cater to students at the Augusta Technical College. The rent is cheap, and it's only fifteen minutes from the school.

Mail found on the coffee table identified the occupant as James Landers. A small stack of AA pamphlets next to the mail rang a bell with Louie, as she remembered Steve saying Joey was out of the Augusta area, and was living with his sponsor. She mentioned this to Holmgren and Farrell, thinking it was too much of a coincidence to be possible.

"This is too good to be true," she said. "What are the odds?"

Farrell, Louie, and Holmgren's partner, Madison, were looking through the smaller of the two bedrooms. Madison was looking in the dresser's top drawer when he found a small stack of papers. In the stack were several paystubs from Walmart, for Joseph Torelli.

"Hey, Farrell. Check this out," he said.

"Well, I'll be damned." Turning to Louie, Farrell said, "Looks like another murder connected to the Torelli case."

Chapter 23

While Landers' apartment was being searched, Sherie had recovered enough to be interviewed by a sheriff's investigator. Though she'd suffered a broken nose, and other facial bones, along with a concussion, Sherie was able to give a partial statement before being transported to the hospital.

Detective Sergeant Amie Colson knocked on the door jamb and stuck her head in. Seeing Sherie sitting up in bed, she walked in, pulled a chair up to the bed, and sat. She frowned as she saw the dark blue bruising around Sherie's eyes and face, and the bandages.

"Hi, Sherie. I'm Sergeant Colson with the Sheriff's Department. Feel up to talking with me? Are you in much pain?"

Sherie sat up a little higher, her hands clasped in her lap. She sighed and said, "The pain isn't too bad. The doctor gave me painkillers. It aches, now."

Sherie saw a 40ish woman--stocky, not fat, dressed in tan slacks, a white button-down collar blouse, carrying a navy-blue blazer. Her badge was clipped to her belt, and her pistol rode high in a holster at her right hip. Her dark hair was cut short, and she wore little makeup. She carried a brown leather portfolio stuffed with manilla folders and loose papers.

"Great. Quite a rough time, eh?"

Sherie looked down and mumbled, "Yes, yes it was."

"I'm sorry you had to go through this." She took Sherie's hand and said, "I promise we will do everything we can to find who did this to you. You sure you feel up to it?"

"Yes. Let's get this over with." Sherie took a deep breath. "I don't know what else I can tell you."

"Maybe something you forgot? What I'd like you to do is tell me everything from the time he parked behind the building until you got to Mr. Johnson's house. Is it OK to record this?"

"Yes." Sherie closed her eyes and was quiet for a minute. While she waited, Sergeant Colson activated her mini-recorder and set it on the tray next to the bed.

Sherie opened her eyes and looked at Colson. "I'm ready."

She related her escape from the ropes binding her to the seat, her flight from the car into the woods, and how she ended up at Johnson's house.

"You told the officers last night he duct-taped your mouth so you couldn't scream, or call for help, right?"

"Yes, why?"

"I've read your statement over several times, as well as Johnson's. He said there was no duct tape over your face, and you were able to yell for help at the front door. What happened to it?"

Sherie looked puzzled, her brow furrowed. "I don't know. I don't remember taking it off, but I must have."

Colson thought for a moment, then stood up. "I've need to make a call. I'll be right back. You relax for a couple of minutes. Think about the duct tape."

Colson left, and Sherie slid down to recline on the bed.

Colson returned in three minutes. When she saw Sherie, she looked like she had fallen asleep.

"Sherie? Are you awake?"

She opened her eyes and said, "Yes, Sergeant."

"Do you remember removing the tape?"

"Not really, I'm sure I would have taken it off soon after running from the car."

"OK, that's a help. I called the investigator who was at Johnson's house. He said he directed two deputies to trace your path back to the car, but didn't find anything they felt was evidence along the way. Is there anything you remember about the suspect that was unusual? An accent, scars, mannerisms, anything?"

"No, sorry."

"That's all right. You've suffered a very traumatic event. Think about it over the next couple of days, and if anything comes to mind, give me a call." Colson took a business card from the portfolio and handed it to her. "Here's my card. My personal cell number is written on the back, and you can call me anytime if you remember anything, no matter how trivial it may seem." Colson took Sherie's hand again, and gently squeezed it. "I hope you feel better soon. You're safe now. There's a deputy stationed outside your room, so rest easy, Sherie. I'll be in touch."

After leaving the hospital, Colson drove to the apartment building crime scene. She saw the detectives standing by Holmgren's car, talking. Driving up to them, she stopped next to the car, rolled her window down, and said, "Any of you want to help in a search of the area?"

Holmgren said, "I thought it was already done?"

"Yeah, last night, but I got a feeling the two deputies didn't do a thorough job." She got out of her car. "The suspect gagged Sherie with duct tape, but no one knows what happened to it. She removed it somewhere between here and Johnson's house."

Louise asked, "Did she say where she took it off?"

"No, doesn't remember. I'd bet she dropped it, or tossed it, as she ran. It's out there, waiting to be found."

"Well, I got nothin' better to do," Holmgren said, grinning.

They formed a line, six feet between each other, and slowly walked toward the woods, scanning the ground. They walked to Johnson's house, turned around and walked back, six feet away from their original path, through the woods and into the field. Farrell, walking on the outside of the line, found the duct tape at the base of a tree at the edge of the field, stuck to the base of the trunk, partially concealed by the tall grass.

After photographing it, Colson used a gloved hand to pick up the tape and put it in an evidence bag. Sealing the bag, she had all three of them put their initials over the sealed flap.

Back at the crime scene, Colson turned the bag with the tape over to the CSI supervisor. "Can I get a rush on this, Dave--prints, DNA, the works?"

"Can't promise you anything, Detective. We're pretty backed up." He smiled at her, stretched his arms and said, "Almost done here, then off to The Happy Hour Saloon for a drink. Care to join me?"

"Can't, sorry. You're not the only one swamped."

"OK," he said, frowning in disappointment. "Maybe next time."

"Next time for sure."

Colson started to leave, but turned back toward him. "Oh, wait. Damn, I almost forgot. There's been strange things going on in the department. Things have turned up on people's desks during the night. There's been boxes of candy, movie tickets, music CDs, among other things. Listen, if something is on your desk in the morning, like, oh I don't know, a bottle of Gentleman Jack, let me know, all right? I'm in charge of finding out who is leaving these unasked-for things and why."

Dave smiled and said, "You'll be the first person I call. By the way, Sergeant, you do know it's a felony to bribe a police official."

Not looking back, Colson raised her hand in a thumbs-up gesture.

Seven miles northwest of Evans a deputy was parked on the shoulder of Highway 104 at a dirt road, awaiting a tow truck. The road led to a burned-out car a half-mile in. Two hundred feet down the dirt road the field was replaced by thick forest, and the road looked like it went through a tunnel.

The deputy was unaware the car could be related to a homicide in Evans. A BOLO had been put out in the early morning for a black car, make unknown, as described by Sherie. The deputy couldn't tell the car's color, as it was totally burnt and covered with greasy, black soot. The license plates and VIN plate were missing.

The car was taken to the sheriff's impound yard for storage, until the registration could be determined and the owner contacted.

Later that afternoon, the swing shift watch commander was reading the previous shift's activity report when he saw the synopsis on the recovery of the abandoned, burnt car.

This could be the car in the BOLO. He thought for a moment, then decided it was better to be safe than sorry. He called the investigations number on the BOLO and advised them of the incident.

Vince was on a plane heading to Augusta. After talking with Louie, he was worried that Steve and Joey were still being hunted, and it appeared the hunter was a contract killer. Vince called and told Steve he was flying in, over Steve's objections. "Don't really need to, Vince. We can take care of ourselves."

"I know, but having a third person there won't hurt."

This time, Vince took his duty weapon with him, packed in his checked luggage.

Vince hired an Uber ride from the airport to Steve's, and while waiting for it to arrive, called Louie's cell. It went directly to voice mail. "Hey, Louie, It's Vince. I flew in and am on my way to Steve's. Give me a call when you get this. Talk to you soon." He then called Steve and told him he would be at the house in a half hour.

"I'd like to get Louie over and talk about the case. We need a strategy to keep safe."

Chapter 24

As Louie and Farrell were getting ready to leave the Evans crime scene, Louie's phone rang. She saw it was from the Narcotics Enforcement Bureau's main office.

"Sergeant Princeton."

"Hi, Louie, it's Sam Mason."

"Hey, Sam. What's up?" Louie had dated him a couple of years ago, for around six months. They were a good match, and spent a lot of their off-duty time together.

Work schedules eventually came between them, and they found there rarely was time they could get together. They mutually agreed to end their relationship. It wasn't working out anymore.

Sam asked, "Remember that snitch that told us about Banjo?"

"Yeah. What about her?"

"I met her last night, trying to set up a controlled buy, and she said word on the street has it that Junior Henderson is wrapped up in the Judge Torelli case."

"Really? Hold on, let me put this on speaker so Farrell can listen." She pressed the button, then said, "Did the snitch say how?"

"No, but it seems he knows who is gunning for the sons. Said it's the mother of a guy the judge sentenced to death for an armed robbery of a deli, during which the owner's wife was killed by one of the suspects."

"Farrell is looking through the judge's past cases, trying to find anyone he sentenced who would be gunning for him. The list is kinda long."

"I'll bet, knowing Torelli's hardcore sentencing history. Anyway, the snitch didn't have a name, but Junior would be a good place to start.

"You still looking for Banjo?"

"Yeah, but he's disappeared. Nobody's seen him for a couple of months."

"OK. Thanks for the tip, and let me know if Banjo turns up. Maybe when things calm down, we can get together for a drink."

"I'd like that. Take care."

"You, too," Louie replied.

Disconnecting the call, Louie turned to Farrell and said, "We need to talk to Junior."

"I'll get his number. We can give him a call and see if he'll meet us."

"OK. We'll keep it friendly and casual. If he is involved, we don't wanna set off any alarm bells."

A quick call to the records department and Farrell had Junior's cell number. He pulled off the highway and stopped in a gas station lot, parking near the back.

"Want me to call?" Farrell asked.

"Better let me. Junior may know I'd talked to his dad after the judge's death, so a familiar name might keep him less wary."

Junior answered on the third ring. Louie put it on speaker.

"Who's this?"

"Hello. This is Detective Princeton. Am I speaking to Junior Henderson?"

"Yeah. What do you want?"

"Don't know if you know my name, but I spoke with your father a couple of days after Judge Torelli was killed."

"I remember. My Dad told me he talked to a woman detective."

"Good. Listen, I'd like to talk to you."

"What about?"

"Your name came up in an investigation. A witness said you might have information that could help with the case."

"What investigation? When did this happen?"

"It was a home invasion and assault that happened two nights ago."

"Huh, I don't know nothing about a home invasion. Don't see any need to talk to you."

"Still, I'd like to ask you a few questions."

"I don't know ..."

"Oh, C'mon. It'll only take a couple of minutes. Are you home?"

"No. Got some business to take care of."

"I'm out and about, too. Where are you?"

"In mid-town."

"OK. Let's meet at the Starbucks at Augusta Square Mall?"

After a few moments of silence, Junior said. "Well, suppose it can't hurt. All right. I'll be there in ten minutes."

"Great. See you then." Louie disconnected the call, looked at Farrell, and smiled.

"Why you silver-tongued devil," Farrell said, shaking his head. "I wouldn't have given you a chance in hell he would agree to meet us."

Louie sat back in the seat and folded her arms over her chest. "Must be my natural charm," she said, smirking.

"Think it will spook him when he sees you aren't alone?"

"Nah. If you're worried about it, you can wait in the car."

"I don't think so."

Farrell grinned as he started the car and pulled out into traffic.

Louie walked into the Starbucks, with Farrell following, and spotted Junior at a table near the back. The rich smell of brewing coffee filled the room, and made her want a cup as she made her way to the table.

"Hello, Junior, or do you prefer Robert? I'm Detective Princeton, and this is Detective Farrell. Thanks for agreeing to meet with us."

Junior glanced at Farrell, but didn't ask, or comment, on his presence.

"Everyone calls me Junior. You said there was a home invasion, and someone told you I might have information about it?"

"Actually, it's a homicide, now," Louie said as she sat across from him.

Junior sat up in his chair, frowned, and said, "Who was killed?"

"James Landers, the roommate of Joey Torelli."

"What the hell," Junior said, a bit too loudly, which caused the customers to look in their direction.

"Who said I knew anything about that?"

"I can't tell you. We think the witness could be involved in the murder, and is trying to divert our attention away from himself."

Junior shifted in his chair, sliding to the front and leaning on the table. He seemed genuinely shocked, looked in Louie's eyes, and said, "I swear, Detective, I'm not involved in it. I don't know James Landers."

"Ya know, Junior. I believe you. I gotta ask--where were you between 11:00 p.m. and 1:00 a.m. last night?"

Without hesitation, he said, "Drinking with a couple of buddies. I can give you their names."

"That would be a big help," Louie said, taking a small notebook from her coat pocket. She slid it and a pen across the table. "Write it down, please."

As Junior picked up the pen, Farrell said, "I'm gonna get coffee. You guys want anything?"

Junior declined the offer, but Louie asked for a grande decaf. While Farrell got the coffees, she made small talk with Junior, who seemed very curious about Landers being Joey's roommate. Louie noticed the perspiration on Junior's forehead and upper lip, and said, "You worried about something?"

"What? Uh, no. Why?" Junior asked.

"You're sweating, and it's not hot in here."

"Guess it's because I don't like talking to cops."

Farrell returned with the coffee, setting Louie's cup in front of her. Louie sat back in her chair and Farrell sat next to Junior, and scooted closer to him.

Junior looked from Farrell to Louie, and back to Farrell. He was effectively boxed in, and his anxiety level increased. "What are you doing?" he said as he wiped sweat from his face with a napkin.

Louie leaned in over the table. "I have to admit, Junior, we haven't been totally honest with you."

"What do you mean?"

"We suspect you were involved in Lander's murder. And right now another detective is getting a search warrant for your house and car."

"You can't do that," he said. "I told you I didn't know the guy, and I had nothing to do with any murder. I swear." Louie could see he was close to tears, wringing his hands and fidgeting in the chair.

"If that's true, why would anyone say you were involved?"

"Who said that?" He thought for a moment, then said, "It was that little rat-fuck Banjo, wasn't it?"

"You know I can't confirm that, but out of curiosity, why'd you name him?"

Junior swallowed hard, coughed, and said, "He called me a couple of days ago. Said he thinks he'd run into Joey. Nobody knew where he was--Joey disappeared a couple of months ago--and wanted to know if I could put him in touch with whoever was looking for him. Banjo thought there might be a reward for the information."

"What did you tell him?"

"I said I had no idea who was after him, and I couldn't help him. That's the last time I talked to him."

On a hunch that Junior was holding back, Louie said, "Who'd you call, Junior. Don't bullshit me. I know about your call, and want you to confirm who it was."

"I didn't call no one."

Louie turned to Farrell and said, "I had enough of him. Let's cuff him and drag his sorry ass to the station."

Farrell nodded, stood up and took his handcuffs from his belt. "Stand up, Junior. I'm arresting you on suspicion of hindering and/or impeding a criminal investigation."

"No, wait," Junior said, raising his arms in front of him as if he was pushing them away. He took a deep breath, lowered his arms and hung his head. "You win. I'll tell you everything."

"Smart choice, Junior. Let's not do it here. How about you come with us to the station, and we can do a proper interview. When we're done, we'll bring you back here, OK?"

"Am I under arrest?"

"Not now."

Chapter 25

After six hours of interrogation, Farrell and Louie had found out all they could from Junior. He was arrested as a conspirator in the murders of James Landers, Lois Sampson, Janice Roberts, and Judge Anthony Torelli. Booked into jail, he was held without bail.

Junior was allowed one phone call after booking. He chose to call his father, who was angry with him for not calling earlier, or asking for an attorney before his interrogation. Junior told him the police already knew most of what he had to say before asking questions.

"I'm tired, Dad, so tired of letting people use me in their schemes. I can't take it anymore."

"I can't help you with this, Junior. The charges are too serious. At least let me send my attorney to see you. He can help you deal with it, maybe get the charges dismissed, or reduced."

"I don't want your help. No attorney, nothing," he said, and hung up.

Over the next two days, based on information from Junior Henderson, the sheriff' department served five search warrants; Mama Peters' house, Billy

Peters' apartment, Clive Rutherford's home and office, and DeWayne White's home. The warrants included any electronic devices--computers, cellphones, and tablets found at the premises.

The search teams were looking for anything that would corroborate the information from Junior. If found, arrests would be made immediately. If there wasn't enough to make an arrest at the time, warrants would be sought after more investigation.

Three texts between Mama Peters and Clive were found on their cellphones, incriminating them in the plot to kill Steve and Joey. One, from Clive to Dewayne, mentioned hiring a person named Ronin to 'take care of the Torellis'.

As the police were arriving at her house, Mama Peters called her son.

"Billy, Clive called and said his office and house were being searched. They're here now, and probably on the way to your place. You gotta get outta town. Now."

Billy fled back to Texas. He was arrested a month later after Louie, Farrell, and the U.S. Marshalls tracked him to a friend's house in Houston.

Mama Peters was arrested at her house, screaming and cursing the whole time. Clive was arrested at his office. Both were charged with the murders of Anthony Torelli, Janice Roberts, and Lois Sampson, and the murder for hire of James Landers, and two counts of the attempted murders of Sherie MacDonald and Joseph Torelli, and conspiracy.

DeWayne White wasn't home when the warrant was served. One of his neighbors called him and said, "The police are all around and inside your house. I think they're searching it."

"Shit. Don't tell them you talked to me. Say you haven't seen me for a few days."

He left South Carolina without going home. Made one quick stop at his bank to close his accounts, then took off for Chicago where he had a few distant cousins. Arrest warrants were issued charging DeWayne with the same crimes as his boss, Clive. He would be found three months later by a task force of U.S. Marshalls and Richmond County Sheriffs.

The warrant for Billy was issued for the attempted murder of Joey Torelli, and the murder of Janice Roberts. He also was listed as a "person of interest" in the disappearance of Chester Williams and Floyd Thompson. They were two known criminal associates of Billy's, thought to be the other shooters in the attack on Joey and Janice. They had disappeared without a trace after the attack.

Several fingerprints were found on the strip of duct tape Ronin used to gag Sherie. Extensive searches through local, county, and Georgia fingerprint databases, and the FBI Integrated Automated Fingerprint Identification System (IAFIS) failed to locate a hit on those prints. The investigation into Ronin's true identity was ongoing.

Vince was able to observe, and hear, the interrogation of Junior from an adjacent room with a one-way mirror. Louie's boss allowed him to watch, as a professional courtesy, and as he was acting as the family's representative. Vince agreed to not share anything he saw or heard with anyone other than Steve and Joey. All of the others arrested invoked their right to an attorney, declining to talk with the investigators.

After four days, Vince returned home and went back to work. He kept in touch with his cousins, and Louie kept him updated on the cases.

Two weeks later, Vince called Louie.

"You ready for Junior's preliminary hearing tomorrow?" he asked.

"As ready as we'll ever be. Truthfully, I'm not feeling good about the hearing."

"Why? You've got his confession, and it fits the timeline of the crimes. That should be enough for the judge to bind him over for trial, right?"

"You would think so, but the D.A. is waffling on Junior's charges. Said the case is weak, and wants to have more investigation into Junior's actual participation before deciding what to file--specifically, she wants witnesses to corroborate the confession."

"You're kidding me. Doesn't the D.A. realize that's what the prelim is for? Once he's bound over for trial, it will be months, if not years, before it starts. How much more time does she need?"

"I know, Vince. I've had that conversation with her. I'd give it a fifty-fifty chance she declines to file the charges."

"Shit. Well, we can only hope. Please, give me a call as soon as you can tomorrow."

"I will. Fingers crossed, my friend, fingers crossed."

"Damn it," Vince said, as the call was ended. Pacing back and forth, he dialed Steve's number. Steve answered the call on the fifth ring.

"Hello?"

"It's me, Steve. Have you talked to Louie today?"

"No. I'm gonna see her tomorrow at the hearing. Why?"

Vince decided not to tell Steve he had talked to her, wanting to hear what Louie told him first. "I'm wondering how the case was going. Maybe I'll give her a call later."

"How do you think it'll go?"

"No telling. Hopefully he'll be held to answer tomorrow, but you never know."

"I'll tell you he better be held for trial. That little weasel helped kill my father, and probably had a hand in the attack on Joey and Janice."

"Slow down, Steve. There's a lot of evidence against Billy Peters, his mother, and the others, but from what I know, it's not that strong against Junior. Anything is possible."

"Huh. If the system doesn't hold him responsible, maybe someone else will."

"Don't say that. Don't even think it."

"What? You think I'm gonna do something? C'mon, Vince, you know me better than that."

Vince paused a moment. "Yeah, I do, Steve. Sorry."

"It's fine, cousin. I'll call you tomorrow after the prelim, all right?"

"Yeah, that's good."

Chapter 26

At 8:00 a.m. Vince's cell rang while he was meeting with Lieutenant Simons, Bobby, and the other homicide inspectors. He quickly silenced the ring, and looked at the caller ID. It was from Louie.

"Sorry, LT, this is important. I gotta take it," he said, as he stood up to leave the room. He answered the call as he walked to his desk.

"Hey, Louie. What's up?"

"Well. It's 11:00 in the morning here, and Junior's prelim was supposed to start two hours ago."

"Ah, damn," Vince said, sitting down, anticipating bad news. "What's going on?"

"I don't know. Everyone was in court, but before we got going, the D.A. asked if she and the defense could approach the bench. They talked for two minutes before the judge called a recess and they all went into his chambers. Haven't heard a word yet."

"Crap. That doesn't sound good. Any idea what they're talking about?"

"Yeah. I think the D.A. is waffling on holding the prelim today. I told you she wanted more corroboration of the confession. That's the only logical reason I can think of for the delay."

"God damn it. I sure hope..."

"Hold on, Vince," she interrupted. "They just came back. Gotta go. I'll call you as soon as I can." The call was disconnected.

Vince called Steve and asked if he was at the prelim.

"Yeah. Something's going on. They're two hours late starting the hearing."

"I know. Louie called me. I'll let you go, but call me as soon as you learn anything."

Steve sat in the courtroom getting angrier and angrier as the Deputy D.A. assigned to the case outlined the reasons for declining to charge Junior.

"At this time, your honor, on the recommendation of the District Attorney, we feel there is not enough to hold Mr. Henderson for trial. We need to confirm Mr. Henderson's involvement through independent witnesses, and right now, we don't have any."

The judge sat back in his chair. "If that's what's been decided by your office, then there's only one thing I can do. The charges against Mr. Henderson are dismissed, with the provision that the prosecutor can refile at a later date." Addressing Junior, the judge asked, "Mr. Henderson, you understand what's going on, correct?"

"Yes, your Honor."

"OK. You are hereby released from custody. Is there anything else from either of you?"

The deputy D.A. and Junior's attorney indicated they had nothing else. Standing up, he rapped the gavel and said, "We are done here."

Steve sat in the courtroom gallery, seething. He could no longer stifle his anger, and followed the deputy D.A. into the hallway.

He walked up behind him, grabbed him by the shoulder and spun him around.

"What the hell are you doing?" Steve shouted in his face. "Junior Henderson helped set up the murder of my father, and gave information to the people trying to kill me and my brother that led to the death of two innocent citizens. I hope you're fucking happy." His shouting drew the attention of Louie and Farrell, who quickly came over.

The D.A. backed up three steps and put his hands up, palms out, toward Steve. "Excuse me, Mr. Torelli. Back off."

"Back off? Or what? You gonna arrest me?"

"You touch me again, and I'll have you in jail on an assault charge."

"Oh, give me a break. If I was gonna assault you, you'd already be on the floor spitting out teeth." Steve took a step toward him and said, "You better fucking hope nothing happens to my brother, or any member of my family. That happens, I'll be coming for you."

Louie and Farrell each grabbed one of Steve's arms and pulled him back a few steps. The D.A. turned and quickly walked away. "OK, Steve, you had your say. Let it go," Louie said, pulling him away.

"I can't believe this, Louie," Steve said. All the anger had drained out of him, and he visibly slumped. "What a joke."

"Come on Steve," Louie said, "Let's go get a drink. I don't know about you, but I sure could use one."

Chapter 27

It had been four months since Junior had been released from jail.

After all the search warrants had been served, and the arrest warrants issued, Louie came over to tell Steve and Joey they were looking for a hitman, hired by Mama Peters through Clive.

"We originally found out about him from Sherie, and during the searches of Clive's and Mama Peter's cell phones some very interesting, and incriminating texts were found. He goes by the name of Ronin."

"Ronin?" Steve chuckled. "You do know what a Ronin is, don't you?"

"Of course. It's a wandering samurai who has no lord or master. I'm confident he's not in the area anymore. He'd be crazy to stick around."

"I hope you're right. I'm anxious to bring my wife and kids back from her sister's, but I don't feel I can until he's in jail, or dead."

"That's gotta be tough. You've been seeing them, haven't you?"

"I have. I meet them two of three times a week, and we've spent a few weekends together away from Augusta, but I want them here, with me. I wish I could be sure they'd be safe."

Louie asked, "Have you thought about selling the house and moving out of the city?"

"Yes, but I don't consider that an option. This is my home. I was born and raised in this house."

"I can understand that, Steve. Wish I could tell you it is safe."

"I know, Louie. You know I don't blame you, right? It's the damn D.A. who owns the blame."

"Well, all I can say is hang in there. Between you and me, we've gotten information from the FBI regarding Ronin. We're getting closer to identifying him, and once we do, it's a matter of time until he's in custody."

Steve was up before dawn. He'd only had a few hours of fitful sleep and felt groggy and drained. He showered, went downstairs to make coffee, and found Joey sitting at the table, staring out the back window.

"Hey, Joey. Want breakfast?"

"No thanks. Not hungry," Joey replied, not looking at him.

"Coffee, then?"

"Sure, that sounds good." Joey turned to Steve. "What are we gonna do now, Steve? It's been months since the arrests, and the D.A. hasn't done anything. Junior has been out of jail and they haven't been able to find Banjo or Ronin."

"I know. I'm as frustrated as you, but there's not much we can do, Joey. We have to trust in the system."

"I can't take it much longer. I need to see every one of them dead."

"I know how you feel, brother."

They sat at the window, silently drinking coffee for several minutes, when Joey pushed back his chair and stood up. "I've gotta get out of the house."

"Where you going?"

"I don't know--driving around. I'll be back in a while. I checked the videos from the security cameras this morning. I know you check them a couple times every day, to be safe."

"OK," Steve said. He turned and looked out the window as dawn broke, admiring the colors in the sky. He never got tired of the view.

Joey walked into the pantry. Steve wasn't paying any attention to him as he took down the rifle down from the shelf and went out the back door to the garage. After five minutes he went to his truck carrying a rolled-up beach towel, backed out of the driveway, and drove away.

Steve spent his time reviewing the videos, not finding anything in them to be concerned about. He was beginning to think that with all the arrests, he and Joey were safer than they had been for months.

Over the last three months, Joey had spent hours watching the Henderson house. Whenever Junior left, Joey would follow him. He recorded where Junior went and who he met in a small notebook. He learned Junior had a favorite bar, The Gator, where he would drink with his druggie friends for a couple of hours. It was in a seedier part of town, and Junior visited there every Friday night, arriving around 9:00 p.m.

Steve didn't know about Junior's surveillance. If Steve asked where he was going, Joey said he was going for a drive, or was meeting a couple of friends, or gave another innocuous reason.

The next Friday, Steve was gone, visiting with his family, and Joey used the opportunity to drive to the Gator bar. The rifle was stashed behind the truck's seat, and if anyone looked inside, all they would see was a couple of inches of the towel.

He drove to the bar, and parked across the street. It was 8:20 in the evening, and, figuring he had plenty of time until Junior arrived, he walked to a 7-11 three blocks away for a cup of coffee. Fifteen minutes later, Joey was back in his truck, watching the front door of the bar.

At 8:45 Joey saw a cab pull up to the front of the bar. A man got out, and in the glow of the street light next to the cab, Joey watched as he handed money to the driver through the passenger window, then leaned in, appearing to talk with the cabbie for a half a minute. When the passenger stood up on the sidewalk, he turned and looked up and down the street. Joey was surprised when the light illuminated his face--it was Banjo.

Joey watched Banjo enter the bar, then, a few minutes later, saw Junior arrive. He settled in, slumping in his seat, waiting for Junior to leave. Joey debated on whether he should call Louie and tell her he had found Banjo. He decided to make an anonymous call to the Sheriff's office.

Joey drove back to the 7-11 and used the phone booth outside to make the call. He dialed 911.

When the 911 operator answered he said, "Listen carefully. A guy called Banjo went in The Gator bar. He's wanted for questioning by Detectives Farrell and Princeton in a murder four months ago. They've been unable to find him. Call Princeton to verify this."

"What is your name, Sir?"

"That's not important," Joey said, and disconnected the call.

Joey went back to his truck, this time parking fifty yards away, and awaited the arrival of the police.

Within five minutes, three sheriff's cars arrived, two stopping out front with the third driving around back. Four deputies went in the front door. After seven minutes, two deputies came out half-dragging Banjo, who was yelling and kicking. They stuffed him in the back seat of one of the cars, and drove off.

Joey smiled to himself, feeling good for the first time since the preliminary hearing. *Maybe now Louie can get enough to have the charges against Junior refiled.* He settled in his seat, and kept watch for Junior to leave the bar.

Chapter 28

Steve's phone rang as he and the family were finishing breakfast. He swallowed his last bite, wiped his mouth with a napkin, and picked up the phone, saw it was Louie, and said," Hey, Louie, What's up?"

"Is Joey there? Got some news--you're gonna like this."

"No. I'm with my family. Tell me you got Ronin."

"No, but we do have Banjo."

"Well, that's good. How'd you find him?"

"I'm embarrassed to say we didn't. Got an anonymous call last night that he was at a dive bar, and patrol was dispatched. Three units responded. As soon as they walked in, Banjo bolted for the back door where he was met by two deputies. He was arrested and taken to the department and put in a holding cell."

"You talk to him?"

"Not long. He said he wanted an attorney, so we stopped the interview."

"Man, too bad the days of rubber hose interrogation are gone."

Louie chuckled. "I think Banjo will cave and spill his guts. We told him we were charging him as an accomplice in three murders, a kidnapping, and the attempted murders of Joey and Sherie. I'm going to let him stew in jail for a day or two, then hit him up with a deal. He'll talk."

"Is he really that deeply involved?"

"No, but he isn't bright enough to realize it. When we offer to reduce the charges in exchange for information, he'll jump at the chance. Maybe get enough to get the D.A. to charge him."

"You sure about that?"

"I am. He was so scared he was crying like a baby. I think he peed his pants. He probably heard something while he was with his dope friends, and wanted to pass on the info to someone, possibly Mama Peters, for a reason unknown to us."

"I hope you're right. Thanks for calling, Louie. I appreciate it, and please keep me updated."

"I'll try, as long as it doesn't compromise the investigation."

"Fair enough," Steve said. "I'll let Joey know you called."

Louie called Vince next and repeated what she told Steve. Vince was excited about the arrest of Banjo, and the info on Ronin.

"Finally, progress. Now that Banjo is in custody, I assume you'll be concentrating on finding Ronin?"

"We will. I want to reinterview Billy Peters. While the U.S. Marshalls were driving him back to Augusta he repeatedly denied being involved in any homicides, or a plot to hire a hitman from Florida. That Florida statement narrowed the search. I have to think Ronin is a freelance contractor, and I'd be willing to bet he is well known in the Florida organized crime family."

"If he is, it will be tough to break that wall of silence."

"I know. We'll keep constant pressure on the mob. If we can convince them we aren't investigating them, that all we want is info on Ronin, they may give us what we want, if for no other reason than to get us and the feds off their backs."

"Might work, Louie. Good luck with that, but be careful. If you put too much pressure on the mob, they'll make Ronin disappear permanently. He's got too much on them."

"I thought that might happen. Hopefully, we can break this case before then."

"I hope so."

Two days later Farrell got a call from Billy's lawyer, a public defender, who told him his client was ready to talk. He said they were interested in making a deal, and Billy had info that may help them find Ronin. Farrell made an appointment to meet him and his lawyer at the county jail in two hours.

"I have to notify the D.A. about this. She might be willing to deal, and may want to send someone along. I'll call you back after I talk with her."

Farrell called the D.A and she agreed to meet with him, and Louie, in a half-hour. He then called Louie's office and told her about Billy wanting to make a deal.

"She agreed to meet, but wants the meeting in a half-hour. Is that a problem?"

"Nope. I'll make the time. I'll leave now."

"Great. See you there."

They both arrived at the D.A.'s office twenty minutes later. Farrell filled Louie in over the phone as he drove, and once in the office, he told the D.A. what Billy's lawyer said.

"He didn't give specifics, but I know he's gonna want to pare down the charges."

The D.A. turned to Louie and asked, "Are you in agreement with this?"

"Yes, Ma'am. It wouldn't be a problem to drop the kidnapping of Sherie, two of the murder charges, and all but one of the attempted murder charges. We don't have enough to prove those, and, honestly, I don't think he was involved at all in the murders of Lois Sampson, James Landers, or the judge."

The judge thought for a few moments, then said, "OK. Since you two agree, go ahead and listen to what Billy's lawyer has to say." She pointed at both of them and said, "Don't agree to anything without notifying me first. Understood?"

"Goes without saying, Ma'am," Louie replied.

As they walked to their cars Farrell said, "We've got time before meeting with Billy and his lawyer. Want to grab lunch?"

"Sure, if you're buying."

Farrell chuckled and said, "OK, my treat."

"Great. Let's go to Calvert's Restaurant. I've been craving a good piece of prime rib."

Farrell laughed. "I'd have to take out a loan to afford that place. How's the Cracker Barrel on Park West Drive?"

"That's fine. You know I was kidding about Calvert's, right?" Louie said, unable to repress her grin.

"I hoped so. I'll meet you there. I've got to call the lawyer and let him know the meeting is on."

An hour before the meeting, Billy was playing cards with five inmates in the jail day room. The previous day Billy had been talking to anyone who would listen about his involvement in the murders. He exaggerated his involvement, trying to impress the others with his importance and criminality, to the point of implying he had information on the mob in Florida.

Unknown to Billy, one of the inmates he talked to--in custody on a drunk driving charge--was a low-level soldier, or *soldato,* with the Florida Trafficante Mafia. He promptly got a message to his *Capo* through the jail pipeline. The *Capo* relayed the message up the chain of command, and two hours later he received a call with instructions on handling the problem. Those instructions were relayed to the *soldato.*

As Billy was shuffling the cards, a group of six inmates approached the table. The others at the card table recognized the group as being mobbed up, and quickly got up and walked away.

Seeing this, Billy stopped shuffling and said, "Hey, where you guys going? We haven't finished our game."

The group of inmates walked close behind Billy, effectively screening him from the guard's view, and the surveillance cameras. The *soldato* pulled a shiv made from a mess hall spoon from his waistband, and, as he passed Billy, jammed it into his neck below the jaw, slicing downward at an angle, cutting the carotid artery. The group walked a short distance away, waited five seconds, then called out for help while rushing back to the table, ostensibly to help Billy. While providing first aid, they became splattered with Billy's blood. Billy bled out and was dead within two minutes.

Deputies flooded the dayroom as the lockdown alarm blared. Orders were shouted to clear the room and return to their cells.

The inmates who rushed to help Billy were isolated for later interview. The blood on them couldn't be described as evidence. Each of them claimed they didn't see the attack. The murder weapon was found on the floor next to Billy's body. No prints were found due to the amount of blood covering it.

Louie made a conference call to Steve, Joey, and Vince.

"Hey, guys. Bad news from the county jail."

"Oh, crap," Steve replied. "What now?"

"Billy Peters was murdered today."

"Shit," Vince said. "What happened?"

"He got his throat cut. From what I learned, Billy was shooting off his mouth about the murder of Steve and Joey's dad, and Janice. Said things that weren't true about how he was connected to the mob, and it was them who ordered the hit on the judge."

"Is that true?" Steve asked.

"Can't be," Louie replied. "Billy was nothing more than a half-wit little punk, living under his mother's thumb. He did nothing unless she told him to. No self-respecting mobster would have anything to do with him."

"If I remember right," Vince said, "There isn't any connection between the judge and the mob. This smacks of a mob hit, though."

"Yeah, it does. We couldn't find Judge Torelli ever came into contact with, or sentenced anyone in the mob. I believe this was a case of the mob being safe rather than sorry."

"What about witnesses?"

"According to the investigators, there are none, even though there were forty guys in the day room when it happened. That includes the five guys Billy was playing cards with before the attack."

"So," Steve said, "No one's talking, right?"

"Nobody will admit to seeing anything. They would be signing their own death warrants."

"Dammit. How does this affect the case?"

"We've lost a valuable resource. Billy might have been a small-time crook, but he knew a lot about the judge's murder. After all, his mother planned the "accident". Speaking of which, Mama Peters has been removed from general population, and now is in protective custody. She hasn't been told of her son's death yet."

"Did anyone interview her?" Vince asked.

"We tried, but she invoked her right to silence immediately. She hasn't said a word, even to other inmates, as far as we can tell. We had her placed in PC, in case she's next on the list."

Joey interjected, "What about DeWayne or Clive? Have they been questioned?"

"Yes, with the same results as Mama Peters, though DeWayne asked questions about making a deal. He didn't specifically say he would talk in exchange for a lighter sentence, but he did leave the door open. Clive isn't talking, either. When he gets wind of Billy's death, I can guarantee his continued silence."

"Shit," Vince said. "Seems like you're losing your potential witnesses, and with it, your case."

"Seems that way. Our best hope now is to find and arrest Ronin. I think we can turn him if we get the FBI involved. They could get him in the witness protection program. What a gold mine Ronin could be in their ongoing investigation into the Florida mob. He might be able to give us enough info to ensure convictions in our case."

"Good luck with that," Vince said. "If Ronin isn't already dead, he will be soon. His body will never be found."

"We're making the assumption here that Ronin works for the mob, right?" Steve asked. "So, if that's the case, why would they kill one of their own? I mean, he's probably done other hits, and as far as we know, he's still walking around."

"Good point. Let's hope you're right, Steve. Ok, I've got a lot of work to do. I'm meeting with the FBI later today to decide how our joint investigation to find Ronin will go down. I'll let you know if there is any new info."

"One last thing, Louie," Vince said. "If the mob did hit Billy, I think the next on the list would be Clive, or DeWayne. Are they in PC, too?"

"Not DeWayne. He is being released on his OR, and will be back on the street soon. Clive, well, that's another story. Yes, he is in protective custody."

"Why is DeWayne getting out?" Joey said.

"We don't have anything that ties him to the murders. The only link is he works for Clive. His attorney requested a bail hearing and made his case, and the judge agreed to release him on his own recognizance."

"When's he being released?"

"This afternoon, around one. Why do you ask, Joey?"

"I'm curious. He's not a danger to us, but it's nice to know when he gets out."

"I hope so." Looking at her watch Louie said, "Shit. I've got a meeting with the FBI in an hour. I'll talk to you guys later today if any new info turns up." With that, Louie ended the call.

Joey asked Steve if he was bringing his family home, after all the time that's passed since the arrests.

"Barbara's been begging me to let them come home, and the kids are homesick, but Ronin is still out there."

"You think he is still after us?"

"That's the problem. I don't know, and I'm not willing to take that chance."

"I can understand that, Steve."

Chapter 29

DeWayne was processing out of the county jail's Charles B. Webster Detention Center. He was being cocky and smirking the whole time. DeWayne had no problem making his hatred for the police well known, insulting and cussing out the deputies. He knew there was nothing they could do about it, and made it as troublesome for the officers as he could.

After changing into his civilian clothes and getting his personal belongings, Dewayne was escorted to the front gate and released. As he walked out, he saw his attorney sitting in a car, waiting for him.

The detention center was away from the city, built in a 400-yard circular field surrounded by trees. DeWayne paused on the lawn outside the gate and was taking a deep breath when the right side of his head exploded from the impact of a high-powered bullet. The sound of the shot followed one second later. Deputies and others in the parking lot were unable to say from which direction the shot came. Five minutes later a search of the woods facing the front gate was begun. No evidence was found.

An hour after DeWayne's death, Joey was putting away groceries he picked up at the supermarket when Steve walked in.

"What took you so long? I thought you'd be home before now."

"I changed my mind. Decided to go to Dragon Express for Chinese. It was really crowded--lunchtime, ya know."

Louie and Farrell were notified of DeWayne's death at 12:20 in the afternoon.

"Gotta be Ronin," Farrell said. "A sniper shot from three hundred yards?"

"I agree. He's out there, cleaning up loose ends. First Billy Peters, now DeWayne. Good thing Mama Peters and Clive are in protective custody."

"That's no guarantee they're safe. If the mob is behind these killings, they can get to them anywhere."

"I know." Louie thought for a moment. "How about we contact Mama and Clive? Tell then the mob is eliminating everyone they think is a threat to them, and they are likely next on the hit list. Maybe we can convince them to cooperate and help us find Ronin."

"Wouldn't hurt to try."

They grabbed their coats and headed out to the parking lot.

"You want to take the lead with DeWayne?" Louie asked.

"Sure. That means you get to handle Mama Peters."

"Damn. That's gonna be fun, eh?"

"I don't envy you," Farrell said, chuckling. "I had the pleasure of dealing with her a few years ago, and she's plain crazy. Hates cops, is foul-mouthed, and generally not a nice person."

The interview with Mama Peters went nowhere. Louie and Farrell waited for a guard to bring Mama Peters in. As she was placed in a chair and handcuffed to a large eyebolt in the metal table, she said, "You two can go fuck yourselves. I got nuthin to say to you."

She was dressed in an orange jail jumpsuit with black six-inch capital letters on the back that read RCSDC--Richmond County Sheriff Detention Center.

The room was a ten-by-ten space with cinderblock walls and a cement floor. The walls were painted a calming light green. The table was bolted to the floor, and a video camera was attached above the door, providing a view of the room to others watching and listening in a nearby office.

Once the guard was gone, Louie said, "We're here to try and help you."

"Help me? How can you help me? Puttin' me in PC? You couldn't help my boy--now he's dead."

"We know," Louie said. "We are so sorry for your loss. We believe your son's death was a mob hit and think you may be next on their list. I would like you to help us out--tell us about the contract on the Torellis, and help us put those responsible for your son's murder on death row."

"Yeah? And what do I get in return, huh?" Mama Peters leaned forward and shouted, "You ain't got nuthin to offer. This interview is over."

"Mrs. Peters, we..."

"Guard, I want to go back to my cell now!" Mama Peters shouted, looking at the camera. She sat back in the chair and turned her head away from Louie and Farrell, trying to hide the tears running down her cheeks. The guard came in, unlocked the cuffs, and led her out. Louie and Farrell were left alone in the room, staring at each other.

Louie shrugged, and said, "Oh, well. It was worth a try."

Farrell leaned back with his arms crossed over his chest and grinned at her, not saying a word.

"Feeling pretty smug, aren't ya?" Louie said, grinning back at him. "C'mon, Clive is awaiting our presence. We'll see how long that shit-eating grin lasts."

Louie and Farrell entered another interview room, identical to the one they'd just left. Clive was already seated and handcuffed to the table.

"Good afternoon, Clive, I'm Detective Farrell, and this is Detective Princeton with the sheriff's office," gesturing toward Louie. He sat across from him and placed a thick folder on the table. Louie took the adjacent seat.

Clive, too, was wearing the standard jail jumpsuit. Though he had been in jail just two days, his face looked gaunt, with dark circles under his bloodshot eyes. Prominent frown lines covered his forehead, and he looked exhausted.

"You probably know why we are here, but I'll remind you anyway. We're investigating the murder of Judge Anthony Torelli, and the attempted murder of his sons, Steve and Joey. During the attempt on their lives, a woman named Janice Roberts was shot and killed." Farrell paused, looked at Louie, then back at Clive, who sat slouched in the chair, with a smirk on his face.

Clive replied, "I had nothing to do with any of that."

Farrell continued. "We don't think you were involved in the judge's death, or the attempt on the sons' lives, but we have evidence you arranged the hiring of a hitman, called Ronin. Ronin is wanted for the murder of two people during his search for Joey Torelli. Both were innocent victims, as was Sherie, a server and friend of Joey's at a small roadside café. Ronin kidnapped and beat her to get information on Joey's whereabouts. We believe he would have killed her, too, had she not escaped him."

"Like I told you," Clive said, "I had nothing to do with that shit."

"We have some questions for you, and before we begin, I want to remind you of your Miranda rights."

"You don't need to do that. I'm well aware of my rights, and I'm not talking to you or answering your questions without my lawyer."

"Fine, Clive. We won't ask any questions, but we have some information we think you should know. You just sit there and listen. First, did you know DeWayne was released on OR around 12:30 p.m. today?"

Clive looked surprised at this and sat up straighter. "Had no idea. How'd he manage that?"

"Got himself a good attorney." Farrell stopped, looked at Louie, and said, "Let's step out for a moment."

When they were in the hallway, with the interview room door closed, Farrell said, "I'm gonna 'suggest' to Clive that DeWayne got out 'cause he might be working a deal with the FBI."

"I thought of the same thing," Louie said. "He looked startled, maybe even a bit worried, when you told him DeWayne was released."

"I noticed it, too. Let's go back in."

"Sorry for the interruption, Clive, had to check my messages. So, where was I?"

"DeWayne getting out on OR," Louie prompted.

"Oh, yeah. Thanks. Back to DeWayne. He took a dozen steps out the front door, and someone blew half his head off."

Clive sat with his mouth hanging open, in shock at the news. He swallowed, and muttered one word--"Ronin."

"Yes, Ronin," Farrell said. "We're wondering if DeWayne might have made a deal with the FBI--release from jail and witness protection--in exchange for information against the Florida mob. Maybe he was going to testify against them, or you and Mama Peters. After all, we have your phone records showing calls to Florida, and texts to DeWayne. Very incriminating stuff, Clive."

Clive maintained his silence, and remained seated, head hanging, while Farrell continued.

"Yesterday, Billy Peters was murdered in the detention center. We believe the mob was behind his death. He was shooting off his mouth, claiming to be a member and having information about the mob's involvement."

"Billy? Murdered, too?" Clive asked, lifting his head.

"Yes. Why do you think we had you put in protective custody?" Louie asked. "You and Mama Peters are the last two threats to the mob," she continued. "Don't think you are safe in PC. They can get to you anywhere. Are you willing to take your chances?"

Clive looked from her to Farrell, worry etched on his face. Having dealt with the Trafficante mob before, he knew quite well what they were capable of.

Farrell stood and said, "We're gonna take a few minutes break, give you a chance to think of your options. You want anything--coffee, water?"

"Coffee, black, would be good."

"OK. Be back shortly."

Farrell and Louie retreated to an empty interview room where coffee, tea, and water had been set up. Grabbing cups and filling them from a large urn, Farrell handed one to Louie, and they sat at a small table.

"Think he's gonna turn?" Louie asked.

"I'd be willing to bet on it. Did you see the look on his face when I told him of DeWayne's and Billy's murders? He knows his life isn't worth spit."

"I'll call the FBI and see if they are willing to go along with the witness protection plan. That's another thing we can tell Clive. Might be enough to get him to help us."

"What about Mama Peters?" Farrell asked.

"Oh, I'm sure Clive will throw her under the bus in a heartbeat. She's the one who started this whole thing. Mama Peters set up the judge's murder, then got her half-wit son to attack Joey. When that failed, she contracted Ronin for the hit on Joey and Steve. She is directly responsible for four murders."

"Well, let's give it a try. You ready to confront Clive?"

"Absolutely. Let's go, and don't forget his coffee."

Chapter 30

Joey's birthday was in two days, and Steve wanted to throw a family party for him at the house. He was on the phone with Vince asking if he could come to Augusta for the event. It had been nearly six months since Vince had been there.

"Sure, Steve. I'll be there. I'll bring Maggie, but the kids won't be coming. They have school and sports commitments. They'll be staying with friends."

"Great. We'll miss the kids, but I understand. The party is on Sunday, here at the house. We'll have a barbeque--ribs, chicken, hamburgers and hotdogs--sodas, water, beer, and wine. I've got a bottle of Maker's Mark stashed away for some selected guests."

"Anything new on the case?"

"Yes. Yesterday, Louie and Farrell reinterviewed Mama Peters and Clive Rutherford," Steve said.

"How'd that go?"

"Not well with Mama, but they convinced Clive his best chance of surviving was to turn state's evidence. Clive's been moved to an FBI safe house. He's agreed to testify that Mama Peters arranged for Ronin to kill Joey and I, and will give the FBI info for their ongoing investigation of the Trafficante family."

"What about his involvement in your dad's death, and the other murders?"

"Louie thinks it was Mama Peters who arranged it, not Clive. Louie said he would plead no contest. He'll avoid the death penalty, and the prosecutor will ask for a sentence of thirty-five years, with no possibility of parole. He will be ninety-two if he lives long enough to complete it."

"As good as a life sentence. Any progress locating Ronin?"

"Not yet. Louie's hoping Clive will have the information they need."

"We'll see. How's Joey doing? Still on the straight and narrow?"

"Yeah. He's come out of his shell some, and isn't as depressed and gloomy. Still working at the warehouse and living here. He's hooked up with some new friends from work--spends a bunch of time with them. They do a lot together, and they're not like that bunch of slime balls he used to hang with. Joey's still off the drugs, and has given up the alcohol. He's clean and sober."

"Great. Glad to hear it. We'll be coming in on Saturday. See you then?"

"Absolutely. Let me know when your flight comes in and I'll pick you up at the airport."

"Will do, Cuz."

Called in to the investigations office for further questioning, accompanied by his lawyer, Junior, once again, gave a statement regarding his participation in the death of Judge Torelli. Still claiming he did only what he was asked to do by Mama Peters, and he had no idea the judge would be killed. He provided the names of the other two guys with him who forced the judge into the street.

Louie was able to locate one of them, Frankie Patterson, in Mobile, Alabama. Soliciting the help of the local PD to serve the arrest warrant, Patterson was currently in custody, awaiting extradition to Augusta. Frankie saw the SWAT team and armored vehicles outside his house, and wisely decided not to resist. He walked out of the house with his hands in the air, giving up meekly.

The other person had been killed in a motorcycle accident two weeks after Torelli's death.

Louie had informed Steve and Joey of the arrest in Mobile and, later, called Vince to tell him.

"He's not fighting extradition, right?" Vince asked.

"No, he's not. We're working on getting the order processed. Shouldn't take more than a week, and he'll be back here, in our custody."

"Did he give a statement to the Mobile detectives?"

"Sang like a bird when he found out the warrant was for conspiracy to commit murder. He's another small-time druggie and hood."

"Did he admit to anything?"

"Nope. He said he was paid a hundred bucks, and given a new suit to stand blocking the sidewalk. He claimed not to know it was a murder setup. Pretty much echoing Junior's statement. Couldn't, or wouldn't, say who paid him."

"Think he's telling the truth?"

"Hard to say at this point. We'll find out more when we interrogate him."

"I'll be in town on Saturday for Joey's birthday party. Can we meet for lunch, or a drink? I'd like to go over some things with you."

"I'll see you at the party. I talked to Steve earlier, and he invited me."

"Terrific. I'll see you then."

Joey's phone rang and he saw it was Steve calling. He let it go to message. He was supposed to be at the movies with a couple of friends and knew Steve would expect him not to answer.

In reality, he was parked in a dark area down the street from The Gator Bar. Fifteen minutes ago, he watched as Junior Henderson arrived with three others and went in.

Through conversations with Louie, Joey knew Junior was one of the three men blocking the sidewalk, forcing the judge to move into the bike lane where he could be hit by the car. It infuriated him that Junior was free, and not facing any charges. Joey constantly thought about avenging his father's death, and plotted how he could accomplish it without anyone suspecting him. He decided it would be too risky in the city. Too many people out and about who could become a witness to a shooting. He decided on an alternate plan.

Joey pulled on a medium length blonde wig, long enough to cover his brown eyebrows, and covered it with a sweat-stained Atlanta Braves baseball Cap. He took off his leather jacket and donned an old field jacket that once belonged to his father. Getting out of his truck, he paused, took two deep breaths, and headed to the bar. Tucked into the waistband of his Levis, at his back, was his father's .45 caliber pistol.

Walked in the bar, Joey had no idea what he was going to do. On one hand, he had a strong urge to walk up to Junior and shoot him in the head. On the other hand, he wasn't sure he could murder in cold blood. Though the night was a cool 55 degrees, and the bar not much warmer, Joey was sweating profusely.

Joey sat at the bar in the dim light, and ordered a Bud Light. His hands shook as he picked up the glass and pretended to sip from it. He saw Junior sitting at a table off to his left with three others. They were talking loudly and laughing, without a care in the world.

I wonder what Junior would do if he knew I was here. Would he realize I came to kill him?

After fifteen minutes, Joey got up and headed toward the bathroom, passing right by Junior's table, his hand on the butt of the pistol at his back. A wave of nausea rolled through him, and he rushed to the bathroom, barely making it before vomiting over and over into a toilet, until there was nothing left to come up.

Joey splashed cold water on his face and neck. Drying off with the flimsy paper towels, he regained his composure. Leaving the bathroom, he walked directly out of the bar. Once in his truck, he broke down, weeping.

Joey was angry with himself for not being strong enough to avenge his father. Pulling away from the curb, he drove a block from the bar, and parked in a dark, unlit alley fifty yards from a shuttered movie theater. It was a place he'd often visited when using drugs. No one was out walking on the sidewalks.

He sat for a moment, wiping the tears away. *Stop it. Stop being such a coward.* With a new resolve, he retrieved a flashlight from behind the seat and made his way down the trash littered, smelly alley, to a side door of the theater. Joey knew the door had been forced open by drug addicts and homeless people who used the interior as a crash pad and shooting gallery.

Joey pulled the door open and stepped inside. Immediately, he was assailed by the stench of urine, feces, and something else--something dead. He pulled the door closed behind him and snapped on the flashlight. Shining it over the interior, he saw a path through the mess of papers, filthy blankets, decaying food, and other detritus all over the floor. Red velvet wallpaper was peeling from the walls, and a filthy dark carpet covered the floor. Several large rats scurried away through the mess when the light hit them. The smells became stronger the further in he went. Joey pulled his handkerchief out and tied it over his nose and mouth, masking enough of the odor to make breathing tolerable.

In the flashlight's beam, he saw a rickety-looking staircase adjacent to the far wall. Taking the stairs two at a time, Joey made his way past a door on the second floor with "projection room" stenciled on it. He saw the stairs continued up, ending at a small cupola at the top. There was a short ladder attached to a wall leading up to a small access panel that Joey surmised allowed entry onto the roof. A window, the glass broken out, was partially covered by shutters. Peering between two missing slats, he had a clear view of the street, and the bar 300 feet away.

As Joey dragged an empty wooden crate to the window, he thought he heard a soft thump. He shined the flashlight around the room, looking for what may have caused the noise. Not seeing anything, he shrugged. *Must be my imagination, or a rat running around.* Joey folded a musty old blanket he found thrown on the floor and, using it as a cushion, sat on the crate. Joey watched the front door of the Gator Bar through the window for the next half-hour without seeing Junior leave. Joey planned to return with the rifle next Friday.

Junior was having a good time. Here he was, free as a bird, and enjoying it. He'd had four whiskey and cokes, backed by two beers, and was feeling no pain. It had been a good night--laughing and talking with his friends. He looked at his watch and saw it was nearing 11:00 p.m.

"Uh-oh. I gotta go, guys," he said, standing up from the table.

"Aw, c'mon, Junior. One more drink, eh?"

"Can't. Gotta get home. Early day tomorrow."

"OK, go on then. See you later."

Junior stopped at the bar, paid their tab, and headed for the door. As he reached it, one of his friends, Jimmy, called out, "Hey, hold up, Junior. I'll go out with ya."

"I'll meet you out front," Junior answered, as he turned and went outside. Standing near the curb, he leaned against the street light and lit a cigarette.

Jimmy came out a few moments later. "Can I catch a ride, with..." his question was interrupted by the sound of a gunshot, and the sight of Junior lurching backwards from the bullet punching into his chest. Jimmy watched, unable to move, as Junior crumpled to the ground. Jimmy stood there in shock, watching Junior's shirt turn red with blood.

He ran into the bar and yelled at the bartender, "Call 9-1-1. Junior's been shot. He ran back out, followed by his friends. As they knelt to help Junior, a police car pulled to the curb. The officer got out and ran to them, asking "What's going on?"

Seeing Junior on the ground, and the blood on his shirt, he radioed he was at the scene of a shooting, giving his location and asking for backup. The dispatcher said she had just gotten a call and was dispatching an ambulance and a supervisor. "How'd you get there so fast?" she asked.

"I was only a half a block away. I heard the shot," he said into the radio, as he ran back to his car to get the first aid kit. Hurrying to Junior, he tried to stem the blood flow. By then, the bar patrons and employees had come out and were standing around, watching. A couple of them were recording the incident with their phones.

Three minutes later a second patrol officer arrived. He slid to a stop behind the first officer's car, shut off his siren, and got out. Gun in hand, he cautiously approached the crowd standing around Junior and the officer.

"Where's the shooter? He asked the officer kneeling next to Junior.

"Long gone by now."

"Anyone see anything?"

"Haven't asked yet. Been kinda busy here. Push the crowd back, would ya?"

"Sure," the second officer said. "Then I'll start getting witness statements." He moved the crowd fifty feet back, then cordoned off the area with yellow police line tape. More sirens could be heard off in the distance, getting louder as more emergency units responded.

Despite the best efforts of the officers and the paramedics, Junior died in the ambulance while enroute to the hospital.

Joey arrived home thirty minutes after the shooting. Rushing into the house, he shouted, "Steve, Steve, where are you?"

"In the kitchen making coffee."

Joey joined him and sat at the table. "I called you a half-hour ago and there was no answer."

"I was out in the backyard. Didn't hear the phone ringing. Didn't you leave a message? There was nothing on the machine."

"No, I didn't. You won't believe what happened tonight," he said, wiping the sweat from his face with his hand.

"Man," Steve said, "You look awful. What is it?"

"Junior Henderson was shot. He's dead."

"What? Who told you?"

"Nobody. I saw it. I was parked down the block from The Gator Bar, and saw him come out the door. Not ten seconds later, I heard a shot, and Junior went down."

"Did you see the shooter?"

"No. Junior must have been shot from some distance away. The cops got there fast. They've got the whole street shut down."

Steve was looking at Joey, a frown creasing his forehead. "What were you doing there."

"Just watching the place, that's all."

"C'mon, Joey. Why that bar? Did you know Junior was there?"

"Yes, I knew. I've been keeping an eye on him for a while."

"Why?

"I don't know," he lied. "It felt like something I had to do. I still can't believe, after all these months, he's hasn't been charged, and is not in jail."

"I don't like it either, but I'm not out stalking him. Do you know for sure he's dead?"

"I walked by and from what I could see--the amount of blood, the paramedics giving him CPR--yeah, I'm pretty sure."

"Anybody recognize you?"

"Nah. I've never been in the bar, and I didn't see anyone I knew in the crowd."

"I hope not. Don't say anything to anybody about being there. It wouldn't look good, and they might start to suspect you had something to do with it. After all, Junior was involved in Dad's murder, and you've told a bunch of people how pissed you are with him not being charged."

"OK. I'll say I heard it on the news, or something."

"Good. I'm gonna turn on the tv, try to catch the latest news. I want see if there is anything on the broadcast. Wanna join me?"

"No, thanks. I've had enough for one night. I'm going to bed."

"All right. Good night."
"Night," Joey said, and went upstairs.

Chapter 31

When Steve left to pick up Vince and Maggie at the airport the next morning, asking Joey if he wanted to go along and stop for breakfast, Joey declined, saying he wanted to relax quietly at home.

Figuring Steve wouldn't return for two or three hours, Joey took the rifle from the pantry and wrapping it in a blanket, went to the garage where he removed the barrel. He planned to replace it with one from an identical rifle he'd agreed to buy from a guy in Swainsboro a week earlier. It was the kind of deal handled strictly by word of mouth--no paperwork, cash only, no questions asked--arranged by a friend of a friend of a friend.

Joey then drove 65 miles south to Swainsboro, population 7,600, paid the seller, and was home in two hours. He made one stop along the way, pulling off the road as it passed through a heavily wooded area between towns. Joey dismantled the new gun, walked fifty yards into the woods and buried all but the barrel. He dug a two-foot-deep hole, placed the parts in and covered them up, scattering leaves and small branches over the freshly-turned earth until it looked like the rest of the area. The chances of anyone finding the weapon were next to zero.

Once done replacing the new barrel on the rifle, Joey thoroughly cleaned it, erasing all evidence it had recently been fired, and placed it back on the shelf in the pantry. He then went upstairs, showered, and changed into clean clothes. He put the dirty clothes in the washer and started the machine. Convinced he had eliminated all the evidence, Joey went to the kitchen and poured himself a cup of coffee. The next day, he threw the original barrel into the Savannah River from the middle of the James U. Jackson Memorial Bridge.

Dinner that night for Steve, Joey, Vince, and Maggie was pizza and salad, delivered to the house from Giuseppe's Pizza, and two bottles of Chianti Steve bought on the way to the Airport. Joey told Vince about Junior's death the previous day. Vince asked him some of the same questions Steve had about why he was there. Neither he nor Steve were convinced Joey was telling them the entire truth, but didn't say so.

For the most part, they had a nice time, talking about Joey when he was growing up. They laughed at the goofy things he'd done, like when at eight he picked a fight with a much bigger twelve-year old at the park. Not wanting to hurt a skinny little kid, the bigger boy picked him up and stuffed him head-first into a garbage can. Joey managed to climb out, smeared with old food and trash, and ran to Steve, demanding Steve beat up the other kid.

Steve, who had witnessed the whole thing from the start, refused, telling Joey he'd acted like a little punk, and deserved what he got. The stories went on, with Joey recounting with the time Steve cornered a skunk in the yard and ended up getting sprayed. Joey told them Steve stunk so bad that, even after a vigorous scrub-brush bath, he still smelled, and their dad made him sleep in the garage for three nights.

After dinner, Steve told them Barbara and the kids were moving back into their home the next day. "I think we're safe. If anything was going to happen, it would have by now. Not to say we will let our guard down, but the months we've been apart have been hard on all of us."

"I think that's a good idea," Maggie said. "I'll bet the kids especially are glad."

"Yeah. They're already planning things we can do together, and I sure missed Barbara. It will be nice to return to some sense of normalcy."

Yawning, Joey said he was beat and was going to bed. After hugging each of them, he said goodnight and went upstairs.

Maggie echoed Joey, claiming jet lag, and made her way to bed. In reality, she could sense, by the Steve's and Vince's behavior, something was bothering them, and wanted to give them the privacy to talk about whatever it was.

When they were alone, Steve got up, walked to the sink, and began washing out the coffee pot. Standing with his back to Vince, he broached the subject, saying, "What do you think about Joey's rendition of Junior's killing?"

Vince took a deep breath, exhaled, and said, "It doesn't make sense. That whole thing of him stalking Junior for no particular reason? I don't know about that."

"I thought the same. I wondered if he had something to do with it. Joey's angry because Junior was released, and no charges were filed. I told him I knew how he felt, and I wished Junior would go to prison for life. Joey said he wanted to see him dead, and I wasn't the only one he told it to."

"You think he's capable of murdering him?"

Steve turned around, wiping his hands on a dish towel. "I can't believe my brother would shoot someone down like that. Tomorrow I'm gonna check his pistol and see if it's been recently fired. Louie will be at the party, and I'm wondering if we should talk to her about our concerns."

"I'm sure she's been notified of the shooting and I'd like to see what she has to say before we tell her."

"OK. Sounds like a plan. Let's enjoy the party, and get with her when we can talk in private."

The day started out sunny and cool, but by 11 a.m. had warmed to a pleasant 76 degrees. Forecast was for a high of 82, with scattered clouds, and a gentle breeze--a perfect day for a backyard party.

Steve's wife, Barbara, and the kids arrived at 10 a.m. to help with the preparations. The kids had fun running around putting up birthday decorations on the house, shrubs and trees in the yard, their laughter and chatter filling the air. Barbara and Maggie were in the kitchen cooking platters of rigatoni, lasagna, and ravioli. The clatter of pots, pans, and dishes filled the room, along with their conversation. A radio on the counter by the sink played soft rock music. Vince helped by making the salad and the garlic bread, getting in the way of the women.

"If you want to help, Vince, stay out of the way," Barbara said, laughing.

"I've been telling him that for years. Hasn't listened yet," Maggie said.

"You will sing a different tune when you taste the garlic bread. I make the best ever, and you will bow down to my culinary skill."

"Yeah, right," Maggie said, throwing a dish towel at him.

Joey was tasked with getting the ice for the coolers, and was at the grocery store piling bags of ice in the back of his truck. Steve was in charge of cooking the ribs, chicken and tri-tip and had fired up the barbeque. He was a master at barbequing, and everything would be cooked perfectly.

Family and friends started arriving shortly before 1 p.m. and the noise level picked up with shouted hellos, conversation, hugs, and laughter. Outside of Steve, Joey, and Louie, none of the family knew Vince and Maggie would be there, and everyone was delighted to see them.

Barbara and two of the aunts brought out appetizer trays, setting them on a picnic table in the center of the patio amidst the plates, forks, and napkins. Vince fetched bottles of wine, and made sure the beer cooler was fully stocked. By 1:30, everyone, including Louie, had arrived and the party was in full swing. It was a typical Italian family gathering--lots of cheeks pinched and kissed, tons of food, loud talking, and promises to keep in touch.

The cake was brought out at 4 p.m., candles ablaze, with the guests singing happy birthday to Joey, who looked happy, and a bit embarrassed by all the attention.

By 5 o'clock, the aunts, uncles, cousins, and family friends were leaving. Barbara and Maggie, with Joey's, Louie's, and the kids help, began clearing the plates, bottles, cups, and cutlery from the outside tables. Barbara was firmly in charge. "Alright, you guys," she said, "let's get busy with the cleanup, and be careful with those dishes and glasses." Louie came to mock attention and saluted her.

When the time was right, Steve asked Louie to join him and Vince in the study, saying they needed to talk.

They were able to leave without anyone noticing and sat on the chairs arranged around a large coffee table. A bottle of Maker's Mark Bourbon was on the table, along with three glasses and a small ice bucket.

Steve took a glass and held it up. "Anyone care to join me?" Vince and Louie both said yes.

After their drinks were poured, Steve closed the door, turned to Louie and said, "There's something we need to discuss regarding Joey. Before we do, though, I'm sure you're aware of Junior Henderson's murder last night."

"Yes. I was notified shortly after the shooting. I got there a half hour later. Why do you ask?"

Steve looked at Vince, and said, "Joey told me about it when he got home last night. He was supposed to be out with friends, but said he was alone, parked down the street from the Gator."

"Really? I don't remember him being on the witness list."

"That's because he left before he could be contacted."

Louie frowned, and said, "What was he doing there?"

Steve told her what Joey said about following and watching Junior.

"He's been doing it for the last two or three months."

"Did he say why he was following Junior?"

"Couldn't give us a good reason. I told Vince what he said, and we both think his story doesn't sound right."

Louie paused a moment, took a sip of her drink, and said, "It almost sounds like you think Joey may have had something to do with Junior's death."

Vince replied, "I wouldn't go that far. We think he's not telling us the entire story. Steve even went so far as to check Joey's pistol to see if it had been fired."

"Yeah, and I found it hadn't."

Louie leaned forward in her chair and lowered her voice. "What I'm about to tell you hasn't been released to the press yet. I'm telling you because I trust you both not to pass it along." Louie looked around to make sure the door was still closed.

"Junior was killed by a sniper. From what we can tell, the shot came from the roof of a closed theater a block away from The Gator. A friend of his was out front with him when he was shot, and said there was no one else around."

Vince looked puzzled. "How do you know the shot came from the theater?"

"When we realized it had to be a sniper, we expanded our search looking for elevated positions from which the shooter might fire. An officer familiar with the old theater went in to search it, and found the sniper's perch--in the cupola at the top. The shooter had set a crate in front of the window. There were smeared footprints all over the floor. It was easy for him to tell where the shooter had walked, and where the crate came from.

"Sounds like Ronin's work," Vince said.

"That's what I thought, at first." Louie yawned, and said, "I've been working this case all night. This morning I had a couple of officers complete a canvas of the street, looking for video cameras. I wanted to see if anybody was lurking about, or vehicles driving by before or after the shooting."

"Have any luck?" Steve asked.

"I did. We have videos from two cameras covering the street and sidewalk a block from the bar. One was on a restaurant a block north, and the other on a pharmacy a block south, same side of the street. Pretty good definition, too. Farrell and I watched the videos from a half hour before the shooting to a half hour after. They confirmed the witness' statement. We saw only a few people walking by the bar, some going in, some coming out, and several cars driving by at normal speeds."

Steve stood and began pacing back and forth. Stopping in front of Louie he asked, "Again, what does this have to do with Joey?"

"Joey wasn't on any of the videos after the shooting. He didn't walk by or mingle with the crowd. What we did see was a truck like his drive slowly past the bar less than five minutes after Junior was shot. We pulled the plate from the video, and sure enough, it came back to Joey."

Steve looked at Louie and said, "Why would he lie about being there?"

"I don't know. I need to interview him tomorrow. Junior's autopsy is at 11:00 in the morning, and I need to be there. We're hoping the bullet can be recovered from his body and it's not badly damaged. Can you bring him to my office around 3:00?"

"Yeah, we'll be there."

Vince chimed in, "I'm going with you, Steve."

Joey, Steve, and Vince arrived at the sheriff's office a few minutes before three and were escorted to Louie's office. She and Farrell were waiting for them.

"Thanks for coming in," Farrell said. "I'm gonna get a cup of coffee. Can I bring you anything?"

They declined the offer, but Louie asked for a diet Pepsi. While Farrell was gone, she made small talk about the party--how much she enjoyed it, and what a great family they have. Once Farrell returned, and they were all seated, she began.

"The medical examiner was able to recover a bullet from Junior's body. It was identified as a .308 caliber, and luckily for us, it was only a bit damaged."

Vince and Steve looked at each other, then looked at Joey, who was leaning forward in the chair, his head hanging. Louie caught the look. *Interesting. I'll have to ask them about it.*

"It has some good markings," she continued. "If we find the rifle, we should be able to get a match."

"How long was the shot?" Vince asked.

"We measured it from the front of the theater to where Junior was shot, and came up with 250 feet. Our police sniper says it would be nearer 275 feet, after adding in the extra distance from the elevated cupola. Damn good shot, if you ask me."

"Jesus," Vince said. "That's a hell of a shot." Looking at Steve and Joey, he said, "I've never taken a shot at anything that far away. You guys ever shoot that distance?"

Joey shrugged his shoulders and said, "Dad used to take us to the range and we'd shoot targets up to a hundred yards. Steve and I have shot deer from that distance. Isn't that hard."

"Easy for you to say, Joey," Steve said, smiling at him. Turning to Louie he said, "Joey was the marksman in the family. Always was the best shot."

Looking at Joey, Louie said, "Best shot, eh?" She turned to Steve and asked, "Did you bring it with you?"

"Yes. It's in the trunk of my car. Want me to get it?"

"No. Give me the keys and I'll have Farrell do it."

"What are you talking about?" Joey asked

Steve said, "I brought dad's rifle here at Louie's request. Yesterday she asked if we still had it. When I said we did, she asked me to bring it in so it could be tested."

Turning to Louie, Joey said, in anger, "You think Steve and I are suspects in Junior's death?"

"No. I don't. It's a matter of being thorough, Joey. I remembered being told about your dad's rifle, a Remington .308, the same caliber as the bullet that killed Junior. I would be remiss in my duties if I didn't check it out. I'm doing it to eliminate it as the weapon, not tie it to either of you."

"Here are the keys," Steve said, tossing them to Farrell.

Farrell caught them and said, "Thanks. Is the ammo with it?"

"Yeah. Car is parked out front."

Farrell stood and said, "I'll be taking the rifle to the ballistics lab. Be back in a while."

After Farrell left, Louie asked Joey to explain why he had lied. "I know you didn't walk up to the scene. We have video of your truck driving by a few minutes after the shooting. You have anything you want to tell me?"

Joey was silent for a few moments, sitting looking down at the floor. He raised his head and said, "OK. I admit I lied. I don't know why, other than I thought it would be better if you didn't know. I've said it before, that I wanted to see him dead, but I didn't shoot him. If you ask me, I'd say it was that Ronin guy."

"You may be right, Joey. Whoever the shooter was, I will find him."

Louie's cell rang. She saw it was Farrell and answered, "Talk to me, Farrell."

"The tests won't be done until tomorrow, but that's not why I called. The rifle has been recently cleaned, I'd say within the last three or four days. You need me there?"

"No. You can call it a day. I'll see you in the morning."

Disconnecting the call, she said to Steve and Joey, "Farrell says the rifle was cleaned recently. Is that true?"

Steve shook his head and shrugged. "That's news to me."

"I cleaned it three days ago," Joey said. "It's been sitting on the shelf for a few months and was all dusty, so I cleaned it. What's the big deal?"

"Could be important, Joey." Louie said. Turning to Steve she said, "The ballistics test will be completed tomorrow. I'll call and let you know the results. I have nothing else for you tonight. Have a good evening."

Later that night Joey lay on his back on the bed, smiling. *I'm not as dumb as they think.*

Chapter 32

Louie called at lunch time the next day. Steve took the call in the study, alone. "Hey, Louie. Did you get the ballistics test results?"

"Yep. A few minutes ago. No match to your rifle."

"Not unexpected," Steve said, "But a relief all the same. All right if I come by this afternoon and pick it up?"

"Sounds good. I won't be here, so I'll leave it with the desk sergeant."

"Thanks, Louie. Talk to you soon."

Joey stood just to the side of the study door, out of sight, listening to the phone call. From Steve's replies, he knew Louie was advising Steve the ballistics test didn't match their rifle. He smiled, and quietly walked to the kitchen to join Vince, Barbara, and the kids for lunch.

Steve came in and told them the good news. "Now Louie can concentrate on finding the real killer."

"I could've told you that," Joey said, as Barbara placed the plate of sandwiches on the table. She came over to Joey and hugged him from behind. "There never was any doubt, Joey. Now, let's eat."

That afternoon, Steve and Vince were sitting out back on the patio, drinking a beer. Vince scanned the large backyard and asked, "When you guys target shoot out here, what do you aim at?"

Steve pointed off to the left and said, "See that group of trees, the ones that grew so close together? We put the targets on one of them."

"You told me there's a hiking trail out there. Didn't you worry someone out walking could be hit by one of your shots?"

"No, not really. The trail turns away from the woods about fifty feet from the trees, and heads back to the road six hundred feet away. Besides, there's a six-foot chain link fence a couple of feet from the trail, paralleling it. It's highly unlikely anyone would be in danger of getting shot. The road doesn't cross behind it, and there are no buildings back there. The woods go a half-mile back from where our targets were, and there are warning signs posted on the fence every fifty feet."

"Hmm," Vince muttered. "How long of a shot is it from the house?"

"About a hundred yards."

Downing the rest of his beer, he stood up from his chair and said, "Take a walk with me, Steve. I want to see the target area."

"Any particular reason why?"

"Just curious. C'mon, grab a couple of beers and let's go."

They spent a half-hour at the trees. Steve sat on the ground dozing in the shade while Vince walked around, looking closely at the tree trunks.

"Hey, Steve, wake up. I'm done. Let's go back to the house."

Steve yawned, got up and stretched. "What were you doing, Vince?"

"Looking around. I saw some bullet holes in a tree, a nice tight grouping, and walked along the fence separating me from the trail. You were right--the target area is far enough away from the trail that there was no chance of a stray shot hitting anyone. Let's go. I need to make a phone call."

Back at the house, Vince found Maggie sitting alone in the study, with a glass of wine, reading a book.

"What're you reading, Babe?"

"Hi, Honey. It's a book Barbara gave me. Said it's a pretty good one. It's a thriller about a serial killer in San Francisco, of all places. I'm only a couple of chapters in, but so far I'm liking it."

"Well, good. Let me know how it turns out. I'll be up in our room for a bit. Got an important call to make."

"OK, Hon," Maggie said, her nose back in the book.

Up in the bedroom, Vince sat on the bed for a couple of minutes and thought about what he would say to Louie. He needed to convince her his request was important and necessary to her investigation. Vince took a deep breath, let it out, then dialed.

"Hi, Vince. What can I do for you?"

Vince chuckled. "What makes you think I want something?"

"Oh, just a hunch."

"Just wanted to know how the investigation's going. Any leads on Junior's killer?"

"Other than the bullet dug out of Junior, we have nothing--no witnesses, no bullet casings, no prints. This isn't news to you, so what do you really want?"

"I might be able to help you out. I have a bullet that should be compared with the one from Junior."

Louie didn't say anything for a moment. "A bullet? Where did you get it?"

"Can't say at the moment."

"Can't, or won't?"

"Please, don't ask me that. If you'll do the comparison, I'll tell you everything regardless of the results--where I got it and why."

"Come on, Vince. I can't do that without more information as to its relevance."

"It may not have any relevance. At least, that's what I'm hoping. Will you do it, as a favor to me?"

"Does this have anything to do with Steve or Joey?"

"I can't say, Louie. Will you test it, or not?"

"I don't know. Meet me at my office tomorrow morning and I'll let you know. Bring the bullet."

"I'll be there by nine. Thanks, Louie."

"Don't thank me yet. See you in the morning."

Steve and Barbara were sitting outside on the backyard patio, watching the sunset. Joey was there too, but was restlessly pacing back and forth.

"Joey," Steve called, "What's the matter with you? Come sit down and relax."

Joey kept pacing, now muttering to himself. It was as if he hadn't heard Steve at all.

"Hey, Joey," Steve said, louder. "Sit down. You're driving us crazy."

Joey stopped and looked at Steve, his eyes bloodshot and brow furrowed with worry. "What?"

"For Christ's sake. Stop pacing."

"Oh, OK. Sorry."

"What's bothering you, Joey?" Barbara asked as he sat next to her.

"Nothing. Just got a lot on my mind."

"Want a drink, or a beer?" Steve asked.

"A beer would be good."

Just then, Vince and Maggie joined them. Vince placed an ice bucket containing six beers on the patio table.

"Somebody call for beer?"

"Wow," Steve commented, "You must be psychic."

"Nah. Just know you guys too well."

Vince and Maggie watched as Joey took a beer, stood up and started pacing again. Vince looked at Steve, pointed to Joey, and silently mouthed "What?" Steve shook his head side to side and shrugged.

"Hey, Joey," Vince said, "Come sit with us."

Without stopping his pacing, Joey said, "No, thanks. I think I'll go upstairs. I've got a lot to think about, and I need to be alone."

"Anything we can help you with?"

"No. I've got to figure out a couple of things, that's all." Joey stopped, turned to the table and said, "See you in the morning."

He placed his untouched beer on the table and started to walk into the house. Joey stopped, turned back to Steve and said, "You know I love you, right?" then went inside.

After Joey left, Steve said, "Well, that was strange. I'm worried about him. I get the feeling he wants to tell us something but can't bring himself to say it."

"I agree, Steve," Vince said. "He's really bothered, that's for sure. He didn't drink any of his beer. You have any idea what's bugging him?"

"Not a clue. He hasn't been himself the last couple of weeks. I hope he figures out whatever is bothering him."

"Maybe we'll find out tomorrow. He'll tell us when he's ready," Vince finished his beer, looked at his watch and said, "I'm going in. Gonna watch the second half of the Falcons and Forty Niners game."

Steve said, "I'll join you."

Maggie and Barbara stayed outside when they went into the living room, where Steve turned the TV on and tuned it to the game. They sat there without speaking, each lost in their own thoughts.

Chapter 33

Vince arrived at the sheriff's department at 8:40 a.m. and was escorted to Louie's office where she was waiting. She had been notified of his arrival by the receptionist and was at her desk with two cups of coffee.

"Good morning, Vince. Want some coffee?" she asked, holding up one of the cups.

"Sure, thanks."

"I convinced ballistics I needed a quick comparison, so, let me see the bullet."

Vince grinned, sat across from her, and said, "So much for the small talk. Here." He pulled a plastic sandwich bag from his coat pocket and handed it to her.

Louie visually examined the bullet inside for a minute. "It's in really good shape. The nose is a bit deformed, but there are clear striation marks. Should be easy to compare." Looking at Vince, she said, "Where'd you get this?"

"Not yet. The deal is I will tell you when the comparison is complete. I'm asking you to trust me on this."

Louie sighed, hung her head, and said, "I can't, Vince." Looking up at him she said, "I need to know where you found the bullet, and why you want it compared with the one from Junior's body."

Vince was silent for a minute, sipping from his cup. He set it down on the desk and said, "You don't know how hard this is for me, Louie. It's been eating me up inside, trying to decide if I wanted to have the comparison done." Vince sighed and took another sip of coffee. "I'm not gonna tell you, and if you won't do the comparison without the info, then so be it."

"What are you hiding? If this comparison is important to solving Junior's murder, then you are obligated as a police officer to tell me what I need to know. Do I have to say you could be arrested for withholding critical evidence in a homicide?"

"I know that, Louie. But maybe the comparison isn't critical evidence."

Louie looked Vince in the eyes for a few moments, then said, "I think I know the answers to my questions. The fact that you have the bullet and don't wanna give up any more information leads me to believe it's somehow connected to your family." Louie thought a moment and said, "OK. I'll have the comparison done. I'll call you and let you know the results tomorrow. Keep this between you and I. We both could be in trouble if it gets to the wrong people."

Vince took a deep breath and sighed in relief. "Thanks, Louie. I owe you."

Louie smiled and said, "Yeah, sure. Where you going from here?"

Vince chuckled. "Gonna take Maggie out for breakfast. We're going home in two days, and I'll be outta your hair. By the way, if you had refused to do the comparison, I would have given in and told you everything. Talk to you soon."

Two Hours later, Vince and Maggie were at the house. They found Steve and the kids watching cartoons Barbara was cleaning up the breakfast dishes.

"Hey, Steve. Enjoying yourself?"

"Shut up, Vince. I remember you watching cartoons when you were in high school."

Vince chuckled. Looking around the room, he asked, "Where's Joey?"

"Have no idea. His truck was gone when we got up. He must have left pretty early. I'll give him a call in a minute. The kids want to go to the zoo today, and he loves that place. Wouldn't miss a chance on going. Barbara and Maggie said they want to go, too, and I'm assuming you do, also. I'll call him now. I'd like to get going soon, and it'll be a nice family outing."

Steve dialed Joey's cell and it rang until the call went to his messages. "Hey, where are you? Call me as soon as you can. We're planning a trip to the zoo, and I know how much you love that place. OK, talk to you soon."

A half-hour later Joey hadn't called back, so Steve packed up the family and left for the zoo.

The next morning as Vince and Maggie were packing for the flight home, Vince's cell rang. "It's Louie, Babe. I'll take it downstairs."

As he descended the stairs, he answered the call. "Hey, Louie. You got anything for me?"

"Yep. The bullet you gave me matched the one taken from Junior's body."

"Shit. That's what I was afraid of."

"Now you going to tell me where it came from, Vince?"

"All right." Vince took a deep breath and began. "I don't believe Joey told the truth about what he did the night Junior was killed. He was there, but I don't think he is involved in Junior's death."

"Why?"

"Remember Steve told us a few days ago Joey has been following Junior around?"

"Yeah. Did Joey say why?"

"No. He wouldn't, or couldn't, give a good reason. Anyway, he hasn't been himself the last few days. Steve and I noticed he's been distracted, like he has something heavy weighing on his mind. He's looks worried. Joey's really upset over his dad's murder, and told Steve he wanted to see Junior dead for what he did to set up the judge."

"We already did a comparison with bullets from his rifle--they didn't match."

"I know. I think he might have switched out the barrel after shooting Junior."

"I don't know, Vince. Joey doesn't strike me as the smartest person in the family."

"That's the impression everyone has of him, but he's no dummy. You obviously checked the serial number on his rifle, and it matched the registration info, right?"

"Yeah, so?"

"I did some research with the Winchester company and found the serial number is stamped on the receiver, not on the barrel. It's not difficult to remove a barrel and replace it with another. No one would know. What I will say, for now, is I don't believe Joey told the truth about what he did the night Junior was killed."

"You really think Joey killed Junior." It was not a question.

Vince shook his head side to side. "Something's wrong with him. I can't say for sure Joey was involved in Junior's death. I hope I'm wrong, but my gut tells me he was. I remember you said the bullet that killed DeWayne White was never recovered."

"Yes. We went over the grounds with a fine-toothed comb, even used a metal detector--no luck." After a moment Louie said, "Oh, c'mon Vince. You're not hinting Joey killed DeWayne, too."

"No, no. I'm sure it was Ronin cleaning up for the Trafficante family, though I would like to know the caliber of the bullet that killed Dewayne."

"Well, that's most likely not gonna happen." Louie paused. "Oh, I see. You want to know if it's the same caliber as the one that killed Junior."

"Just curious. Seems too much of a coincidence that both DeWayne and Junior were killed by a sniper."

"In both cases that sniper could have been Ronin, though I think it's unlikely he killed Junior."

"Yes, it could. I'm not ruling it out. I just want to know for sure. Since you mentioned it, any progress finding Ronin?"

"Not much. I've been in touch with Sonny Refugio, explained what I wanted, and assured him I was not investigating him, nor his businesses. He didn't admit to knowing anyone called Ronin, but said he would ask around. He also said if I didn't hear from him within a week, it meant he has nothing for me."

Vince grinned. "We both know he has Ronin on retainer, and can contact him anytime."

"I'm sure. I think he's going to check me out before deciding what to do. I'm running out of leads, Vince. The investigation has stalled. I don't even have a suspect. Sure, there's a few persons of interest, but some have alibis, and others can't be placed at the scene, or tied to the murder--there just isn't any evidence."

"Been there, Louie," Vince replied. "All I can say is shang in there and keep at it. You eventually will get the break you need."

"This case is getting mighty cold. I'll keep plugging along hoping for the best."

"Good. Well, I'll say so long for now, my friend. Steve is taking us to the airport tomorrow early morning. You take care of yourself, and be careful out there. Let's keep in touch, OK?"

"You bet. Who knows, someday you may see my face at your door."

"Anytime, Detective Louise Princeton, anytime."

Three weeks later Vince got a call from Steve. "Hey, Steve. How ya doing? Everything all right with the family?"

"Yeah, all's well. The kids miss their aunt and uncle and have been asking when we can go to California for a visit."

"Anytime. I haven't heard from Louie for a while. She called ten days ago to tell me there's nothing new on your dad's murder. Said Mama Peters' trial is scheduled for next month, and I may be needed to testify."

"She told me that last week, too. Called me two days ago about Junior's murder. Said she suspects Joey killed Junior, and might have killed DeWayne, too. The problem is she has no evidence to prove it. The slight circumstantial evidence connecting Joey is not enough to seek a warrant for his arrest."

"That's good news. Louie is smart, and I'd bet she ends up finding out who really killed Junior." Vince breathed a sigh of relief. *Thank you, Louie, for not telling Steve about the bullet comparison I asked for.*

"I can't believe my brother could kill anyone, especially like Junior died."

"Speaking of Joey, how is he doing? Is he feeling better now that Junior's dead?"

"Yeah. In fact, he took off four days ago to go deer hunting with a friend. Headed up to Kentucky. His buddy has a cabin near the Daniel Boone National Forest. He's supposed to be back next week."

"That's great. He's in a better place now?"

"Yep. Well, that's all the new for now, Cuz. I'll talk to you later. Gotta pick up the kids from school."

"Alright. Give our best to Barbara, and tell the kids I've got a room for them when you come out here."

"Will do. Bye."

Vince saw it was 3:30 in the afternoon, which made it 6:30 in Augusta. He called Louie after disconnecting from Steve, and when she didn't answer, left a message. "Hey, Louie. Just talked to Steve, and I want to thank you for not telling him about the ballistics test. I don't know how I could've explained it to him, or Joey for that matter. Thanks again."

Chapter 34

Two days after talking to Steve Vince got a call from Louie.

"Sorry I didn't get back to you Vince, but there are things going on here regarding the shooting of Junior Henderson. I've been working around the clock. This is the first time I've gotten a break, so I thought I'd call you and fill you in."

"Big news, huh?"

"Yes. Three days ago, I had an anonymous message on my office phone. It said there was a body buried in the woods in Euchee Creek Park. Gave directions to finding it, and sure enough, we did."

"Who was It? What does it have to do with the Henderson case?"

"I'm getting to that. The body was in a state of moderate decomposition--the medical examiner estimates the victim died four to five weeks earlier. He was able to roll some prints by removing the fingers on one hand and soaking them in a sodium carbonate solution until they were sufficiently re-hydrated."

"Were you able to get an I.D. from them?" Vince asked.

"As a matter of fact, we were. Want to guess whose body it was?"

"Oh, no. You gotta be shittin' me. It was Ronin's, wasn't it."

"Bingo," Louie said. Vince could almost see the smile on her face as she talked.

"Any idea who made the call?"

"No, but I'm betting the Trafficante's had something to do with it."

"How did you know to compare the prints with Ronin's?"

"I have no idea how the caller knew, but he said to look at the prints we recovered from the duct tape used to bind Sherie MacDonald."

"Scary. Think there was someone on the inside helping them?" Vince asked.

"Hard to say for sure, but how else would the caller know that?"

Vince thought a few seconds. "That puts Ronin's death before Junior was murdered," Vince said.

"Yes, it does. Rules him out for Junior's murder, but not for DeWayne's. It sure throws a twist into this investigation."

"On the one hand," Vince said, "I'm glad Ronin's out of the picture. On the other hand, it makes me think Joey killed Junior. Did the M.E. determine Ronin's cause of death?"

"During the autopsy, he found two bullet wounds to the back of the skull, and fragments from two small caliber bullets in the skull--he believes they were .22 caliber."

"A hitman's favorite weapon," Vince said.

Louie didn't say anything for a few moments, then said, "Being honest with you, Vince, I also believe Joey killed Junior. He could have replaced the barrel, as you suggested. There's no other explanation why the bullet you gave me matched."

"Yeah, I know. Steve told me of your conversation. At this point, I don't know what to think."

"There is one good thing about knowing Ronin is dead--it closes a part of the investigation into DeWayne's murder. Now I can devote more time to your uncle's and Junior's deaths."

"What are you going to do next?"

"I'm going to re-interview Joey--put on some pressure to try and pry the truth out of him."

"Good luck with that. I'll bet he shows up with a lawyer advising him to not answer your questions."

"I hope he doesn't, but I think you're right. We'll see. I gotta go, now. You take care."

"You too, Louie."

Vince disconnected the call and sat at his desk, phone in hand, thinking. Bobby, seeing the frown on his face, came over, sat on a corner of Vince's desk and said, "Bad news? Is it about your uncle's murder?"

Vince had been keeping Bobby up-to-date on the investigation into Junior's murder and filled him in on the latest news from Louie.

"Damn," Bobby said, "It's not looking good for your cousin."

"I hope he's smart enough to bring his lawyer with him when Louie calls him in. Right now she doesn't have any solid evidence Joey was involved. Since the rifle was ruled out as the murder weapon, all she has is him driving by the scene a few minutes after the shooting, and a couple of comments about wanting to see Junior dead."

"That ain't nothing," Bobby said. "Bet Steve had the same thoughts, and you, too."

Vince smiled, and didn't answer.

Louie and Farrell sat across from Joey who was accompanied by his lawyer, Sam Winston. An officer came in carrying a tray with four cups of coffee, sugar and creamer packets, and wooden stir sticks. Setting it on the table, he asked Louie, "Anything else you need, Detective?"

"No, thanks, Jenkins."

When he left the room Louie passed out the coffee. Sitting back in her chair she said, "Joey, you know why I asked you to come in today, right?"

"Yes, Ma'am," Joey replied, holding his coffee in both hands. When he raised it to take a sip, Louie noticed they were trembling.

"Before we start, as a matter of procedure, I'll be reading you your rights. This interview is being recorded."

Louie recited the Miranda warning, had Joey check the box that said he understood it, then sign the card. Sam Winston sat quietly, stirring his coffee.

"OK. Four days ago a body was recovered in a shallow grave at Euchee Creek Park. The M.E. determined the victim had been dead four to five weeks. We were able to lift prints from it and identify him as Ronin." She paused for a moment, gauging Joey's reaction to the news. "Do you have any knowledge of this body?"

Joey's lawyer interrupted her. "Are you accusing my client of being involved in Ronin's death Detective Princeton?"

"No, Sir," Louie replied, "But I do consider him a person of interest in another homicide we thought Ronin committed." Louie started to give Winston a brief background on Ronin, however, Winston interrupted her again, saying, "My client has already briefed me on Mr. Ronin."

"All right, then. The other homicide I mentioned was the shooting death of a participant in the murder of Joey's father. We have statements from a half dozen witnesses to whom Joey said he wanted to see him dead for what he did."

"And is that all evidence you have?"

"No, I also have video of him driving by the murder scene a few minutes after the shooting, and a bullet taken from where Joey had been target shooting matched the bullet that killed Junior."

Joey started to speak before Winston could stop him. "I already told you, I had nothing..."

Turning to Joey, Winston said, "It is my advice that you not answer any questions." He turned back to Louie and said, "It is my understanding that Joey's rifle was test fired, and that bullet didn't match. So, unless you have more linking my client to the murder, we are leaving."

Louie addressed Joey directly, saying, "That's your right, Joey, but if you have more information on Junior's murder, now's the time to come clean."

Joey looked at his lawyer and said, "I think I'll listen to Mr. Winston."

Louie sighed, and said, "If that's what you want, then this interview is over."

Winston stood up and said, "Thank you for the coffee, Detective. We'll be leaving now. If you want to talk to my client in the future, call me first. C'mon Joey, let's go."

As they started for the door, Louie said, "You're making a big mistake, Joey."

Joey stopped, turned toward Louie and said, "I know," before Winston took his arm and ushered him out of the room.

As Louie and Farrell were walking back to their office Louie said, "I know in my gut Joey killed Junior. The one thing that really bothers me is how he did it."

"It's been bothering me, too," Farrell said. "We know it was a .308 bullet, and the Torellis have a Winchester rifle in that caliber, but ballistics confirmed the bullet that killed Junior didn't come from their rifle."

"Vince suggested Joey may have replaced the barrel after he shot Junior, in case we wanted to test his rifle. I'm now thinking that's not such a far-fetched idea, but I'm not convinced Joey is smart enough to think of something like that."

"Well, Ya never know, Louie, ya just never know," Farrell said.

Chapter 35

It had been nine months since Junior Henderson was gunned down. Louie had relegated DeWayne's murder to the cold case office, and, though she was still investigating Junior's murder, she was no closer to solving it.

Dozens of calls to the sheriff's tip-line lead to over a hundred potential witness interviews and six search warrants, all without finding evidence that pointed her to a viable suspect, or connected Joey further to Junior's murder.

She served a search warrant at the Torelli house which included the garage, and grounds, looking for a .308 rifle other than the one she knew they owned. The warrant included parts of a similar rifle, specifically looking for another barrel. She had the forensic team go over the grounds with a metal detector in case such items had been buried, and a half a dozen cops and CSI techs thoroughly searched the house and garage to no avail.

Louie had visited Steve and Joey every couple of weeks to keep them informed of the lack of progress in the investigations. She phoned Vince several times with the same information, though he normally got it from Steve after she talked with him.

Vince had not needed to testify at Mama Peters' trial a month earlier. With the amount of evidence Louie had amassed on Mama, the jury found her guilty on all counts after a three-week trial, deliberating only six hours before reaching a verdict. She was sentenced to death by lethal injection, and awaits her fate on death row. Her lawyers have filed an appeal which has yet to be decided.

Clive took a deal, agreeing to plead guilty to arranging the murder for hire. In return, he testified against Mama Peters, and avoided the death penalty, receiving a life sentence without parole.

After the trial and sentencings, Joey told Steve he was going away for a while, to help put everything behind him. In answer to Steve's questions about where he was going and how long he would be gone, Joey replied, "I don't know. Wherever my whims lead me. Maybe I'll go visit Vince in California. I don't know when I'll be back."

The next morning, Joey packed his suitcase and loaded it in his truck. He said his goodbyes to Barbara and the kids. Steve walked him to the truck.

"Give me a call now and then, Joey, to let me know you're OK. Here," Steve said, taking a thick envelope from his back pocket. "There's five grand in here."

Joey started to protest, but Steve cut him off. "Take it. You'll need it. If you run out, let me know and I'll wire you more."

Joey took the envelope, then hugged Steve tightly and whispered "I love you, Bro." Breaking the embrace, he got in the truck, started the engine, and backed down the driveway. Before he drove away, he looked at Steve and gave a single wave, then drove down the street. Steve watched him until he was out of sight. Once he was gone, Steve slowly walked into the house.

Six weeks later no one had heard from Joey. He hadn't called Steve, or showed up at Vince's house. He seemed to have vanished.

Another week had passed when Vince received a letter at his house, postmarked Madison, Wisconsin. There was no return address. He opened it, took the letter out and recognized the unique scrawl of Joey's handwriting--half printing interspaced with cursive.

Hey, Cousin. Guess you're surprised to hear from me. There are a couple of things I want to get off my chest that I couldn't tell you in person. You'll understand why as you read more.

First, I'm somewhere no one would think to look for me. This letter was mailed by a casual acquaintance who doesn't know my real name. I asked him to mail it when he got home, as I wanted a postmark far from my real location.

First, Louie will never be able to get the evidence she needs to charge me with Junior's murder--mainly because I didn't kill him. Lord knows I wanted to, in the worst way. On the Friday he was shot I went to the bar and parked a half-block away. I went in, disguised, and sat at the bar, watching him living it up with his friends, not a care in the world.

I had my .45 with me, and walked by his table, with every intention of killing him. I couldn't do it, not that close up. I left and drove to the old theater, looking for a place from which I could shoot him with a rifle. I found the cupola was perfect--a clear view of the bar entrance. I set up a perch, planning to use it the next Friday.

As I was making the sniper nest, I heard a thump on the roof above me, but didn't think anything of it. A couple of minutes later, I hear a shot. A half-minute later the access door to the roof was pulled open, and I saw the legs of someone starting to climb down the ladder to the cupola.

"Sona of a bitch," Vince murmured to himself. He took a deep breath, and continued reading.

I hid behind some crates in a corner of the room along the front wall. It was pretty dark as I watched a guy climb down the ladder. He was carrying something that could have been a rifle.

When he got down the ladder, he walked to the window and looked out. I could see his face in the dim light leaking in from the street. I was startled and shocked to see it was Steve.

Steve turned and headed to the stairs. As stunned as I was, I stood up and said, "What have you done, Steve?"

He spun around and lifted the rifle, pointing it at me. I guess he recognized me 'cause he didn't shoot. I shined the flashlight on my face, as he asked me what I was doing there. Long story short, when we left, I drove by where Junior was. I knew from the amount of blood around him he was dead.

When I got home, I took the rifle and cleaned it. I'd switched out the barrel a few days before Junior was shot. Since I planned to kill him, I didn't want to chance a ballistics test would match a bullet fired from our rifle.

So, now you know what really happened that Friday night. Everything I did was done to protect my brother. He's the pillar of our family now, and not a threat to anyone else. Junior was the last person involved in my father's death to avoid justice.

I'm sure you will let Louie know about this letter, and that's OK. Wouldn't expect anything else from you. She has a little evidence connecting me to the crime, but nothing to connect Steve.

Who knows, Vince. Maybe I'm lying and making this up to cover my own ass. If I'm every found and arrested, I will confess to the murder, and plead guilty at my trial.

It's useless to try and find me. I have a new name, and the documents to support it, and have changed my appearance. I doubt you would recognize me if we passed on the sidewalk.

I sent Steve a letter, too. So long, Vince. Do what you have to do.

Wishing you all the best. I will miss you, and I love you.

Joey.

Vince carefully folded the letter and placed it back in the envelope, then put it in a plastic baggie. He knew he had to call Louie and that she would want the letter. He placed it in the desk drawer in his office, then wiped the tears from his eyes on his sleeve. He took a few minutes to compose himself, before calling Louie.

Epilogue

It had been a year since Joey disappeared. In spite of Louie's efforts to find him, he was never located. He might as well have been a ghost.

She never found enough to file charges against him. Though there was little to nothing more she could do, she kept the case active. Every few weeks she would read through the report, hoping to find something she missed before.

Louie interrogated Steve, confronting him with the letter Joey wrote to Vince. Steve steadfastly denied having anything to do with Junior's murder, and denied having received a letter from Joey. Without a shred of evidence against him, he was released. Louie stubbornly kept him listed in the report as a 'person of interest'."

Louie never had any doubt she would solve the case.

If you enjoyed this author's book, then please place a review up at the site of purchase, and any social media sites you frequent!

You can find ALL our books up on our website at:

http://www.writers-exchange.com

All our mysteries:

http://www.writers-exchange.com/category/genres/mystery-thrillers-suspense/

All John's Books:

http://www.writers-exchange.com/john-schembra/

About the Author

John Schembra was born Jan. 3, 1948 and raised in the San Francisco Bay Area.

He retired Feb. 2001 from a small northern California police department as a Sergeant after almost 30 years' service.

Prior to becoming a police officer, he was a Military Policeman assigned for a year to the 557th MP Co., Long Binh, Bien Hoa, South Vietnam, where he had several "adventures" that provided the basis for his first novel, *MP*.

He has earned a B.A in Administration of Justice and an M.A in Public Administration. He spent his retirement time writing as well as teaching other police officers emergency vehicle operation/pursuit driving through the Contra Costa County Sheriff's Office and Police Academy. He also instructs officers in the driving simulators, is a train the trainer for emergency vehicle/pursuit/ simulator instructors, and has been recognized as a Subject Matter Expert by the State of California in emergency vehicle operations/pursuit driving.

He has had several trade articles published in law enforcement magazines such as *Law and Order, Police Officer's Quarterly*, and *The Backup*. He is also a member of the Police Writers Association, a very supportive writers' group for anyone affiliated with any type of law enforcement organization.

In his spare time (what little there is) John enjoys reading, fishing, and most of all, spending time with his family.

John's personal website is: http://www.jschembra.com

You can keep track of John's work on his author website: http://www.writers-exchange.com/John-Schembra/

If you want to read more about other books by this author, they are listed on the following pages...

A Vince Torelli Novel

{Historical: Vietnam War}

MP - A Novel of Vietnam (War: Vietnam)

As Vincent Torelli stepped off the plane at Bien Hoa Air Base, South Vietnam, in June 1967, he was almost overwhelmed by the stench in the hot, humid air. Drafted into the armed forces five months earlier, he still can't comprehend how he ended up in this place, now a Military Policeman assigned to the 557th MP Co. at Long Binh Post just outside Bien Hoa City.

His year-long tour of duty in Vietnam changes him from a somewhat naïve young man to a battle-hardened veteran. Through unlucky chance, Vince becomes involved in the ferocious '68 Tet offensive, barely surviving the night. He sees and experiences things he could never have imagined before ending up in Vietnam.

This is Vince's story... survival, coping with the hell he's facing, the sorrow of lives lost, and the friendships he formed.

Publisher: http://www.writers-exchange.com/MP-A-Novel-of-Vietnam/

A Vince Torelli Mystery

A former soldier who becomes a San Francisco police homicide investigator after the war, Vince Torelli is dedicated, intelligent and highly principled--all skills that serve him well given the difficult, almost impossible murder investigations he's assigned to handle that force him to the razor edge with equally resolute, extremely ruthless masterminds.

Book 1: Retribution (Mystery: Serial Killer)

There's a vigilante killer loose in San Francisco, and when the justice system fails, he doles out his own brand of justice.

Homicide Inspector Vince Torelli has handled some of the city's worst murders, but this case has him baffled. It seems no matter what he does, the killer manages to stay one step ahead of him, anticipating his every move. The false clues and trail the killer leaves keeps Vince chasing shadows as the body count rises. Will he discover the killer's identity and will he survive long enough to bring him to justice?

Publisher: http://www.writers-exchange.com/Retribution/

Book 2: Diplomatic Immunity (Mystery/Thriller)

There are sixty-six Consulates and Embassies in San Francisco and a very talented, deadly sniper is targeting the Consul Generals seemingly at random.

San Francisco Homicide inspector Vince Torelli has a reputation for solving the toughest cases in the city, but this one is unlike anything else he has faced. The killings make no sense, lack motive, and appear to be unrelated but Vince knows there has to be a link between them. As he struggles to find the connection and identify the suspect he becomes a target himself. This can end only one of two ways: Either he solves the case...or he becomes a victim himself.

Publisher: http://www.writers-exchange.com/Diplomatic-Immunity/

Book 3: Blood Debt

San Francisco Homicide Investigator and Vietnam veteran Vince Torelli strives to clean up the violence in San Francisco but, after a suspect in a double murder is killed during an attempted arrest, he finds himself also protecting the police officers of the city he considers family. His efforts put him in the line of fire when he's targeted. The brother of the suspect victim wants revenge on the officers responsible and he'll stop at nothing. He kidnaps Vince, a man obsessively loyal to his job as well as those he works alongside, a man as smart and committed to his principles as the criminals he catches almost without fail. Vince knows best, though, a blood debt always demands payment...

Publisher: http://www.writers-exchange.com/Blood-Debt/

Book 4: The List

A recently mutilated, naked corpse is found in an early 19th century tunnel under San Francisco. With no forensic evidence, solving the crime seems impossible.

After San Francisco Homicide Inspector Vince Torelli begins investigating, notes from the killer, addressed to him, start showing up. Vince realizes this murder may be the first of several, leading Vince on a deadly multi-state investigation.

Publisher: http://www.writers-exchange.com/The-List/

Book 5: Southern Justness

When his uncle, a Superior Court Judge in Georgia, is killed in a hit-and-run accident, San Francisco PD Homicide Inspector Vince Torelli travels to Augusta for the funeral.

While there, it is discovered the judge's death was no accident, and Vince gets caught up in a deadly vendetta against his family. Unofficially working with Detective Sergeant Louisa "Louie" Princeton, Richmond County Sheriff's Department, several suspects are eventually identified. Louie and Vince are determined to bring them to justice, but someone is frustrating their attempts with deadly results.

Publisher: http://www.writers-exchange.com/southern-justice/

An Echo of Lies

The prospects for recovery for Officer Bob Kelly were not good. Shot twice during a traffic stop, the emergency room doctors had worked feverishly to save his life. Four weeks later, to the doctor's surprise, Kelly walked out of the hospital and went home. He felt good--no pain, fully alert, and strong. Little did he know the terror and struggle that awaited him as the demon who possessed him took more control.

Publisher: http://www.writers-exchange.com/an-echo-of-lies/

Sin Eater

{Supernatural Murder Mystery}

The shocking murder of a professor at San Donorio State College brings the city police to investigate with Campus Police Officer Sarah Ferris acting as college liaison. Sarah's friend, Nico Guardino, a history professor at the college, gets drawn into helping her investigate. As Nico and Sarah struggle to find the murderer, the killing continues.

Drawn inexorably deeper into the investigation, Nico begins having visions and deep feelings of dread he knows somehow connect to the murderer. He feels the connection becoming stronger, but the how and why remain frustratingly unknown even as the visions and feelings become more disturbing.

"A fascinating page turner. Every chapter builds on the next and brings the reader to an unpredictable, satisfying climax. A great (summer) read."

~ Thonie Hevron, award winning author

Publisher: http://www.writers-exchange.com/Sin-Eater/

www.ingramcontent.com/pod-product-compliance
Lightning Source LLC
Chambersburg PA
CBHW060908140726
47996CB00001B/159